Someone had been here

And judging by the open decanter, she knew who. Maybe she had changed everything else, but Elizabeth still kept the best whiskey in the Waterford.

"What the hell are you doing here, Rafe?" she asked, not raising her voice. Wherever he was, he would have been watching her since she'd entered the kitchen.

"You've cut your hair."

He always noticed things like that. Maybe too much. Still, the fact that he had noticed caused an unwanted thickness in her throat.

From force of habit, her hand rose to rake the chin-length hair that had once been long enough to tangle around his bare, sweating shoulders as they made love.

At the memory, a jolt of sexual heat seared along nerve pathways that had seemed atrophied. They weren't. Painfully, unexpectedly, she knew that now.

Steeling herself, she walked into the living room. After five years, she was in the same room with Rafe Sinclair. Something she had thought would never happen again.

Dear Harlequin Intrigue Reader,

We've got what you need to start the holiday season with a *bang*. Starting things off is RITA® Award-winning author Gayle Wilson. Gayle returns to Harlequin Intrigue with a spin-off of her hugely popular MEN OF MYSTERY series. Same sexy heroes, same drama and danger...but with a new name! Look for *Rafe Sinclair's Revenge* under the PHOENIX BROTHERHOOD banner.

You can return to the royal kingdom of Vashmira in *Royal Ransom* by Susan Kearney, which is the second book in her trilogy THE CROWN AFFAIR. This time an American goes undercover to protect the princess. But will his heart be exposed in the process?

B.J. Daniels takes you to Montana to encounter one very tough lady who's about to meet her match in a mate. Only thing...can he avoid the deadly fate of her previous beaux? Find out in *Premeditated Marriage*.

Winding up the complete package, we have a dramatic story about a widow and her child who become targets of a killer, and only the top cop can keep them out of harm's way. Linda O. Johnston pens an emotionally charged story of crime and compassion in *Tommy's Mom*.

Make sure you pick up all four, and please let us know what you think of our brand of breathtaking romantic suspense.

Enjoy!

Sincerely,

Denise O'Sullivan
Associate Senior Editor
Harlequin Intrigue

RAFE SINCLAIR'S REVENGE

GAYLE WILSON

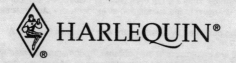

HARLEQUIN®

TORONTO • NEW YORK • LONDON
AMSTERDAM • PARIS • SYDNEY • HAMBURG
STOCKHOLM • ATHENS • TOKYO • MILAN • MADRID
PRAGUE • WARSAW • BUDAPEST • AUCKLAND

ISBN 0-373-22685-3

RAFE SINCLAIR'S REVENGE

ABOUT THE AUTHOR

Five-time RITA® finalist and RITA® Award winner Gayle Wilson has written twenty-seven novels and two novellas for Harlequin/Silhouette. A former high school English and world history teacher of gifted students, she has won more than forty awards and nominations for her work. Recent recognitions include a 2002 Daphne du Maurier Award for Romantic Suspense.

Gayle still lives in Alabama, where she was born, with her husband of thirty-three years and an ever-growing menagerie of beloved pets. She has one son, who is also a teacher of gifted students. Gayle loves to hear from readers. Write to her at P.O. Box 3277, Hueytown, AL 35023. Visit Gayle online at http://suspense.net/gayle-wilson.

Books by Gayle Wilson

*Home to Texas series
**Men of Mystery series
†More Men of Mystery series
‡Phoenix Brotherhood series

FOR YOUR EYES ONLY

CIA
AGENT PROFILE

NAME: RAFE SINCLAIR
DATE OF BIRTH: JANUARY 18, 1964
ASSIGNED TEAM: EXTERNAL SECURITY

SPECIAL SKILLS: Trained in counterterrorism
and in interrogation methods; hand-to-hand combat
expert; top-notch marksman; speaks fluent Arabic

AGENT EVALUATION: Recipient of the agency's
highest citation for valor above and beyond the call of
duty.

STATUS: Resignation accepted

CURRENT ADDRESS: Unknown...

FOR YOUR EYES ONLY

CAST OF CHARACTERS

Rafe Sinclair—Five years ago this ex-CIA operative hunted down and executed a terrorist responsible for the deaths of hundreds of innocent people. Now the agency is telling Rafe that Gunther Jorgensen not only isn't dead, he's bent on revenge. The problem is Rafe may not be his target.

Elizabeth Richards—Once a member of Griff Cabot's elite antiterrorism team, Elizabeth has a new identity and an ordinary life, one that is about to be disrupted by a couple of ghosts from her past. One of them is hunting her. The other, former partner and lover Rafe Sinclair, is determined to become her protector.

Gunther Jorgensen—Is the terrorist mastermind alive or dead? And if it's not Jorgensen who is stalking Elizabeth, then who is it?

Griff Cabot—What secret knowledge does Griff possess that makes him agree to let Rafe set out alone on a suicide mission?

John Edmonds—Was Edmonds really sent by Cabot or does The Phoenix operative have his own agenda?

Lucas Hawkins—The legendary assassin of the External Security Team may hold the answer to questions about Rafe that Elizabeth has puzzled over for more than six years.

To BJ
who makes me incredibly envious of her talent.

Prologue

The man Griff Cabot had come to find was carefully turning a piece of wood on a spindle sander. Dark, long-fingered hands handled the object with a skill that was nearly graceful, despite the strength and masculinity that was apparent in their every movement.

The workshop where he was working had been attached to the back of a small log cabin, which sat in a clearing on the side of Sinclair Mountain. When no one had answered his repeated knocks on the front door, Cabot had been drawn around to the back by a sound he hadn't then been able to identify. Now he could.

When he lifted his gaze from the workman's hands, he realized with a sense of shock that the passage of six years had had as little effect on the face of the man he was watching as on those hands. The striking blue eyes were hidden, intent on whatever he was shaping, but the austere, almost forbidding features were exactly as he had remembered them.

"You should never sneak up on a man who's holding a gun," Rafe Sinclair said without glancing up. "I would think you, of all people, would know that."

"Out of practice, I guess," Griff acknowledged, his mouth relaxing into a smile. "Besides, I didn't realize that was a gun."

"This is only the butt. But when it's finished..."

With a tilt of his head, Sinclair indicated the rosewood box that lay open at the end of his workbench. He still hadn't made eye contact with his visitor.

Cabot understood that was deliberate. As deliberate as had been his unannounced arrival. If he had told Rafe Sinclair he was coming, he would have found the North Carolina mountainside deserted.

Griff stepped into the shop, crossing over to the rosewood case to which he'd been directed. The inside was lined with black velvet, still rich if faded with age. Nested against that darkness was a single dueling pistol, incredibly beautiful and yet also obviously, almost obscenely, deadly.

Despite the indention in the lining where a matching pistol should rest, there was only the one. Cabot raised his eyes, examining with renewed interest the object Sinclair was now holding up to the light.

"You're repairing the mate to this?" Griff asked.

"I'm *recreating* the mate."

Cabot looked down again on the weapon in the box. The curved wood of its handle was the same glowing rosewood as the case. Its sides were covered with intricately chased silver, the soft gleam of that precious metal outshining the baser metal of the long barrel.

"You can do that?" he asked. "Duplicate this one?"

"Of course," Sinclair said, looking directly at him for the first time.

The crystalline-blue eyes hadn't changed either, Griff realized. And for some strange reason he found that comforting.

"The only difference between them," Rafe went on, "is that this one will be accurate. If you'd ever fired the one you're looking at, you'd wonder why they bothered with duels. If you needed to be sure of killing your opponent, you'd have been better off beating him to death with it."

Griff laughed, his own knowledge of the notorious inaccuracy of early nineteenth-century firearms affirming the truth of what Sinclair had said. Just as his knowledge of the man who was in the process of reproducing a two-hundred-year-old pistol confirmed that he would do exactly what *he* had claimed.

Rafe Sinclair would build a weapon that would be perfect in every detail, identical to its mate, except for its increased accuracy. That demanding perfectionism, inherent in every task he undertook, had always been this man's gift. Ultimately, it had also been his curse.

"Where did you get them?" Griff asked, in no hurry to broach the subject that had brought him here.

"They belonged to an ancestor of mine. Sebastian Sinclair, who supposedly dropped the missing pistol of that pair into the Thames while he was rescuing his Spanish-born wife."

Griff wondered if that might be where his friend had acquired his Christian name. The source of that "Rafael," always spoken with a true Iberian accent, had always seemed as enigmatic as the man himself.

"Bloody careless of him, if you ask me," Sinclair said, his deep voice lightened with a sudden amusement, "but I don't suppose they were nearly as valuable then as they would be now."

"English," Griff guessed, bending closer to the remaining pistol to examine the workmanship.

"And very fine for the period."

"Just not…fine enough for you?" A smile hovered at the corners of Cabot's mouth as he posed the question.

"It isn't enough to be merely beautiful."

Beautiful *and* deadly. He had thought exactly that before, Griff realized, looking down on the lone dueling pistol.

And the word "deadly" would just as well describe the man before him. At one time Sinclair had been an extremely valuable weapon in the war Griff's division of the CIA had waged against international terrorism. Although the External Security Team had eventually been disbanded by the agency, Sinclair's own departure from the EST had occurred long before that decision had been made.

"What are you doing here, Griff? I thought we had an understanding."

The question brought Cabot's eyes up to focus on the man he had come to see. The inquiry was inevitable, of course, considering who and what they were.

"I'm not here about the Phoenix, although the offer to join us is still open."

The Phoenix Brotherhood was a private organization that had been formed by Cabot and a few of his ex-operatives. No longer under government direction, they set their own agenda, bringing the skills they once had used in the defense of their country to bear on all manner of private problems. As much as he'd like Sinclair to be a part of what they were doing, however, that hadn't been his purpose in seeking him out.

"You were never much inclined to social visits, so…" Rafe walked over to the rosewood box to compare the curve of the handle he'd just created with the original.

"There's something I thought you should see."

Cabot reached into the breast pocket of his blazer and pulled out a folded sheet of paper. He didn't bother to open it before he held it out to Sinclair.

There was a hesitation, long enough that Cabot had time to wonder what he would do if Rafe refused to read the information contained in the security alert. After all, Sinclair had been adamant about leaving the agency, so much so that eventually Griff had been forced to stop arguing against it or risk their friendship.

Finally the blue eyes lifted from the unopened paper. They studied Griff's face for a few seconds before Rafe's lips compressed. Then the same long, scarred fingers that had delicately shaped that piece of rosewood reached out to take the alert.

Sinclair unfolded it with a flick of his wrist, holding the document out between them. His eyes rose again—briefly—as soon as he saw the heading.

Griff could read the question in them, but he didn't bother to respond. There would soon be other questions that would have to be answered.

After a moment Rafe's gaze returned to the alert that had been clandestinely, and illegally, passed on from one of Griff's contacts within the CIA. Carl Steiner had thought this was something he ought to know. As soon as Griff read it, he had called to reserve a seat on the first flight out of Washington.

"Why are you showing this to me?" Rafe asked.

"You're the expert on Jorgensen. I thought if you could shed any light—"

"He's dead," Sinclair said flatly.

There was no overt emotion in the phrase, but his hatred for the man the pronoun referred to permeated each syllable. The force of it held Griff silent for a moment.

"The signature of those last two bombings has been the same. It's distinctive enough that the agency's experts—"

"Screw the agency *and* their experts. I'm telling you Jorgensen is dead."

"There's always the possibility—"

"I watched the bastard die. Whoever this is, it isn't Jorgensen."

Without denying what Rafe had said, Griff let the silence stretch again. The tension it produced grew as the slow seconds ticked off, their eyes locked.

Finally, Griff asked, "And you're willing to stake *her* life on your certainty of that?"

The blue eyes changed, darkening as they always did when Sinclair was angry. Of course, that wasn't all he was seeing in them now, Griff acknowledged. He had known this man too long and too well to be mistaken about what was there.

"You bastard," Rafe Sinclair said, the words so soft they were almost a whisper. "You conniving bastard. You haven't changed at all, have you? You're still doing their dirty work. They sent you here—"

"Nobody sent me," Cabot interrupted, his own anger flaring unexpectedly. "Least of all the agency. I assure you they no longer have the power to send me anywhere." Rafe should know better than that. He should know him better.

"You're here strictly out of friendship." The tone this time was mocking. Sardonic.

"I'm here because I thought you should know about that," Griff said, gesturing with an upward tilt of his chin toward the CIA document. "What you do with the information is up to you. Good luck with the pistol," he added before he turned, striding across the workshop to the outside door.

He had almost reached it when Rafe's voice stopped him.

"If I'm wrong about your motives, I apologize. I'm not wrong about the other. Jorgensen is dead. You can tell Steiner that I guarantee it. Tell him that whoever this is was probably a protégé. An admirer perhaps. Imitation is still the sincerest form of flattery."

"There have been a couple of sightings," Griff said without turning. "One in Bern. Another in Prague."

"There are always sightings. How many times has someone reported that they've seen Mengele?"

It was an apt analogy, given the death and destruction Gunther Jorgensen had been responsible for.

"I thought you should know," Griff said again. "For what it's worth."

He took another step, the next to the last that would carry him out from under the artificial light of the workshop and into the daylight. Automatically, the force of habit too deeply ingrained to deny, his eyes surveyed the panorama spread out before him. Somewhere in the distance a thrush sang. There were no other sounds.

"You ever get the urge to say 'I told you so'?" the man behind him asked.

"Occasionally. I try to resist."

"I'm not sure I'd be able to," Rafe said. And then he added, the mockery wiped from his tone, "Thanks for coming."

There was another long beat of silence.

"Do you know where she is?" Griff asked, and then wished he hadn't.

"Of course," Sinclair said simply.

Unconsciously, Cabot nodded, the movement subtle enough that the man behind him was probably unaware of it. He took a deep breath and stepped through the doorway and out into the slant of late-afternoon sunshine.

He walked to the car he had rented at the Charlotte airport and climbed in without looking back. He was aware almost subliminally as he turned the wheel to pull onto the unpaved drive that Sinclair was standing in the doorway of the workshop, watching him.

And he knew, because they had once been as close as brothers, that the far-seeing gaze of those blue eyes would follow his car until it had disappeared into the twilight haze that gathered over these ancient mountains.

Some things never change.

Chapter One

The woman known as Beth Anderson lifted her hand from the key she'd just inserted into the ignition to adjust the rearview mirror of the SUV, pretending to check her makeup. As an added bit of play-acting, she touched her index finger to the small indention in the center of her top lip as if wiping away a smudge of lipstick.

Not that she could see her lip, since the mirror was focused on the line of cars behind her in the grocery store parking lot. And there was nothing suspicious about any of them. No one suspicious.

With the late-afternoon heat, there was almost no one in the parking lot at all, which made her feel more than a little foolish. It was a feeling she was becoming accustomed to.

She reached up and readjusted the mirror, putting it back into driving position. *Old habits die hard,* she thought. In this case, it was more like a resurrected habit. Resurrected from a life that was long dead.

She couldn't remember making such a conscious effort to be aware of her surroundings in years. All week long, however, she'd had the sensation that someone was watching her. Maybe even following her.

In the quiet, summer sombulance of Magnolia Grove, Mississippi, that was patently ridiculous. And that was exactly what she'd been telling herself since the first flutter of that "eyes on the back of her neck" feeling had drifted along her spine.

She'd been out of the game too long for anyone to be interested in her. Her current position as the junior partner in a two-person law firm had once or twice evoked an angry response from someone she'd gone after in court. No one, including Elizabeth herself, could believe that any of her current cases might generate enough heat to cause someone to trail her around.

The whole thing was ridiculous. There wasn't a single, solitary reason under the sun for anyone to be remotely interested in her daily routine.

Routine. The word reverberated in her consciousness, producing a nagging sense of guilt.

That was one of the first things you were taught. Never establish a routine. Vary your route to and from work. Vary the times you travel it. Vary everything in your existence so that no one can know where you'll be or what you'll be doing at any given moment of the day or night.

She was a little amused at the clarity of her memory. The problem with following those instructions, even if there had been any legitimate reason for doing so, was that there was only one route from her office to the bungalow she'd bought here three years ago. And she didn't exactly set her own hours. She could vary the time she headed home, as she had today, but she was the one who opened the office every morning, promptly at nine o'clock.

She didn't live her life by a routine, she thought, as she released the mirror to turn the key. She had slipped past routine and straight into rut. Small-town rut.

And there's nothing wrong with that, she told herself determinedly, backing quickly out of the parking place. She had had enough excitement to last her a lifetime. All she wanted now was peace and quiet.

Not exactly all, she admitted with a touch of bitterness

as she guided the car out onto the two-lane. Because after all, peace and quiet Magnolia Grove offered in abundance. As for the other…

What was it that Paul Newman had said? Why settle for hamburger when you have steak waiting at home? The analogy didn't quite fit her situation, but she hadn't met anyone in Magnolia Grove remotely interesting enough to compete with her memories.

And that's a hell of a note, she acknowledged.

Maybe that's why she'd been imagining someone following her. Loneliness. Routine. Rut. Boredom.

All of which were why she was here, she reminded herself. This place ranked at the top in the all-time boredom ratings. That's exactly why she had chosen it. Just because she was now having some kind of midlife crisis—

Midlife? Her eyes left the road, lifting to the mirror. Although she had to shift her position in order to accomplish it, this time they examined the reflection of her face, which was reassuringly the same.

Slightly crooked nose, hazel eyes, faint chicken pox scar on her left cheekbone. And, she assessed critically, only a few more lines around her eyes than had ever been there before.

Thirty-four was hardly "midlife." Even if this peculiar sensation of being watched was the product of some sort of dissatisfaction with her present existence, she couldn't legitimately put it down to middle-age angst, thank God.

Her gaze returned to the blacktop stretching before her. Heat waves rose from the asphalt to shimmer and distort the horizon. There wasn't another car in sight. A quick glance in the rearview mirror revealed there was no traffic behind her either.

Nobody was following her. Nobody was the least bit interested in anything she was doing. The idea that someone might be was probably just wishful thinking.

And that's pretty pathetic.

Her mother used to say, ''Be careful what you wish for because you might get it.'' She had wanted peace and quiet and security. And now that she had it…

Pretty damn pathetic, she thought again, pressing her foot down on the gas pedal to take advantage of the long, deserted straightaway that stretched in front of her.

SOMETHING WAS SUBTLY different about the house. She had known it as soon as she opened the back door. Certainly by the time she'd set the groceries she'd picked up on the way home down on the counter.

Her eyes sought the light on the answering machine first, but there were no messages. Even if there had been, that wouldn't have triggered whatever she was feeling.

She was sensitive to atmosphere, as most women were, but she certainly didn't claim to be clairvoyant. Whatever change she sensed here was physical. Something had been moved, perhaps, so that its being out of place made the room feel strange. Or maybe it was a smell. Something that was different from the normal aromas of her home, so familiar that usually they would go unnoticed.

Her gaze traveled slowly around the room. She had opened the kitchen curtains before she'd left for work this morning. Late-afternoon sunlight spilled through the windows over the sink, slanting across the checkerboard pattern of the black-and-white tile floor. Its brightness seemed to belie her uneasiness, which despite any tangible cause was increasing by the second.

She glanced through the doorway that led into the dining room. It was darker in there, at least beyond the reach of the sunlight pouring into the kitchen. Its reflection made the worn hardwood floor just beyond the open doorway gleam.

Nothing in the dining room seemed out of order. No more than it had in here.

She laid her car keys down beside the sack of groceries and took a step toward the front of the house. As she did, it occurred to her that the smart thing to do would be to go outside, to get into her car and to drive back into town to the sheriff's office.

And tell him what? *Something isn't right at my house. I don't like the way it feels.*

She could imagine what a charge the deputies would get out of retelling that story. The sheriff would probably send someone back with her, and when they discovered there was nothing here…

She made her feet take another step and then another, crossing the kitchen with determination if not alacrity. There was no reason for this apprehension, she reiterated doggedly. It was ridiculous. No one knew she was here. And no one here knew who she was.

She had changed her name. Changed her appearance. Changed her life. She wasn't about to go through any of that again because something about this place was suddenly giving her the willies.

She stopped at the dining room door, reaching out to flick the switch for the overhead light. As it scattered the darkness to the periphery of the room, nothing out of the ordinary was revealed.

She took a deep, calming breath. The comforting smell of lemon oil surrounded her. And underlying that—

Her eyes found her collection of antique decanters on the sideboard. One of them was open. Its crystal stopper lay on the polished surface of the buffet. And a tumbler was missing from the silver tray beside it.

At least now she had a rational explanation for what she had been feeling since she'd entered the house. Someone had been here. Or was here.

And judging by his choice of that particular decanter, she knew who. Maybe she had changed everything else about her life, but she still kept the best whiskey she owned in the Waterford. *Routine.*

"What the hell are you doing here, Rafe?" she asked, not bothering to raise her voice. Wherever he was, he would have been watching her since she'd entered the kitchen.

"You've cut your hair."

He always noticed things like that. Maybe too much. Still, the fact that he had noticed, that it mattered enough to him to mention it, caused an unwanted thickness in her throat.

She had spent a very long time without anyone around to notice those things. Not her hair or her clothes or the condition of her soul.

From force of habit, her hand lifted, fingers spread, to rake the chin-length hair back from her face. When she realized what she was doing, she forced her hand down, away from the strands that had once been long enough to tangle around his bare, sweating shoulders as they made love. Long enough to occasionally catch in his early-morning whiskers, the feel of them so sweetly abrasive against her skin.

At the memory, a jolt of sexual heat seared mercilessly along nerve pathways that had seemed atrophied. They weren't. Painfully, unexpectedly, she knew that now.

"What are you doing here?" she asked again, ignoring those unsettling emotions.

He always managed to suck her in that way. Noticing. Caring. Being aware.

So damn aware. Aware of every aspect of her existence, as no one in her entire life before she'd met him had ever been.

Steeling herself to face him, she walked across the dining

room and through the wide double doorway that separated it from the living room. She always kept the French doors open between the two, so that they were really one.

Which meant, she supposed, that after more than five years, she was once more in the same room with Rafe Sinclair. Something she had thought would never happen again.

"And you've lost weight," he added softly.

His voice had come from the shadows near the fireplace. He was standing in the darkest corner of the room, and with the drapes pulled against the force of the afternoon heat, it was very dark indeed.

His left arm was lying along on the top of one of the built-in bookcases that flanked the small fireplace. Sometime in the past a tenant had painted them a glossy white. That paleness provided a stark contrast to the dark gray shirt he wore. It was long-sleeved, buttoned at the cuff, despite the heat.

As her eyes gradually adjusted to the room's dimness, she was able to discern other details. In his left hand, the one resting atop the bookcase, he held the tumbler that had been missing from the sideboard. It was still half-full.

His right arm hung loosely at his side, the fingers of the hand curled slightly inward. He seemed perfectly relaxed, exuding the same aura of confidence that had always been such a part of him.

She hadn't found the courage yet to look at his face. She would have to, of course, but she needed a few seconds to prepare.

He had had that time. He had obviously been watching her since she'd come in through the back door. The place where he was standing gave him the perfect vantage point to do so.

His position had been carefully thought out. That was a lesson he had taught her—to use every advantage your adversary allows. He had given himself both time and opportunity to study her, while she had been completely unaware of him. Unaware and unprepared.

Except she hadn't been. He had at least played fair in that respect.

That's why he'd poured the whiskey. Why he'd left the decanter unstopped. To let her know he was here. She just hadn't figured it out as quickly as she should have.

Out of practice, she acknowledged.

"I asked you a question," she said instead of responding to his comments about her appearance.

That was certainly none of his business, but that wasn't why she didn't respond. There was something too personal about discussing those things with him. Too near an intimacy neither of them wanted.

"Griff came to see me."

Of all the things he might have said to her, that was the last she would have expected. Rafe had made it as clear to Cabot as he had to her that the part of his life that had included them was over and done. She had gotten the message. Maybe Griff had a thicker skin.

"About what?" she asked, beginning to get her equilibrium back.

Her first reaction to his presence had been strictly visceral. Given their history, that was probably inevitable. It didn't mean she couldn't bring her intellect to bear on the reason he was here.

All she needed was a bit of detachment. Surely after nearly six years that would be possible.

"Someone at the agency passed along a security alert. They think Jorgensen may still be alive."

She tried to decide from his tone what he felt about that. As always, it was impossible to read anything from what he'd said. Not unless he wanted her to.

"Griff thought you should be made aware of the possibility," he continued.

Griff thought you should be made aware...

"So why didn't he call me?"

"I assume because he doesn't know how."

"*You* did."

There was no answer. In the dimness she watched as he brought the glass to his lips and took a long swallow of her whiskey. She wondered, feeling slightly vindictive, if he needed it.

"So how did you know how to find me?"

The more important question was, of course, why would you still know how to find me?

"I know how your mind works."

She thought about that for maybe ten seconds. "That's not an answer."

"I trained you."

"Don't you think I might have learned anything after you left?"

There was a small movement at the corner of his mouth. "Probably not."

She resisted the urge to tell him to go to hell. At least she had learned when he was deliberately goading her.

"Okay, so now I'm aware that the company thinks Jorgensen could be alive," she said. "Anything else?"

"I like your house."

"A little place in the suburbs. Isn't that what we all dreamed of?"

"Is it? What you dreamed of, I mean."

You're what I dreamed of. As much as she hated admitting that, she could no more have stopped the thought from forming than she could have stopped herself from entering this room once she had known he was here.

"I guess that would have depended on which day you asked me," she said.

"How about today?"

Inexplicably the tightness in her throat was back. She couldn't think of a single sufficiently cutting thing to say to him.

"I have to put my groceries away," she said instead, the suggestion that he should leave so she could get on with it obvious.

He let the silence lengthen a moment before he broke it.

"They're wrong, but don't take any chances. This may be someone copycatting Jorgensen's agenda. Which might mean they are also targeting his enemies."

"Then why should he be interested in me? I didn't have anything to do with Jorgensen."

"I did. That would have been enough for him. Whoever this is—"

"Couldn't have found me," she broke in. "Not if Griff couldn't. And if you're so concerned, why take a chance on leading him to me?"

"I wasn't followed." He was obviously amused by the idea.

That wasn't based on arrogance, but experience, and as such, she accepted it. Actually she hadn't been worried about Rafe leading him—whoever he might be—to her. She was more curious about why he had come, especially in person. Despite the excuse he had just offered, there must be something more to this visit.

Wishful thinking? She denied that idea, too, as soon as it was born. She had a perfect right to be curious about why Rafe Sinclair would all of a sudden show up on her doorstep after an absence of nearly six years.

"So what are you doing now?" she asked. "Working for Griff?"

"You know about the Phoenix?"

"Rumors," she said, choosing the word with care. She didn't want her feelings about that to be evident.

"They invited you to join."

They hadn't, but since he didn't seem to know they hadn't, she couldn't see any point in telling him.

"Did *you?*" she countered.

He laughed. The sound, low and pleasant and so damned familiar, evoked more memories.

"I think I'm too old to play hero. Somewhere along the way it all seemed to lose its charm."

Somewhere along the way. And she knew exactly where that had been.

"I'll let you get back to your groceries," he said.

In spite of the fact that she had made that suggestion only seconds ago, perversely she had discovered she wasn't ready for him to leave. Not yet ready to let him walk out of her life for perhaps another six years. Perhaps forever.

That would be the smart thing to do, of course. Just let him walk away. Where Rafe Sinclair was concerned, however, she had never managed to do the smart thing. Why start now?

"Have you eaten?"

Even in the dimness she was aware that his eyes widened. He recovered quickly, but no one could completely control that kind of involuntary physiological response. That he had reacted to the invitation at all was promising.

Promising of what? she wondered, disgusted with her near-Pavlovian response to his every action.

"Today?"

"Dinner," she said patiently.

"Is that what's in the sack?"

"It could be."

"And you're suggesting that we sit down and have dinner together?"

"It isn't all that complicated. I'm going to fix something to eat for dinner. Do you want to join me?" she asked, still feigning patience.

That same movement she noticed before touched the corner of his mouth. "Actually, it might be better if I waited until after dark to leave. Since you're concerned about security."

"I'm not concerned about security. I just wondered why you aren't."

"I told you. I wasn't followed."

"Then there's no reason to wait until after dark to leave, is there?"

This time he laughed. And again that small frisson of sexual reaction stirred deep within her lower body.

"You're a damned ungracious hostess, Elizabeth. Whatever happened to Southern hospitality?"

"I don't know. I'm not Southern."

"I swear there's a trace of an accent."

"Hardly," she said dismissively. "Are you staying or not?"

She could tell he was fighting another smile, which made her regret her impulsive invitation. Maybe he would refuse.

"Of course I am. I can't tell you how long it's been since I've had a home-cooked meal."

Chapter Two

"You never told me what you're doing now," she said, lifting her wineglass to rest the globe against her cheek.

It was something he had seen her do a hundred times. One of a dozen gestures that had been achingly familiar during the few short hours they had spent together.

He couldn't explain why he'd accepted her invitation to dinner. No more than he imagined she could have explained why she'd issued it.

Curiosity, perhaps. A longing to recapture something that had been lost. And he refused, even to himself, to articulate what that was.

At least her tension, which had made the first few minutes difficult for both of them, had gradually dissipated. The wine they'd consumed while he'd watched her cook and during the course of the meal might have had more to do with that than any relaxation of the strain their long separation had caused.

After all, he rarely drank, and Elizabeth had never had a head for alcohol. It was one of the small, endearing cracks in the facade of absolute control she'd assumed while she was with the CIA.

It must have been hard being one of the few women on the team. Not that she'd ever had any reason to apologize to any of them for her femininity.

"This and that," he said aloud. "Consulting mostly."

"Privately?"

"Of course."

He had no desire to be at the government's beck and call. In his opinion, what the agency had done to Griff's people had bordered on the criminal, which was why the idea that Steiner had been the one who had passed on the information about Jorgensen nagged at him. He didn't buy altruistic motivations from anyone at the CIA. Not any longer.

"How about you?" he asked, lifting his own glass to finish the remaining swallow of wine it contained.

"You know what I'm doing. Why pretend that you don't?"

He looked at her over the rim before he lowered the glass, allowing his lips to slant into a smile.

"Convention," he suggested. "It's not considered polite to spy on people."

"Unless you *are* a spy, of course."

"Of course," he agreed calmly.

"So why spy on me?"

"I told you. Griff wanted you to know that the company thinks Jorgensen's alive."

"But you weren't totally sure I needed to know that."

"Because I'm totally sure he's dead."

"Did you kill him?"

No one else on the team would have asked him that question. Not even Griff. For a split second he considered refusing to answer it, but in some oblique way she was the one person who had a right to know.

"Yes," he said calmly, setting his glass back on the table.

She nodded as if that confession were only what she had expected. "Did it help?"

Had it? At least the bastard wasn't blowing people to shreds anymore.

Except, according to Steiner, he was. Or someone using his methodology was.

"There's always someone willing to take their place."

With the change in pronouns, he had broadened the discussion to include not only the German-born terrorist he'd killed, but all those who preyed on innocents to advance their various and sundry political causes.

"Or yours."

"That *has* occurred to me."

It took her a second, but then she had always been very bright. "You think Griff is using you? Because you were their expert on Jorgensen?"

"I think *Steiner* is using *him*."

"Griff isn't anyone's fool. Not even the CIA's."

She put her glass back on the table without finishing her wine. Then she stood, the movement abrupt. She laid her napkin down and picked up her plate and flatware. As she reached across the table to remove his, she met his eyes.

"You aren't going after whoever this is, are you?"

"It isn't my job," he said.

She completed the motion she'd begun, stacking his plate atop hers before she looked up at him again.

"There was a time when it wouldn't have been 'a job.'"

There had been, he thought, but it had been almost too long ago to remember what that felt like.

"There was a time when we wouldn't be sitting here acting like a couple of strangers forced to have an uncomfortable dinner together," he said. "Things change."

She held his eyes a few seconds before she nodded. Then she turned, carrying the dishes into the kitchen.

When she disappeared through the doorway, he leaned back in his chair, taking a breath to relieve the sudden tightness in his chest. It wasn't the only constriction he was aware of. Although his jeans were well worn, their fabric thin with age, they were suddenly uncomfortably restrictive.

The strength of his erection was unexpected. And unwanted. There could be few things as embarrassing as the undeniable physical evidence of how much you still wanted the woman you had walked out on.

There was a time when we wouldn't be sitting here acting like a couple of strangers forced to have an uncomfortable dinner together.

That had been a hell of an understatement. From the day they'd met, they had both been aware of the sexual pull between them. They had later admitted knowing even then that it would eventually lead to intimacy. What neither of them had suspected was how strong that attraction would prove to be. Or how powerfully addictive it would become.

Which was why he hadn't trusted himself to see her in all these years. If things had been different...

They hadn't been. They weren't now.

"I could make coffee."

He glanced up to find her standing in the doorway. They had eaten by candlelight, something that was ritual. She had turned on the light in the kitchen when she'd carried the dishes there, and she was now silhouetted against its glow.

She *had* lost weight, he noticed again, although there had always been something about her figure, at least when clothed, that hinted at the slim, almost boyish fitness of a well-conditioned athlete. The short sun-streaked hair now emphasized that quality without making her seem any less feminine.

With their history, there was probably nothing that could do that. Not for him.

"I have to go," he said, pushing up from the table before he remembered the too revealing tightness of his jeans.

Perhaps it wouldn't be obvious if he stayed in the candlelit dimness of the dining room. Of course, that wasn't the only reason he should resist the urge to close the distance between them.

During dinner he had occasionally caught the faintest hint of her perfume, its fragrance released by the warmth of the sultry Mississippi night's humidity against her skin. It had been evocative of nights when that same scent had filled his nostrils while his lips trailed kisses over the silken smoothness of her body. There was no need to add the temptation of physical nearness to the potent force of those memories.

"Thank you for bringing me Griff's warning," she said formally.

She raised her hand, pushing back the hair that had fallen over her forehead. The gesture was quick, hinting at nervousness. It seemed that the earlier strain was back, although her voice had been perfectly level.

Then she held the same hand out to him. He might have been amused at her offer to shake hands with him if he hadn't still been dealing with all those other emotions. Ones that didn't lend themselves to amusement.

It would be far better to stay on this side of the room. To ignore the proffered hand.

Better perhaps, but not possible.

He pushed his chair back and took the four or five steps that would bring him to stand directly in front of her. There was enough difference in their heights that she had to tilt her head to meet his eyes.

As she did, he took the hand she held out to him. After dealing with the assault of his own emotions, it should have been gratifying to find that her fingers were both cold and trembling.

It wasn't. It made him want to fold them into the warmth of his or to press them against his suddenly increased heartbeat. Or, even more tempting, to use them to draw her to him. To put his arms around her and hold her close, comforting whatever made her tremble, if only for a moment.

As it always had with them, however, one thing would surely lead to another, even after six years. They had come too far to destroy whatever peace of mind either of them had achieved in that time. That wasn't why he had come.

"Be careful," he said without releasing her hand.

"I have been. I just didn't know why. Not until you showed up."

Tonight her eyes were more green than hazel, he decided, examining her face in the revealing light spilling from the kitchen. And the years had wrought remarkably few changes there. Maybe the lines at the corners of her eyes had been graven a little more deeply and the delicate curve of her cheekbone had become slightly more pronounced.

Her nose was still crooked, having been broken in some high school soccer game. There was a small patch of sunburned skin across its narrow bridge, emphasizing the freckles she never bothered to conceal with makeup.

"Thank you for inviting me to dinner," he said.

"Thank you for staying." This time her voice was touched with humor.

Hearing it, he smiled at her. Then, the commonplaces taken care of, neither of them seemed to know what to do next.

It had almost been easier the first time he'd walked away, he thought before he recognized that for the lie it was. There had been nothing harder than that in his life. And nothing more necessary.

He released her hand and quickly pushed past her through the doorway. It was narrow enough that his body brushed hers, his shoulder turning hers slightly.

He didn't look back as he crossed the kitchen. As a precaution, he flicked off the light, using the switch beside the back door to plunge the room into darkness. Then he stepped out into the honeysuckle-scented night, closing behind him a door he should never have reopened.

ELIZABETH HAD STOOD in the kitchen a long time before she finally walked back into the dining room. The candles had burned long enough that they were beginning to sputter, wax pooling at the base of the holder.

In the darkness after she'd extinguished them, she put her palms flat on the surface of the table, leaning forward tiredly, her head bowed. She didn't understand why she was so exhausted. After all, nothing had happened. Nothing at all.

Rafe had been given a message for her from Griff, and he had delivered it. Other than his comment about a couple of strangers forced to have an uncomfortable dinner together there had been almost nothing of a personal nature in their conversation.

Not unless you considered her question about whether he had killed Jorgensen personal. He hadn't seemed to. He had reacted to that exactly as he had to everything she'd said the last time she'd talked to him. Contained. Controlled. Cold.

That coldness had been one of the things that had been so hard to accept. She could understand his anger with the agency, but not why it had also been directed at her. As she'd reminded him tonight, she'd had nothing to do with Gunther Jorgensen.

She straightened, the same questions that had circled endlessly through her brain all those years ago there again. She had found no explanation for what he had done then. Nor was she likely to now.

Why the hell had he shown up here now? she thought with a surge of fury. And why the hell had she invited him to dinner? It seemed that in the silent darkness she could still feel him, just as she had been aware of him watching her all week without understanding what she was feeling.

Now the sense of him was here. Inside her home, her sanctuary. A physical invasion that stirred more memories than she was prepared to deal with.

She turned her head, looking across the dark kitchen to the back door, reminding herself of the reality of his departure. She walked over to that door, turning the latch and hooking the chain into its slot.

She didn't look out into the night revealed through the panes of glass that comprised the door's top half. Rafe had known as well as she did that if he had wanted to stay, she wouldn't have refused.

He hadn't wanted to. And that in itself should be a sufficient answer for all the questions she had wrestled with since the last time he'd left her.

"DAMN IT TO HELL," she said, the expletive muttered under her breath. Not that there was anyone to hear if she had shouted it, which was what she felt like doing.

She'd overslept. Considering the number of hours she'd spent tossing and turning before she'd fallen asleep, that was hardly surprising. On top of that, she had forgotten to set the alarm. And now she was faced with the nearest thing to a morning rush hour Magnolia Grove had to offer.

A logging truck had pulled out onto the two-lane just ahead of her. The red flag at the end of the longest trunk it carried fluttered directly in front of her car as the heavily ladened truck slowed to pull the grade. She glanced at her watch, realizing that despite how much she had hurried to get dressed and out of the house, she was going to be at least a quarter of an hour late in opening the office.

No big deal, she told herself.

Unless he was in court, Darrell never showed up before ten or eleven, his summer seersucker already rumpled from the twenty-mile drive in from the antebellum home the Connell family had lived in since it had been built. Neither of them had any appointments scheduled for this morning. There would be no one waiting for her, so she couldn't quite figure out why she was so upset by the idea that she was going to be late.

Maybe because Rafe Sinclair could simply waltz back into her life after six years and throw everything about her well-ordered existence into disarray. Not only emotionally, but professionally as well. She didn't like admitting he had the power to do that.

She eased across the center line, trying to see if she could pass the truck on the straightaway leading down the other side of the rise they'd just topped. Typical of her morning, there was a line of cars approaching from the opposite direction.

She moved the SUV back into position behind the dangling logs, reconciling herself to the reality of the situation. She was going to be late, and it was ridiculous to let it upset her.

It wouldn't have, she admitted, if she hadn't already been thrown by last night. And she couldn't understand why she had been. It wasn't as if they'd spent the meal talking about old times. That was something they had seemed to agree on—tacitly, of course. There was no point in dredging up the past, not even the good parts of it.

There had been plenty of those, she admitted. Enough that what had followed had been painful in the extreme.

After the embassy bombing in Amsterdam, Rafe had been furious with the government's restraint in going after the people responsible. Since he had been on the scene of the attack, dealing with the cost of that particular act of terrorism up close and very personally, she certainly couldn't blame him. None of them did.

Not even for his decision to disassociate himself from an

agency that refused to let him track down the killers of those dozens of people. Griff had tried to reason with him, arguing that despite the agency's restrictions in this case, he could do more by working with the team, which had been expressly created to deal with those problems, than from without.

Nothing Cabot could say had changed Rafe's mind. And she had never blamed him for that decision. It was the one that followed that she'd never been able to understand or to forgive. The one to disassociate himself from her as well.

It made no sense. It hadn't then, and it didn't now. She had even offered to leave the CIA with him, something which, looking back on that time from a distance of several years, caused a wave of humiliation to wash over her.

That offer had been against every principle she'd ever thought she held. After all, it hadn't been easy reaching the level she had attained in that male-dominated agency. She had been one of the few women Griff tapped for the team, and she had proposed to give it all up to be with a man.

A man who had thrown the proffered sacrifice back in her teeth, disappearing without any explanation of why he didn't want her to come with him. And apparently without any regret.

She took a breath, deliberately loosening the death grip her fingers had taken around the wheel. *Water over the dam. Over and done with a long time ago.*

If so, why the hell had he come back into her life?

Nothing of what he'd said had rung completely true, she thought again as she turned off the two-lane onto the road that led into town. That was one of the conclusions she'd come to during those sleepless hours last night. There was more to this reappearance than Griff's warning.

There was nothing on the road ahead of her, but despite its emptiness she didn't pick up speed. Unconscious now of the fact that she was going to be late in opening the office for the first time in three years, she went over again in her mind all the things Rafe had said last night. And the way he'd looked as he'd said them.

It wasn't that she didn't think he was telling the truth, she reaffirmed, slowing for the first of the three stoplights that regulated traffic on Main Street. It was that he wasn't telling the *whole* truth.

There was something she wasn't getting about this, just as she had always known there was something she hadn't gotten about his disappearance six years ago. Something about both that didn't quite add up with what she knew about Rafe Sinclair.

She slowed, pulling into the familiar parking space in front of the office. It wasn't marked Reserved, but it might as well have been. No one in town would have thought about parking in her spot or Darrell's.

She glanced at her watch again. It was nine-twenty, the office wasn't open, and the world hadn't come to an end. She needed to remember that the next time she got so damned anal.

She picked up her purse and the papers she'd taken home with her last night. Not that they had gotten read.

Of course, there was no hurry about that, either. That was part of the charm of living here. This compulsion to get things done on some kind of schedule was all hers.

She opened the door, stepping out into the heat that would become more oppressive as the day wore on. It was going to be a scorcher, as they said down here. A good day for staying inside by the air conditioner, she decided, skilled by now at evaluating the potential heat index.

It would also be a good day for finding enough work to keep her mind occupied with something besides the events of last evening. Or, rather, she amended, the nonevents of last evening.

She slammed the car door, pressing the auto-lock button

on her key. At that exact instant a blast of heat and sound roiled upward from the heart of the law office, tearing it apart.

The resulting shock wave threw her backward. Her head and shoulders slammed against the pavement with enough force that for a moment she could neither breathe nor think. And then the debris of the building she should have been inside at least twenty minutes ago began to rain down around her.

Chapter Three

Rafe awakened, as he had a thousand times, to the sound of the explosion. His body jerked upright in bed, his heart trying to beat its way out from under the sweat-drenched skin of his chest. He opened his mouth, attempting to draw air into lungs compressed by the force of the blast.

It's just a dream. Plain vanilla, garden-variety nightmare.

He had had enough of those, God knew, that he should be able to tell the difference. As horrific as they were, they were a million times better than the other.

Finally, shaking all over, he managed to take a breath. It seemed he could smell the smoke. He could almost taste it on the cotton dryness of his tongue.

Just another dream, he reassured himself.

He opened his eyes, slitting them against the painful stab of sunshine pouring through the crack he'd inadvertently left between the halves of the motel's plastic-backed drapes when he'd closed them last night. He ran his tongue around parched lips as his heart rate began to slow.

As soon as the frantic pulse of blood through the veins in his ears eased, another sound replaced it. Distant at first and indistinct, within seconds an identification of what he was hearing roared into his consciousness. *Siren.*

He listened, again not breathing. Sometimes he couldn't

tell, but he would have staked his life that what he was hearing now was real. A real siren, and therefore… *Real smoke?*

He tore at the sheet, frantically trying to free his legs from its tangling hold. He staggered a little when his feet touched the floor, but that was only reaction to the flood of adrenaline coursing into his bloodstream.

When he reached the window, he lifted his arm, intending to sweep the curtain aside so that he could see out. He couldn't force his hand to grasp the material. It was as if the muscles were literally paralyzed.

Cop chasing a speeder, he told himself. Or an ambulance carrying some poor bastard with a heart attack to the hospital. Whatever is outside these windows, it won't be what was there before.

Sweat beaded his forehead as he willed his fingers to close over the fabric of the drapes, jerking them to the side. Light flooded the room, forcing him to close his eyes. When he opened them, the pillar of oily black smoke was all he could see. All his mind could grasp.

Smoke. Fire. Explosion.

It hadn't been a dream. The evidence of its stark reality was right before him.

Except he had long ago learned not to trust "reality." Not his. Not about something like this.

He closed his eyes, deliberately holding them shut as tightly as he could for a few seconds before he opened them again. Nothing had changed. The column of smoke still obscured the sky, and that first lonely siren had now been joined by a chorus of others.

He lowered his gaze, examining the rest of the scene revealed by the opened curtain. Parking lot. Cars, most of them recent models. A motel sign.

One he recognized from having glanced at it last night

when he'd checked in. Reassured by that recognition, he lifted his eyes again.

The smoke seemed to be billowing upward from behind the row of buildings across the street. Which meant that the fire was at least a block away, he decided, feeling the adrenaline rush begin to ease. Maybe two. No more than that.

Of course, in Magnolia Grove two blocks was practically across town. Almost—

With the realization, his heart rate, which had almost returned to normal, accelerated like a trip hammer. He ran across the room, scrambling through the sheet he'd thrown aside, trying to locate his jeans.

He dragged them on, hopping awkwardly on one foot and then the other. He pushed his feet into his shoes, not bothering to find his socks. On the way to the door, he grabbed the shirt he'd worn yesterday off the chair where he'd thrown it down on his way to bed.

As soon as he stepped outside, a wall of heat hit him, almost forcing him back. His first response, emotional rather than intellectual, was that it was from the fire. *Just like before.*

It took a few seconds to realize that what he was feeling was simply a typical Mississippi-in-August heat. The air, however, was thick and acrid with smoke. Just as it had been in his dream.

Or maybe this time there hadn't been a dream. Maybe what had awakened him had been a real explosion, one that had started this fire. And if so...

He was already running toward the source of the smoke, and he wasn't the only one. People were rushing out of the surrounding buildings, heading toward the wail of the sirens and the black cloud that seemed to fill the sky.

Despite his lack of familiarity with the town's landmarks, his usually unerring sense of direction led him straight to his destination. As he neared it, he knew with a wave of terror that he hadn't been wrong.

The office where Elizabeth worked was on this street. The same street from where that ominous pillar of smoke was rising.

As he rounded the corner, he made a quick visual assessment. Despite the widespread effects of the blast, there was no doubt in his mind that the structure on fire was the law office of Connell and Anderson.

And with a renewed sense of panic he realized he had no idea what time it was. No idea what time Elizabeth normally arrived at work.

Then his searching eyes found her. She was standing, talking to a fireman or paramedic. There was no blood on her clothing, but even from here he could tell her face was completely without color, the scattering of freckles stark against the milk-white skin.

Still, she was standing. Talking. Not bleeding. Apparently unharmed. His knees almost gave way with the force of his relief.

He closed his eyes in an unspoken prayer of thanks. It was a mistake, but by the time he was aware of that, it was too late to do anything about it. Images began to unwind, like the flickering frames of an old newsreel, against the blackness behind his lids.

They weren't from any newsreel, of course. And they were all in color. The vivid, shocking brightness of freshly spilled blood. The grotesque black of skin that has been charred, peeling off the arm of a woman whose mouth was open, silently imploring him to help her.

At that moment someone running down the street careened into him. The force of collision was enough to turn him, causing him to stumble against the side of a building.

The impact of his fall or the roughness of the brick as his cheek scraped against it was enough to tear him out of the flashback. He opened his eyes, seeing in front of him the scene he had been watching before it began.

Elizabeth was still in the center of his vision. Mouth moving, she was pointing toward the line of cars parked in front of the burning building. They were close enough to the fire that the paint on their hoods was starting to blister. Just like—

He jerked his mind from that comparison, concentrating instead on Elizabeth. *Not the woman in the embassy,* he told himself doggedly. *This was not the same situation. Nothing about it was the same.*

He started to run again, feeling as if he were moving through quicksand. The distance between them seemed vast and immeasurable, but he never took his eyes off his goal. Never allowed himself to think about anything other than reaching it. Reaching her.

He knew the exact second when she became aware of him. She had been talking to another of the firemen, but when her eyes locked with his, her mouth stopped moving, remaining open as if frozen in midsentence.

At her sudden silence the two men standing beside her turned to stare at him as well. One of them moved between him and Elizabeth, the gesture obviously protective.

Rafe's response was nothing short of murderous. *Get the hell out of my way, you son of a bitch.* He didn't say that. He had no breath, and his mouth was too dry to form the words.

Elizabeth moved from behind the fireman, quickly taking the last few steps that would close the distance between them. There could have been nothing more natural than to take her in his arms. He had wanted to do that last night, despite everything he understood about how unwise it would be for both of them. That wasn't what stopped him now.

There was less than two feet between them when their

forward motion ground to a halt. She was again looking up at him, her head slightly raised because of the difference in their heights.

A cone of silence descended around him, blocking out the noises of the sirens, the pressure hoses, the shouts from the firemen fighting the blaze. All he could hear was his own breathing, harsh and panting from the exertion of his run.

Terrifyingly, the smell of the fire was all around him. The heat of it.

Elizabeth didn't say a word, widened eyes searching his face. He couldn't imagine what he looked like. Deranged, perhaps. Maybe even dangerous. Enough like a lunatic to cause the fireman to edge closer again.

She lifted her hand. For an instant he thought she intended to touch his face, but instead she pressed the tips of her fingers, trembling as they had been last night, against the center of his heaving chest.

"Rafe?"

God, he wanted to touch her. Just to take her hand as he had last night.

He didn't, of course, because he was afraid that if he gripped her arm, her skin would slip off muscle and bone to lie in his hand as it had before.

That wasn't here. Not Elizabeth. Not now.

"What the hell happened?" he managed to rasp.

She shook her head, her eyes never leaving his face. "I don't know. It just…blew up. They think maybe there was a gas leak."

He laughed, the sound a breath, devoid of amusement. "They'd be wrong."

Her eyes changed, understanding of what he meant invading them as he watched.

"You think…" The sentence trailed. Once more she shook her head, the gesture small, denying. Her mouth worked and then she tried again. "You can't possibly believe—"

"Come on," he ordered.

He didn't touch her, although by now the few words they'd exchanged had reoriented him. He knew where he was. And there was no doubt in his mind who she was.

Still, he didn't dare put his hands on her. Not yet. No matter how much he wanted to.

"Come where?"

"Away from here."

"I have to talk to the chief. There are questions that have to be—"

"Screw the questions. They'll figure it out. They don't need you to do that."

"Rafe," she protested.

She'd been out of this business too long. Her instincts were to respond to something like this in a rational way. Despite the time that had passed, his were not. His were all of the get-the-hell-out-of-Dodge variety.

The authorities could sort through cause-and-effect to their bureaucratic heart's content. Meanwhile, he'd have her safe somewhere a thousand miles from here. Somewhere this time where that frigging terrorist bastard could never find her.

"Ms. Anderson?"

Elizabeth turned, removing her fingers from his chest. It was as if his connection to the present had been unplugged. He felt the familiar disconnect start and fought it, concentrating fiercely on maintaining contact with her and what was happening.

Her mouth was moving, but for a few seconds he couldn't make sense of the words. He concentrated on doing that, forcing his mind to remain focused on the here and now.

It was a struggle, given the stimuli provided by the sights

and sounds around them. He couldn't afford to think about those. Not about the heat of the fire or the smells of it or the sounds of the sirens.

He forced himself to think only about Elizabeth's mouth until eventually the words she was saying to the man he'd identified as Magnolia Grove's fire chief began to form a pattern. To make sense.

"…a friend of mine from out of town. He was naturally concerned for me."

Because I'm the only one who knows what the hell is going on here.

"We just need to ask you a few more questions, ma'am. Then Tommy thinks you ought to ride on in to the hospital and get checked out. You could have a concussion."

"I'm fine."

"You can't be too careful with a head injury."

Head injury. She had a head injury?

Cautiously, Rafe allowed his gaze to leave Elizabeth's mouth, focusing on her head. Her hair was full of ash, but there were no bruises visible under the strands that fell forward over her forehead.

"You hit your head?" he demanded, his voice more normal.

She turned her attention to him, drawing the chief's there, too. "The blast knocked me flat on my back. I think I hit it on the pavement. I remember looking up at the smoke. Then things were just falling out of the sky…"

As explanations went, it was fairly disjointed. Reassuringly normal.

She'd been the one at the center of the firestorm this time. She was bound to be affected, emotionally if not physically. And there was always the possibility that there *was* some injury. A lot of head stuff didn't show up until it was too late.

"How far's the hospital?" he asked.

The chief answered, his eyes still evaluating him. "Thirty miles or so. Mostly interstate."

"Okay," he said.

"I don't need to go to the hospital," Elizabeth protested.

Maybe it would be better just to put her in his car and take her somewhere. Anywhere. Any emergency room would do. After all, he couldn't see any sign that she was concussed.

That meant zilch with a head injury. He'd seen men walking around one minute and keel over the next from the pressure of internal bleeding. Or go to sleep, believing they were perfectly fine, and never wake up.

It wasn't a chance he was willing to take. Not with Elizabeth.

"You need a scan," he said. "That way—"

"I don't *need* to go to the hospital," she said, raking her hair back with characteristic impatience. "Don't you think I'd know if I were injured?"

"No," he said. The word was unequivocal, as was the demand in its tone.

Her mouth tightened, but she didn't argue. She turned back to the chief instead. "What else do you need to know?"

The fireman's eyes met Rafe's, holding on them briefly before he answered.

"Nothing we can't get later," he said. "The fire marshal will need to examine the scene after we get the blaze controlled and things cool down. That'll take a couple of days. We can always get back to you if we have other questions then. You go on now and get that scan. Smartest thing you can do."

"Come on," Rafe said again.

It would have been easier to take her elbow and physically insist she get into the waiting ambulance, and it should have been okay by now to do that. He didn't risk it. Not with the sounds and the smells associated with the fire still going on in the background.

He had successfully locked them out of his consciousness, but there was no guarantee that something wouldn't happen that he wasn't prepared for. Something that might trigger another flashback. That also was not a risk he was willing to take.

He debated asking the driver to wait until he could get his car so he could follow the ambulance. That way they could leave from the hospital without coming back here.

There were a couple of problems with that. He wasn't willing to leave Elizabeth alone even for the time it would take for him to run back to the motel. And he doubted she'd be willing to leave town with only the clothes on her back. Especially if they were telling her that the explosion had been the result of a gas leak. Especially if she believed them.

He didn't, not for one minute, but there wasn't much point in arguing the theory with the chief. That was something the fire marshal could sort out when he arrived.

By the time he had, he and Elizabeth would be long gone.

Chapter Four

"I told you," she said.

She still looked like warmed-over death, but according to the emergency room attending, the CT had revealed nothing troublesome. They'd been given the general precautions, but thank God, precautions were all they were.

"You never could resist saying 'I told you so,'" he said, taking her elbow.

He didn't even have to think about the wisdom of doing that now. It was strange, but a hospital, despite the time he'd spent in a couple of them after the bombing, had never been a trigger for the flashbacks.

"I didn't get the opportunity nearly as often as I'd have liked," she said.

"So no chance to develop any willpower."

"This isn't the way—" she began, pulling against his direction.

He put his hand against the small of her back, applying pressure. "It's the way we're going."

"But the front is that way."

"Exactly," he said, steering her in the opposite direction.

He knew the scan had been a necessity, but it had also increased the risk that the terrorist would have time to zero in on their location and to make other plans. Of course, if he were typical, he would have been watching them from the first. Especially staying around to watch the fireworks. They could never resist that. Not even the best of them.

"You really think someone set off that explosion?" she asked, finally giving in and allowing him to guide her.

"Let's just say the timing seems coincidental."

"Between Steiner's warning and this?"

He nodded, not bothering to articulate the obvious.

"But you didn't know he was here when you came."

"How could I?"

He opened the door to a corridor marked Authorized Personnel Only, directing her down it as if he knew where he was going. He did have a fairly good idea, having studied the fire exit chart in the emergency room while they'd waited.

"I thought that's why you were here."

"I was here to deliver Griff's message."

"And it took you a week to decide to do that."

He was trying to figure out which way to go since the corridor they'd been following had come to an abrupt dead end. What she had just said didn't register for a moment.

"I told you. I knew Jorgensen was dead."

Actually, it hadn't taken him an entire week to finish the dueling pistol. The whole time he'd worked, the chilling words of that security alert haunted him, warring with his certainty that whoever had blown up the barracks in Greenland and the ambassador's residence in Madrid, it hadn't been Jorgensen. In the end, despite his surety, he had come to deliver the warning. He had known he'd never be able to forgive himself if there was anything to Griff's concern. Apparently there had been.

"So you hung around here just watching me?"

"I didn't get into town until yesterday," he said, confused by her questions.

He'd driven all night and most of the day yesterday, but

he liked to drive. He especially liked it at night, when there was little traffic and long stretches of darkness and silence.

She stopped, pulling against his hold. He turned his head and found that although her gaze was on his face, it seemed unfocused. She was obviously thinking about something other than his features.

"What's wrong?" he asked.

"*Someone's* been following me. I could feel them. All week. When you showed up last night, I naturally assumed it had been you."

"You saw somebody?"

She shook her head, her gaze still contemplative.

"Nothing. Not a sign of anyone. I put it down to paranoia *because* I never saw them. When you came to the house—" She broke off the explanation, her eyes lifting to his, seeing him this time. "I thought I hadn't seen anyone *because* it was you."

If someone had been following her all week, then he hadn't led them to her, which was a consolation. He had taken every precaution he could think of, and as she had intimated, he was very good at what he did. Still, there had been a niggling guilt in the back of his mind that he might have been responsible for giving away her location.

"Is it possible this *is* Jorgensen?" she asked.

"No," he said, urging her forward again.

He had told Griff the truth. He had watched the bastard die. He was willing to concede this might be a protégé or a colleague, someone Jorgensen had trained, but it couldn't be the man himself. He was sure of that.

The fact that whoever it was had been watching Elizabeth all week was significant, however, because nothing had happened until he'd shown up. Whoever this was had been waiting for him to arrive.

The explosion had been for his benefit. Arranged so that when Rafe heard the noise and smelled the smoke, he would believe exactly what he *had* believed—that this time Elizabeth had been the victim.

"Then who set off that explosion?" she asked.

"Someone who wanted me to think you were inside that building. If this had been Jorgensen, believe me, he would have made sure."

There was a small hesitation, and then she said, "I should have been."

"What?" He had been only half listening, wondering if the bomber could possibly know why his ruse had been so successful.

"I should have been in the office this morning. He knew that because he'd been watching me all week. He knew what time I get there every day. And then...this morning I was late."

A coldness settled in Rafe's stomach as he began to understand the implications of what she was saying.

"It should have been deliberate," she went on. "Being late, I mean. I thought yesterday that I'd fallen into a routine. They always told us that was dangerous."

It was. *If* you had any reason to believe you might be a target for someone. After all these years Elizabeth shouldn't have had reason to believe that. He hadn't.

"He could have set his damn watch by me," she said bitterly. "I turn the key in that lock every morning at precisely nine o'clock. Except this morning—"

"You were late," he finished for her, beginning to accept the idea that the explosion might not have been for show. Perhaps the bomber *had* been waiting for him to arrive, but maybe what he had prepared for Rafe to see wasn't what had occurred.

Elizabeth's mouth tightened. "I couldn't sleep. I forgot to set the alarm. And then a logging truck pulled out onto the highway ahead of me. Normally there would have been plenty of time despite that, but this morning..." Again her voice faded. "I should have been there," she said softly. "In the office. I would have been if it hadn't been for that truck."

And if it hadn't been for him showing up at her house yesterday. She wouldn't admit that, but the truth of it had been revealed by her admission that she hadn't slept and by her failure to set the alarm. He didn't really need to hear her confess the reason those two things had happened.

It would be a step back to the personal. Back to things he didn't want to talk about any more than she did. Back to the need for some explanation of why he'd left.

He could make one. He could tell her all the things that he'd never been willing to share before. He had thought about doing that a thousand times.

Even if she knew, even if she understood, it wouldn't change a thing. Nothing could.

He had always known that one night, as he took her into his arms, feeling the sensual slide of sweat-moistened skin against his, she would suddenly become the woman from the embassy. The woman with the silent scream. The woman who had died in his arms.

And when that happened, she would know everything he had come to know about himself. That was the one thing he had known he couldn't live with—what would be in her eyes when she looked at him then.

THE CAB he'd called before they left the emergency room had been waiting at the back entrance when they finally made their way through the maze of hospital corridors. The driver, an elderly black man, had been eager to talk about the explosion in Magnolia Grove.

According to him, everyone was buying into the fire chief's explanation that it had been caused by a gas leak. From their perspective, that was probably a good thing, Rafe decided.

It wouldn't stand up to an arson investigation, of course. And he'd be willing to bet that the methodology used in this bombing, the so-called signature of the bomber, would be identical to that used in those that had precipitated the CIA security alert Griff had shown him.

By the time that had all been determined, he'd have Elizabeth away. With the care the CIA had taken in destroying any link between the people on Griff's team and the agency itself, no one would ever connect Magnolia Grove, Mississippi, or Beth Anderson to those acts of terrorism.

Rafe had every confidence that he could keep her safe. The most dangerous aspect would be getting her out of town, simply because that's where the terrorist was. Or maybe he was wrong about that. Maybe this guy wasn't one of those who waited around to glory in the results. *And maybe pigs can fly.*

"Drive around the block," he instructed the cabbie as they approached the motel.

Despite the ongoing excitement a couple of streets away, the parking lot looked reassuringly empty in the early-afternoon heat. Most of the cars that had been there when he'd pulled aside the drapes this morning had since disappeared, moving on to their next destination.

His own sat fairly isolated among the remaining vehicles. It looked the same as it had when he'd parked it there last night. Of course, looking the same and being the same were vastly different.

All kinds of things might have been done to it in that time frame. Something could have been attached to it, for example. A device set to explode when he turned the key in the ignition. Or when he unlocked the door.

"Want me to drive around again, boss?" the cabbie asked after he'd made the slow circuit of the block.

Not much point, Rafe decided. There was only one way

to tell if the room or his car had been tampered with. "That's okay," he said. "Pull up near Room 18."

"You got it."

The cabbie maneuvered his ancient sedan into one of the parking spaces that had opened up in front of the room since Rafe had left it on foot this morning. Rafe added a generous tip to the fare and handed it to the driver across the bench-type front seat. "Thanks for coming all the way out to the hospital."

"Glad to do it. Ain't nothing else happening around here. Not with all that commotion going on. Least the air-conditioning in the car works. Cooler here than at home," the old man said, carefully folding the bills and putting them in the breast pocket of his cotton sports shirt.

Rafe didn't argue the point, although the air inside the cab wasn't appreciably cooler than that he stepped out into. He had thought it was hot this morning, but the afternoon's heat was a physical assault.

He glanced at Elizabeth's face as she slid across the cracked vinyl seat and climbed out, using his hand for support. The nearer they had gotten to town, the quieter she had become. Now her expression was closed, her face still colorless, the features pinched with the strain of the last few hours.

She waited until the cab had driven away before she revealed what she'd been thinking during the ride back. "I need to call Darrell. If this is what you think it is, then I'm responsible for what happened to the office."

"Your partner?"

She nodded. "Semiretired. I handle most of the cases now. It's what he intended when he took me into partnership. He's been very good to me, Rafe. At the very least I owe him some explanation—"

"You don't owe him anything," he said harshly, taking her elbow and urging her toward the room.

"He owned that building. It was an investment. And if what you believe is true—"

"He'll have insurance. If he doesn't, he's an idiot. And if he's really ready to retire, the explosion was probably a blessing. He won't have to fool with selling the place."

"I'm not sure *he'll* think that," Elizabeth said.

He could tell she wasn't pleased with his lack of sympathy for her partner's loss. He was still having trouble dealing with the realization that she was supposed to have been inside that building when it blew. Somehow, in light of that information, he couldn't be too concerned about the fate of bricks and mortar.

This wasn't Jorgensen, but whoever it was had already proved that he valued human life no more than his role model. And proved that he was out to make a personal rather than a political statement.

"Stay back," he ordered when they reached the walkway in front of the motel.

"You think he's rigged something up in your room?"

"I think we don't know who or what we're dealing with," he said, "and until we do..."

He flattened his hand to fish the key out of the front pocket of his jeans. It was the old-fashioned metal kind, which was rare these days. Of course, there was probably little cause to worry about theft in this setting.

As little as there had been to worry about an act of terrorism. Until today.

"You're just going to stick that key in the lock and turn it in an effort to find out?"

Her sarcasm was born of anxiety. He understood that. She would be feeling the same sickness in the bottom of her stomach that he'd experienced rounding the corner this morning and verifying that the fire was in her office.

Something about her words nagged at him, however. *You're just going to stick that key in the lock...*

"Is that what you did?" he asked, turning to look at her. "What?"

"Is that what triggered the bomb? When you turned the key in the office door?"

She didn't answer at once, her eyes again losing their focus as she thought about the sequence. "I never made it that far," she said finally. "I didn't get close enough to the building to put the key in the door. Not before it blew."

That news wouldn't make him any less cautious. Someone like Jorgensen—someone using his methods—didn't employ the same trick again. That was the genius of how he managed to do what he did, despite the strictest security precautions. He always came at you from a different direction.

Reminded of that, Rafe bent to examine the lock. There was nothing to hint it had been tampered with. No scratches on the surface. And it was a standard metal door, which would provide some protection from an explosion.

"Rafe," Elizabeth said softly.

He couldn't quite read the tone, but it seemed strange. Not caution. Not anxiety. He glanced at her over his shoulder and knew immediately from her expression that she had just thought of something she knew was important.

"I hit the autolock, and it blew," she said. "It was keyed to my remote. They never *meant* for me to be inside."

They. The one word that was the most revealing in what she'd said. The most riveting. *They.*

"Steiner." The name sounded like an obscenity.

"You can't know that for sure."

"The hell I can't. Damn it, I *knew* there was more to this. The CIA doesn't give a rat's ass if somebody blows you or me to kingdom come. They wouldn't bother warning us. Not unless they thought they could get something out of it."

"They want you to go after whoever this is," she said,

her thinking paralleling his. Maybe because she knew them as well as he did. "That's what this is all about. That's what it's been about from the beginning. Somebody is doing what Jorgensen did, and they can't get to him. They think you can. You were the expert on Jorgensen. You got him. They want you to get this guy."

"I guess I'm supposed to be flattered at their confidence," he said savagely.

"You're *supposed* to take care of *him*. Like you took care of Jorgensen."

Under strict congressional sanctions against political assassinations, the CIA had refused to allow Rafe to go after the German-born terrorist. He had been forced to do it strictly on his own, without any of the resources the agency could have provided.

It had taken him more than a year to hunt down and execute Jorgensen. A year in which more innocent people had died. Now that the CIA was once more back in the game of tracking down terrorists, they were attempting to use Rafe to do the dirty work they had once professed to have no interest in.

The only remaining question was whether or not Griff had known what was going on. Or was Cabot simply another discarded weapon the agency had decided to pick up and point at a target they hadn't been able to get by any other means?

"Then this should be safe as a church," he said.

An impulsive rage was another by-product of the day at the embassy. Another thing he was constantly forced to try to control. He didn't succeed this time.

He inserted the key and turned it, throwing open the motel room door. As he'd expected, absolutely nothing happened.

After all, they couldn't afford to let something happen

to him. He was a tool they needed. Elizabeth had been as well, only she had been used to lure him into the game.

If the trigger of the bomb this morning had been keyed to the frequency of her car remote, there was no possibility she would be hurt. Those sons of bitches had probably calibrated exactly how much C-4—or whatever the hell they were using these days—it would take to blow that building spectacularly without risking damage to someone standing where Elizabeth did every morning when she got out of her car.

She might have been hit by falling debris. Steiner would probably have been genuinely sorry if that had happened, but it wouldn't have mattered in the grand scheme of things.

Elizabeth's death would still have had the effect they were hoping for. They wanted Rafe to react just as he had reacted to the embassy bombing. They wanted him to go after the bastard who had done it. To hunt him down and kill him as he had killed Gunther Jorgensen.

And if one of their own got injured or killed in the course of convincing him to do that, it was a loss the CIA was willing accept. *Just a little collateral damage.*

Conniving bastards, he thought again, leading the way into the cool darkness of the motel room.

All along they'd been laying their emotional traps, starting with Griff's question. *And you're willing to stake her life on your certainty of that?*

There was nothing else on earth that would have gotten him involved in this, and Griff, of all people, knew that. Just as he'd known that once the suggestion that someone might try to harm Elizabeth had been made, Rafe wouldn't be able to leave it alone.

That was all the excuse he needed. It had taken him a few days to reach the decision, but in the end he had done exactly what they'd expected him to. He'd come here to find Elizabeth. And they'd been waiting for him.

Waiting to turn the screws. Waiting to up the stakes by making him believe that the explosion this morning had been an attempt on her life. Waiting for him to jump through their carefully arranged hoops all over again.

Except this time, he vowed, *you sons of bitches are in for a huge disappointment.*

Chapter Five

"Now what?" Elizabeth asked as they headed down the narrow two-lane that led to her house.

It had taken Rafe only a few minutes in the motel room to gather his belongings. His fury had been apparent with each motion. She couldn't blame him for being angry, of course. He had been used. They both had.

Besides that, Darrell's property had been destroyed and her life had been endangered. The agency would say it hadn't been, but the more she thought about it, the less willing she was to accept that assessment.

A dozen things could have gone wrong this morning. There was no way anyone could guarantee that the explosion and the resultant fire would play out as it had. Not even the agency's vaunted specialists.

Or if Rafe was correct in his suspicions, maybe those had been Griff's specialists—the men she had worked with during her years on the EST. They would certainly be capable of rigging something that would work with the kind of precision demonstrated in this morning's explosion. The question was whether they would be willing to put a former colleague at risk.

If Griff asked them to, she acknowledged. Especially if he made the reason compelling enough.

Maybe he had reminded them of the reality of the situation. If they didn't do it, the agency would. And the CIA wouldn't be nearly so careful as would the members of the team. If Griff had presented them with those options, they would undoubtedly have agreed to set the explosives.

"We contact Griff," Rafe said.

"You really think he was involved in this."

"I think he played me like a fish. And you said it yourself. He isn't a fool."

"That doesn't mean he can't *be* fooled."

"After all," Rafe said, "I was. And look how clever I am."

"What I want to know is why you were fooled."

"What the hell does that mean?"

"Griff came to you with a request. You could have refused. You *should* have refused, based on your certainty that Jorgensen was dead. Instead, you came here. I'm asking you why."

Anything less than the truth would be ridiculous, given their situation. Still, it would be hard for him to openly articulate that he still cared about her, if only as a friend. Hard, no matter how obvious his actions had already made it.

"If anything happened to you, I would have felt responsible that I hadn't passed on Griff's warning."

Not a lie, but far less satisfying than she'd anticipated.

"Then maybe Griff acted for the same reasons," she said. "Would that be so difficult to accept?"

"What's difficult to accept," he mocked, "is that with all his resources he couldn't verify Jorgensen's death. It doesn't wash. And if Griff *knows* this isn't Jorgensen, then he also knows that neither of us is in danger. Except, apparently, from the agency."

"Maybe—"

"Whatever their reasoning," he interrupted, unwilling to listen to anything that might offer excuses for what had been done to them, "whatever their motivation, they have no right to manipulate either of us. We aren't their hired guns anymore."

She had never felt like a "hired gun," and she couldn't believe Rafe had either. At least not in the beginning.

The embassy bombing and its aftermath seemed to have changed him in some fundamental way. Even in the way he viewed the world and those he used to work with.

"Did a lot of people die in those bombings? The ones whoever they think is Jorgensen committed."

"I'm not responsible for their deaths," Rafe said.

He wasn't, but that unfeeling pronouncement was so foreign to who he was that it held her silent. Rafe Sinclair had been the kind of man who believed evil must be fought, even if fighting against it meant you were sometimes forced to employ its methods. For him, there had been no shades of gray. Not about that.

And he had always accepted the full weight of responsibility for the battle they all waged. Maybe too much of the responsibility, she conceded. Especially if there were failures, as inevitably there were.

"I never said you were responsible," she said. "I never meant to imply that. I'm not trying to convince you to do what they want, Rafe. I guess I'm just trying to understand Griff's role in this."

"That's why I'm going to contact him. Besides, even if he's not involved, he's the only one who can call off the dogs."

Call off the dogs? For a moment she couldn't make sense of the expression. And when she had, she realized with dismay that Rafe could be right.

He was assuming the agency would continue to try to get him to undertake the job they wanted him for. Maybe the pressure would escalate into further acts of violence, even more direct than the explosion this morning.

And the only way Rafe had of letting the CIA know that what they were planning wasn't going to work was to go through Griff Cabot. The only way—no matter what Cabot's original role in this had been.

THAT HE STILL HAD the phone number said something, Rafe supposed, about his previous relationship with Griff Cabot. A couple of years ago Griff had approached him about joining the Phoenix. Despite the fact that he had turned down the offer, he had slipped the business card Cabot had given him into the back of his wallet. It was still there.

He laid it and the Glock on the counter in the kitchen of Elizabeth's bungalow. He studied the information printed on the face of the card for a few seconds. He was surprised to find there was nothing in the wording on the card to hint at the purpose of the Phoenix, an organization Griff had built from the ashes of the elite team the CIA had destroyed.

He picked up the phone Elizabeth had left on the counter after she'd called her partner to tell him she was all right but was going to be taking a few days off. Rafe hadn't been in favor of that, but had given in to the argument that if she didn't make some explanation of her absence, the old man was liable to file a missing person's report.

Receiver in hand, Rafe hesitated, tamping down his anger. He shouldn't judge until he'd talked to Griff. After all, he could be wrong in his assessment of what was going on.

He *could* be, but his gut told him he wasn't. And through the years if there was one thing he'd learned, it was to trust his instincts.

As he tried to impose control over his emotions, he could hear an occasional sound from the back of the house where, at his insistence, Elizabeth had gone to put a few things into an overnight bag. If he didn't get some kind of satisfaction from the call he was about to make, it was an absolute certainty that he wasn't leaving her here. Not alone.

If Griff couldn't or wouldn't make it clear to Steiner that the agency's ploy wasn't working, the quicker he got Elizabeth out of Magnolia Grove, the better. He wasn't taking any chances that someone might get carried away and do something stupid. Or something unconscionable.

He took a breath, finally punching in the number. He listened to the distant ringing a couple of times before he thought to glance at his watch.

Twenty after four, which meant it was after business hours on the east coast. Cabot had never been the kind to adhere to a time clock, however. He worked until whatever project was at hand had been completed. Maybe he'd get lucky. Maybe Griff was still in the office—

"Phoenix."

The voice that answered wasn't one he recognized. Certainly not Griff's. Nor did he think it belonged to any of the operatives he'd worked so closely with during his years at the agency, although that was hard to tell from only one word.

"Griff Cabot, please."

"Griff's out of town for the weekend."

Silence stretched across the line after that exchange of information. Although Rafe waited, there was no offer to take a message. No question about the purpose of his call. Maybe that was SOP for any organization that did the kind of work the Phoenix handled.

"Is there a number where he can be reached?"

"May I ask who's calling?"

The series of questions and answers had given Rafe more opportunity to compare the voice on the other end of the line to those in his memory. It still didn't ring any bells. Someone who hadn't been with the team, which made him reluctant to give out any more information than he had to.

And what the hell can it matter? he thought. It wasn't as if he had a lot of choices.

"Someone who used to work for Griff," he said.

Again a few seconds elapsed before the response.

"Worked for him in his *former* capacity?"

"You could say that."

"Are you in…some kind of difficulty?"

Rafe resisted the urge to laugh at the euphemism, although he hadn't found anything else about this day the least amusing. In the back of his mind was the image of Elizabeth's colorless face when he had rounded the corner this morning.

"I need him to give Steiner a message for me."

"I'm not sure I can help you with that."

"Tell him I don't like being used. Tell him I don't work for the company anymore. They're going to have to do their own dirty work."

Another hesitation. "Is there a number where Griff can reach you?"

"Not this one," Rafe said, knowing they would already have it traced. "We won't be here. You can tell him that as well."

"'We'?"

"She doesn't like being used either. Of course, she's a little more tolerant of this kind of betrayal than I am. She's still trying to find some excuse for Griff's role in all this."

"If you're implying that Griff Cabot has in some way betrayed you, then you don't know him as well as you suggest you do. You certainly never worked for him."

That confidence in Griff's integrity where his own people were concerned should make him feel better, Rafe thought.

Except I'm no longer one of his people.

"Maybe he was used, too," he said. "I really hope that's the case. If he was, tell him to take it up with Steiner. *After* he tells the bastard to find himself another boy. This one isn't going to play."

"I need a number where Griff can reach you."

"I don't know where I'll be. Somewhere Steiner won't be looking. Just see that Griff gets the message."

"If you'll—"

Rafe didn't wait to hear the rest. He put the phone back on the counter, imposing a strict control to keep his hand from slamming it down. The call had been wasted effort. The man he'd just talked to couldn't do anything. Not on the weekend. Not with Griff out of town.

All he could hope for was that whoever had answered at the Phoenix would do what he'd been asked to do and pass on the message when Cabot returned. In the meantime...

He realized belatedly that the sounds from the back of the house had faded while he'd talked. No drawers were being opened and closed. No coat hangers slid along the metal bar in the closet. No footsteps crossed and recrossed the wooden floors.

The quality of silence that had fallen bothered him. If Elizabeth had finished packing, she would have come back in here, interested in finding out the result of his call.

He picked up the gun he'd removed from the trunk of his car, the solid weight of it reassuring. He had checked out the house before he'd let Elizabeth go to the back, but he hadn't checked the locks on the windows. It was possible someone had left one of them open to provide themselves with a way in.

Actually, anything was possible considering the people he was dealing with. That was something he couldn't afford to forget.

He moved across the kitchen tiles without making a sound. A couple of boards in the dining room creaked revealingly under his weight, but then, his hearing was probably hypersensitive.

All his senses were. Sharpened. On edge. Ready to confront whatever or whoever had put a stop to Elizabeth's preparations to leave.

He stopped at the doorway that led into the hall, automatically shifting his weapon into firing position, left hand under the right. He eased far enough around the frame of the door to see down the hall and into Elizabeth's bedroom.

There was no sign of her. Nor could he see anyone else. All that was visible was a dresser against the wall, one of its drawers still open, and the foot of the bed, the disordered spread spilling off onto the floor. Unmade, because she'd been running late this morning.

He tiptoed down the hallway, his gun trained on the bedroom doorway. When he reached it, he paused to listen again. There were faint noises coming from inside the room. Nothing he could identify.

Breathing, maybe? The sound of two people breathing, one holding the other captive as they silently waited for him to enter the room?

He weighed his options, limited as they were. He could feel adrenaline rush into his bloodstream, a physiological reaction he couldn't prevent. Nor could he prevent the psychological reaction that might well result from it.

That was the wild card in any situation involving stress and danger. He never knew when something would send his brain spiraling back to the day of the embassy bombing. And the longer he delayed now, the more chance there was that something here would set that sequence into motion.

He took a couple of long strides, carrying him through the doorway and into the bedroom. At the same time he brought the muzzle of his gun around to point toward the corner of the room from which the noises he'd heard had seemed to originate.

And realized he had been wrong in every surmise. Elizabeth was alone. There had been no sounds of packing because she had already finished and was in the process of changing out of the clothes she'd worn to work this morning.

Her shock seemed as great as his. She brought the bra she'd just removed back up against her body in an unsuccessful attempt to cover her breasts.

Despite the adrenaline coursing through his system, the images evoked by this present reality had nothing to do with the horrors of the embassy bombing. They revolved instead around the endless hours the two of them had spent making love.

Once he'd known the contours and textures of her body as well as he knew his own. Better, since he had never fantasized about his. He had certainly fantasized about hers, especially through all the long, empty years of their separation.

"What's wrong?" she asked, her eyes dilating in shock.

He lowered the gun, straightening from the slight crouch he'd assumed when he'd entered the room. He'd been prepared to face an intruder. He wasn't prepared to face this.

"I thought somebody was back here."

She shook her head, denial or confusion, but she didn't ask why he would believe that.

"I needed to get out of those clothes," she offered, glancing down at the garments she had removed.

They lay on the floor around her, exuding the faintest hint of smoke. His gaze followed hers, and then, without his conscious volition, it focused on her feet.

They, too, were bare, narrow and high-arched. The nails had been painted a dusty beige-rose. Above them, her ankles were slim and elegant, the left marked by a small, very discreet tattoo of a heart.

He had run his tongue over it a hundred times. Dropped kisses along the shapely calf above it. Continued upward to press his lips against the sensitive skin inside her thigh.

He was powerless now to prevent his eyes from retracing that sensual journey. Other than her first unthinking reaction in raising the bra, she had made no attempt to cover herself. She didn't now. And he was incapable of tearing his eyes away.

"Elizabeth," he said softly, taking a step nearer.

Despite the stench of smoke that lingered in the fabric of the clothing at her feet, the fragrance of her perfume was suddenly all around him, as familiar to him as the process of breathing. Underlying that was the subtle scent of her skin, woman-sweet, intensified by the heat and humidity.

"Don't," she said.

He lifted his eyes to hers, mentally acknowledging her wisdom in warning him off. There were far too many memories between them. And their emotional intensity was unabated, despite the meaningless encounters with other women in which he'd indulged during the last few years.

Those had been nothing more than fruitless attempts to erase the remembrance of this. Of her. He knew now, if he had ever doubted it, how miserably he had failed.

His entire world had changed in the matter of hours one day in Amsterdam, but nothing had changed about this. Nothing was any different than it had ever been in the way he felt about this woman.

He shifted the Glock to his left hand. It would be no help against the threat he faced. He had no weapons against the danger that loomed like a pit before him. He had never had any defense against the way she made him feel.

"Please go," she said, the words little more than a breath.

Instead of obeying, he reached out to place the tips of his fingers on the curve of her breast. She didn't flinch or turn away, not even when he allowed them to slide slowly downward.

She was still clutching the bra to her breasts with both

hands, but there was room enough for him to slip his palm beneath the weight of the small, perfect globe. He allowed his thumb to trail over the nipple. Despite her lack of any outward response to his touch, it began to harden.

Emboldened, he moved his thumb up and down over the nub, watching it grow more and more taut with each slow stroke. She made a sound, deep in her throat, something between a gasp and a sob. It brought his gaze quickly back to her face.

Her eyes met his, but there was no warmth within their depths, darkened with an emotion he couldn't read. It was clear, however, that it was not invitation. He supposed that was all that mattered.

"Please go," she said again.

Then she swallowed. The movement was strong enough that he could trace it visually down the long, slender column of her throat. Despite her seeming calm, he realized this was no easier for her than for him.

They stood at the beginning of a path they had traveled together more times than he could count. She had been the instigator as often as he had. Her needs as openly expressed. Her body as eager. He knew that if he ignored her request now, moving forward to take her into his arms, she would relent.

She had begun to tremble. He could feel the slight vibration against his palm, still cupped beneath her breast.

Fear or need? he wondered. Disgust or desire?

Whatever emotion she felt, she had every right. He was the one who had left. The one who had offered no explanation.

Even while acknowledging that, he didn't move away. Instead, he allowed his fingers, their surfaces calloused from hours in his workshop, to close around the incredible softness of her breast.

He would not have believed the pupils of her eyes could

expand any farther into the rim of color surrounding them. They did now. Her mouth opened on a quick inhalation. Taking that as a signal, he began to lean forward, his head lowering and his lips parting to fasten over hers.

As he did, the phone in the kitchen rang. For a long heartbeat, neither of them moved. And then it rang again.

His inclination, based on more than what was happening between them, was to ignore it. It would be the fire chief with some unanswerable questions. Or Elizabeth's partner.

Whoever it was, there was no need for her to talk to them. The fewer people who knew they were here—

"Griff?" she suggested, finally taking a breath. It was deep and quick as if she were winded.

She was right. It *could* be Cabot. If whoever had answered at the Phoenix was even halfway competent, it *would* be.

Reluctantly he opened his hand, turning away in the same motion. By that time the phone had rung again.

He began to hurry, remembering that he'd told the man at the Phoenix they wouldn't be at this number. Now that he'd realized who this must be, he understood how important it was not to miss this call.

By the time he reached the hall, however, the answering machine had already picked up. Along with the caller, he listened to Elizabeth's recorded message, hoping Griff wouldn't hang up before he could get to the phone. He was almost to the counter when the tone sounded, signaling it was time for the caller to leave his message.

He reached for the receiver, his hand beginning to close around it when the words came over the line. And with the first syllables, he froze in midmotion.

"So, my friend," Gunther Jorgensen said, the resonance of tone and the accent exactly as Rafe remembered them, "it seems our game begins anew."

Chapter Six

He was torn between grabbing up the phone, screaming into it the kind of profanities Jorgensen deserved, or pulling his hand away from any possible contamination that being near the receiver might give. The latter was prompted by sheer revulsion, an almost superstitious reluctance to have any contact with the man who'd ordered that bombing in Amsterdam.

As well as the more recent ones Griff had told him about?

When the hollow click indicated the caller had hung up, Rafe began to shake his head, moving it slowly from side to side in attempted denial. Jorgensen was dead. He knew that. He had watched the bastard bleed to death on a street in Paris.

If he's dead, then who the hell was that?

"Rafe?"

At the sound of Elizabeth's voice, he drew a long, shuddering breath. He moved his hand up and then away from the receiver, struggling to put the nightmare aspects of the call into some kind of perspective.

That wasn't Jorgensen. It couldn't be. No matter what it had sounded like.

"Was that Griff?"

Obviously she hadn't been in time to hear the message.

For a second or two he considered keeping the contents from her. But she had to be told because if anything happened to him...

He rejected that possibility, turning toward her. She hadn't taken time to dress, pulling on a pale blue velour robe instead. She was in the process of belting it around her waist. At whatever she saw in his face, her fingers hesitated in the act of tightening the knot.

"What is it?"

Without answering, he reached over and pushed the play button on the answering machine. Again the accented voice delivered its taunting message.

"Is that...?" The question trailed as she struggled to make sense of what she'd heard. "Was that *Jorgensen?* You said he was dead. You said—"

"I know what I said, damn it."

He didn't need to be reminded of the strength of his conviction. The images of the terrorist's death had been replaying through his brain like a videotape being rewound and then fast-forwarded through the same part over and over again.

"I watched him die," he said, working to modulate his tone so it would be more reasoned.

"Then...who the hell was *that?*"

"I don't know," he admitted. "Some kind of tape. Bits and pieces of his voice that have been spliced together."

There was little use in denying, even to himself, that it had been Jorgensen's voice. As he offered the explanation of how that could be, his mind grappled with the concept. Was it possible the message had been pieced together?

So, my friend, our game begins anew.

As threats went, it wasn't much. Despite his overreaction. And it told him virtually nothing about Jorgensen's plans.

He tried to decide if the words fit with what he knew

about the German's psychological profile. Although it had been almost six years, he hadn't forgotten anything about the man he had studied so carefully.

And, he conceded, there was nothing about this message that rang false. It was arrogant enough to fit with the murderer he had hunted down and assassinated. *Or had he?*

"Could they do that?" Elizabeth asked.

She meant could the CIA splice together that message. They could, of course. There was very little in the way of technological wizardry they couldn't perform.

"If they had the tapes."

"From some kind of surveillance, you mean? Or from conversations the satellites intercept?"

The latter was a more likely possibility. As far as he was aware, they had never infiltrated any of the cells Jorgensen controlled. The National Security Agency, however, listened in on millions of communications. If what they had just heard *was* a tape, maybe the agency had gotten some of the stuff from the NSA.

"I don't even know that it *was* a tape," he said aloud. "Maybe it was someone with a gift for mimicry. I don't know who that was or what the hell is going on. I do know that whatever it is, we aren't going to sit around here waiting for Act II."

"WHAT MAKES YOU THINK Griff will be there?"

Elizabeth didn't look at him as she asked the question. Despite the hours they'd spent together in the car, she couldn't seem to move past the few moments before Jorgensen's call.

They had seemed frozen in time as his mouth slowly lowered to hers. Those endless seconds were caught in her memory so that she had wondered again and again what she would have done if the phone hadn't rung.

"He may not be. We have to go somewhere."

Rafe had said nothing about what he was thinking during the journey. He'd done most of the driving, letting her take the wheel only when fatigue demanded he catch a few hours of sleep. And as she had driven through the Carolinas last night, the dark, silent miles clicking off while he slept, she'd tried to make sense of all that had happened during the past forty-eight hours.

In the blink of an eye she had gone from bemoaning the boredom of her existence to sheer unadulterated terror. Back to a world she thought she'd left far behind.

At the same time, the only man she'd ever loved had moved back into her life. *And almost back into her bed.*

She turned her head, studying his profile. In the strong morning light she could see a faded scar at his temple, nearly covered by the way he now wore his hair. She had already noticed the faint discolorations, all that were left of those scars that marred his hands.

He had never told her about the embassy bombing. What she knew, that he had saved several people who had been trapped in the rubble, she had learned from other sources, including the official citation for valor the agency had awarded him.

And she also knew that what had happened in Amsterdam that day was in some way connected to what had come between them. He had sent word by Griff asking her not to come to the hospital there. She would always wonder if it might have made a difference had she disregarded his wishes.

"Even if Griff's not at the summerhouse, we should be safe there," he said. "At least long enough to figure out what to do next."

He pulled his gaze from the road to look at her. She nodded, and after a few seconds, he turned his attention back to the traffic on the crowded interstate.

As she watched, unable to tear her eyes away, his fingers

tightened over the steering wheel, stretching the scarred skin on the backs of his hands. The memory of those same fingers drifting over the curve of her breast yesterday was suddenly in her head. It seemed she could still feel his thumb teasing her nipple. Sensation stirred within her lower body, evoking other memories. Other touches.

"I'm sorry," he said.

Her eyes came up to find that his lips had flattened. A muscle tensed and then released along his jawline.

"For what?" Rafe Sinclair had never before apologized for making love to her. Why would he now?

"If it weren't for me, you wouldn't be involved in this."

"His information seems woefully out of date."

The blue eyes again focused on her face. Questioning.

"If he's trying to get at you by threatening me..."

"It isn't Jorgensen," he said, choosing not to comment on what she'd just suggested about their relationship.

"Why would the agency think they could manipulate you that way? I mean now," she added.

There had been a time when Rafe would have taken action against anyone or anything that put her in danger. His feelings for her then probably hadn't been a secret. Nothing ever was in a group as close-knit as the EST.

Griff had almost certainly known. Probably his superiors at the agency had as well.

She doubted she and Rafe were the only members of the team who had ever indulged in a more-than-professional relationship. And she had never been certain Griff disapproved. What the team did was both covert and highly dangerous. Neither of those elements of their work encouraged the formation of emotional liaisons, especially with outsiders.

Yet they were normal men and women in the prime of life. With normal sexual appetites. To think that there wouldn't be physical attachments between some of them would be naive. Griff Cabot wasn't.

"Steiner's never been accused of being too bright," Rafe said dismissively.

"And Griff?"

"I thought you believed he wasn't involved."

"I don't know what I believe. Not anymore. All I know is that I'll be glad to get out of this car."

"A couple of hours," he said, glancing toward her again.

"And if Griff's *not* there?"

"We hole up until he's back in the office on Monday. Whatever's going on, he's still our best bet for finding out the truth."

"Are you sure you can get into the house?"

"I know the codes. If they haven't been changed, it shouldn't be a problem."

"And if they have been?"

"Then we pay the Phoenix a visit," he said, the muscle in his jaw working again. "I wonder if they'll be glad to see us."

IT WAS APPARENT that Rafe had been in Cabot's summerhouse, probably on numerous occasions. Not only had he known the security codes that had gotten them in the front door, but he was obviously familiar with the arrangement of the rooms.

"You've been here before," Elizabeth said, looking into the formal rooms they passed, the furniture protectively draped with Holland covers.

"Of course."

He didn't follow up his answer with the question she'd been expecting. *Haven't you?*

She hadn't. She had heard about the huge old Victorian house Griff Cabot owned on the Virginia coast, of course, but she'd never seen it.

Supposedly it had been in his family for generations. Through the years of Griff's service with the CIA, it had served as both a safe house and an operations center for the team on more than one occasion. Elegant and isolated, it was also equipped with the best security devices that money and the agency's cutting-edge technology could provide.

"Hungry?" Rafe asked, putting her bag down by the staircase that led up to the second floor.

She was, she realized. They had existed on what they could pick up in the service stations where they'd stopped to get gas. Nothing that would qualify as real food.

"There's a well-stocked pantry, I suppose."

"There always was," Rafe answered, leading the way toward the back of the house.

The decor, even in the informal rooms through which they passed, was very different than that of any beach house she had ever seen. She suspected a lot of what was here Griff had inherited along with the house. Old money, and lots of it, she thought.

She had known that about Cabot. As a result, she had often wondered how, and more importantly why, he'd ended up doing the thankless government job he had handled with such skill. Of course, service to one's country had always been a tradition among the Southern aristocracy. Maybe that was handed down along with all that money and places such as this.

"What sounds good?" Rafe asked.

"Almost anything but peanut butter crackers," she said, remembering the packages of those he'd tossed into her lap at the last stop for gas.

"I think we can manage something more substantial." He opened the double refrigerator, examining the contents briefly before he closed the door. "It must have been a while since anyone's been here."

He crossed to a door on the opposite side of the kitchen. Opened, it revealed a deep pantry full of canned goods, packages of staples, and a variety of mixes and boxed meals.

"Something easy," she said, leaning on the counter to watch him. That was still a pleasure, she admitted. As much as it had ever been.

She knew he was self-conscious about the scars by the fact that he took the trouble to hide those he could. Judging by the ones that marred his hands, he probably shouldn't be. She couldn't imagine that those on his body—

Dangerous territory, she decided, forcing her gaze away from the broad shoulders of the man examining the contents of the pantry to take in her surrounding. The kitchen had been redone at some time in the last few years, she realized, the redesign incorporating all the modern conveniences.

"There's some gourmet marinara sauce in a jar. If jar and gourmet aren't a contradiction in terms."

It probably wouldn't be here, she thought.

"Pasta?" she asked.

"Take your pick."

His voice sounded slightly hollow coming from inside the shelf-lined room. What he'd just said seemed to suggest that she join him in there to make that decision.

She didn't relish being that close to him. Not in such a confined space. At least not until she'd had time to recover her emotional balance after what had happened between them.

What had almost happened, she amended.

Since nearly twenty-four hours hadn't been enough to do that, she wondered how long she thought it would take. Of course, she had never managed to put her feelings about Rafe Sinclair into any sort of balance during the past six years. What made her believe she could now?

"I'm not hard to please," she said, deciding discretion

was definitely the better part of valor. "Whatever you decide—"

She stopped because he had reappeared in the doorway,
a jar of sauce in one hand and a package of pasta in the
other. He tossed the latter to her, making a preliminary
throwing motion as a form of warning before he released
it.

"Twenty minutes?" he asked as he set the jar down on
the counter she'd been leaning against.

"About that," she agreed, skimming the instructions
printed on the back of the pasta.

"Then I'm going to take a shower."

She looked up to smile at him. "Somehow I'd gotten the
impression you were going to cook dinner."

"Have you ever known me to cook, Elizabeth?"

"I thought you might have learned *something* in the last
six years."

"Many things, but not that."

"Care to enlighten me?" she asked.

His mood had changed completely since they'd been
here. The cold, angry man she had ridden beside through
a half dozen states seemed as relaxed in this environment
as when he'd been standing beside her fireplace, drinking
her best whiskey as if that were his right. As relaxed as he
had been during the initial team meeting she'd attended.

That was the first time she'd seen him, and despite the
wealth of interesting personalities Griff had gathered
around him, her eyes had immediately been drawn to the
man who had been introduced as Rafe Sinclair. They still
would be, she admitted.

"Enlighten you about what I've learned?" he clarified.

"I'd be interested," she said, removing a pot from the
line of those hanging on the rack above the state-of-the-art
stove.

"Why?"

Because I've always been interested in everything about you.

"Because we were friends," she said aloud. "Because it's been a long time since I've seen you. A long time since we've had a chance to talk."

She walked over to fill the boiler with water at the sink and then carried it back to the stove. It took her a second or two to figure out which button controlled which burner. When she had, she looked up to find he was watching her.

"Don't start something you aren't willing to finish," he said softly.

Clearly a warning to stay away from the personal. The fact that he felt compelled to warn her off both angered and embarrassed her. She could feel heated blood stain her neck.

"What is that supposed to mean?" she asked bitingly.

"That we're going to be stuck in each other's company for God knows how long until I get this figured out. And right now, I don't have a clue what's going on. I don't have a clue who set off that blast in your office or why. I'm not completely sure anymore that it wasn't intended to kill you."

His voice was low and intense, just as it had been years ago when he'd talked about the responsibilities of the duty they had accepted by joining the team.

"I'm not going to let that happen, I promise you," he went on, "but I'll promise you this as well. Neither one of us is going to be pleased with what will happen if you start trying to catch up on old times."

She could feel the blush spreading upward into her cheeks. What he had said was nothing less than the truth. That he had so quickly recognized what she was doing was humiliation enough. That he had called her on it was much worse.

"You're an arrogant son of a bitch," she said.

"That was never exactly a deterrent."

"Rest assured, it will be now."

"Then at least we understand each other," he said. He held her eyes for long heartbeat before he turned on his heel and recrossed the room.

You arrogant son of a bitch, she thought again.

And he was even right about that. It never *had* been a deterrent.

Chapter Seven

She glanced at her watch as she set the second wineglass on the table. It had taken her a little longer than the prescribed twenty minutes to put the meal together.

Not that it was much of a meal, she conceded. She had searched the refrigerator for something to make a salad out of, but Rafe was right. Apparently it had been a while since anyone had stayed here. There was no fruit or produce in the house, other than the canned variety.

She had found rolls in the freezer, which were now browning in the oven. And she had unashamedly raided Griff's wine rack for a nice merlot.

A jug of wine, a loaf of bread—and thou... There was still a part of that poetic equation missing. She resisted the urge to look at her watch again. She listened instead.

At some point in the dinner preparations she had become aware of the sound of the shower running upstairs. Now there was only silence. Of course, she could always do what Rafe had done yesterday and go up to check on him.

Not in this lifetime.

She stepped back to look at the place settings laid out on the small breakfast table, which sat beside one of the wide windows. As she worked, she had been aware of the breathtaking view spread out beneath it.

The beach at dusk was incredibly beautiful. As the waves

rolled to shore, they displayed a dozen variations of greens and blues and browns until they foamed whitely over the dark rocks below. Almost as romantic as the poem she'd just remembered.

Don't start something you aren't willing to finish.

She stepped toward the table and began to gather up items. She crossed to the kitchen's central island to put the plate, silverware, and napkin down before one of the bar stools. Then she returned to the table to pick up the other place setting.

Her eyes again found the scene below. By the time Rafe came downstairs and they finally sat down to eat, it would be fully dark. Nothing outside these windows would be visible. Surely he couldn't question her motives then.

And what if he did? She couldn't believe she was spending all this time worrying about where to put the damned dishes because she was afraid Rafe might think she was trying to initiate something. As if she had no more pride than to do that when he'd made it perfectly clear he wasn't interested.

Except he hadn't really *said* he wasn't interested. He had said she shouldn't start something she wasn't willing to finish.

And because of that, she was acting like a sixteen-year-old virgin who's never been alone with a man. Maybe that was the problem. She had been alone with this one. And they'd *never* left *anything* unfinished.

Nothing except the relationship, she reminded herself. This was the guy who hadn't even bothered to phone in his goodbyes before he'd disappeared.

''Separate tables?''

She turned to find Rafe leaning against the island, an elbow propped casually beside the place setting she'd moved there. She hadn't heard him come in. When her eyes followed the length of long, muscled legs, clad in a pair of fresh jeans, she discovered he wasn't wearing shoes.

There was something unbelievably sexy about a man's bare feet, she thought. Something almost vulnerable. Definitely intimate. She forced her eyes up to meet his.

"I thought that was the whole idea."

One dark brow arched. "Whose idea about what?"

"You know. Yours about not starting anything."

Without waiting for his response, she walked over to the stove and turned off the heat under the pasta. She lifted the pot and carried it to the sink, where she'd already placed the colander. She poured the contents of the boiler into it, breathing in the fragrant steam.

"What can I do to help?"

Not exactly the response she'd been hoping for.

"Pour the wine," she suggested without turning.

She pretended to concentrate on the pasta, but she was aware of every move he made. Every breath he took.

And any minute now I'll break into song.

"Is something wrong?" he asked.

Typical male question.

They had once known every inch of one another's bodies. Every pore. Every heartbeat.

They had been both friends and lovers. Best friends and better lovers. And then…

"Why didn't you call me?"

Typical female question.

She hated hearing it come out of her mouth, but dear God, she needed to know. Maybe then she could get on with it. Just get on with her life.

The silence lasted long enough that she finally turned to face him. Wine bottle in one hand and the corkscrew she had laid out beside it in the other, Rafe was simply standing there. Watching her.

"I deserved to know," she said.

"Yes, you did."

She waited, but he offered nothing more.

"And?" she prodded.

"You deserved to know, and I didn't call you. Mea culpa."

"That's it? That's all you're going to say?"

"What could I possibly say, Elizabeth, that would matter to you after six years?"

"I don't know," she said, feeling her anger build.

Most of it was self-directed, but she didn't want to examine the reality of that too closely. After all, she had plenty of anger to go around. Six long years' worth.

"Whatever it is," she said, "I'd still like to hear it."

"I'm sorry."

"Sorry for leaving or sorry because you aren't going to tell me why you did?"

His mouth tightened. "Sorry for both, I suppose. Is that what you want to hear?"

"What I want to hear is a reason. I know it had something to do with what happened in Amsterdam. Maybe even with what you did afterward. I understood you were going to have to hunt down Jorgensen. You did that, and then—"

She was forced to stop because she had never known what came next. Rafe had recovered from his injuries. He had found and killed the man responsible for the bombing. And then he hadn't come back. Not to the team and not to her.

Maybe he had done what she had eventually. Gone on with his life, pretending he was living. Or maybe, and this would be a much harder thing to learn, maybe *he* hadn't had to pretend.

"This won't help," he said, his tone compassionate.

"It might," she argued. "You said it yourself. We're going to be stuck together for God knows how long."

The blue eyes remained on hers for a silent eternity. The breath he took before he spoke lifted his shoulders.

With resignation? she wondered.

"I knew that nothing between us could ever be the same."

Nothing between us could ever be the same...

"After Amsterdam?" she asked. "Because of Amsterdam?"

He nodded, his face like a mask.

"Why?"

"Because *I* wasn't the same."

She had known that. She had known that the bombing changed him. It had robbed him of his profession. It had sent him on a mission of vengeance that had occupied more than a year of his life. And it had cost him what they had once had together.

She wanted to believe that had mattered to him. That it was the loss he regretted most.

"People change," she said. "Life changes them. Relationships adjust."

"Or they don't."

"Or they don't," she agreed. "You never gave me a chance."

"I didn't mean you."

Which meant...

"*Your* feelings for *me* changed," she said, interpreting that the only way she could.

There was a small silence.

"*I* changed," he said finally.

"Was there someone else?"

Another female question. One she hadn't had any idea she was going to ask until the words were there, naked and exposed.

His mouth moved, the corners tilting minutely. Sickness

crawled into her throat as she watched them. Then he turned and set the bottle and corkscrew down on the island.

"Enjoy your dinner."

"You're *leaving?*" she asked, her voice rising. She hated the sound of it, but that didn't prevent her from adding, "You're just going to walk away?"

"Again." He added the word she hadn't said.

"You damn coward," she said bitterly.

He had taken the first step toward the door, but it stopped him, as she had intended it would. He looked at her over his shoulder, eyes hard and cold.

"That's a weapon you would never have thought about using six years ago. Apparently I'm not the only one who's changed."

He held her eyes, giving her an opportunity for rebuttal. There was nothing she could say, of course, because he was right. The woman she had been then would never have thought about making that accusation.

"I'm sorry."

She was. Sorry she had started this. Sorry she had revealed how much he had hurt her and how long and carefully she had nursed that pain.

He nodded again, and then he turned and crossed the room, disappearing into the darkness beyond the open doorway.

SHE HAD GONE through the motions of eating dinner after he left. She had put pasta on her plate and covered it with sauce. She had remembered to take the rolls out of the oven, although they were too hard and dark by then to be appetizing. She had even opened the wine and filled one of the glasses.

Then she had sat on the stool at the island and prodded the food on her plate with her fork. She couldn't remember eating any of it.

All she could remember were the things they had said to one another. Things they would never have said six years ago. Things *she* would never have said, she amended.

She was the one who had stepped over the line. She had accused him of leaving because he was afraid. The truth was he had sought to escape questions she had no right to ask.

She lifted the wineglass whose stem her fingers had been idly playing with and found it empty. She couldn't remember drinking from it. Not the second glass she'd poured, at any rate. Or maybe she'd never poured that second glass.

And maybe you're too drunk to remember.

She pushed the glass away. She climbed off the stool and stood. The room swam a little before it settled into focus.

Too little food. Too little sleep. A glass of wine on an empty stomach. If she weren't careful, she'd make a fool of herself. As if she hadn't already.

It could have been much worse, she decided, picking up her plate and carrying it over to the sink. The rest of the pasta was still there, cold and congealed in the colander.

Screw it, she thought, setting the plate down on the counter. She'd clean up in the morning. Or if this offended Rafe's sensibilities, he could clean up. Screw him, too.

An unfortunate choice of words, she admitted.

She turned away from the sink and surveyed the room to make sure there was nothing she needed to do down here before she climbed the stairs. As she did, she was aware of a subtle sense of disorientation.

Disbelief that she would be sleeping in the same house with Rafe Sinclair. Disbelief that it was Griff Cabot's house they were sharing. Disbelief that they were hiding from a madman.

And surrounded with the reality of those things, all she

could talk about was why he'd deserted her. That's exactly what it had felt like, she realized. Desertion.

Except there had never been any vows or promises between them. Neither of them had felt they were free to make any. Not given the dangers inherent in what they did for the CIA.

It would almost have been easier if he had died in Amsterdam, she thought, hating herself for that admission. At least then she could have grieved. She could have believed she had mattered to him. This way...

In this way lies madness.

At some point during that terrible first year she had realized that. She had gone back to law school, taken the bar, and gotten on with her life. She had done those things because she had had no choice. Nothing had changed now. She still had no choice.

Or maybe she did. *Don't start something you aren't willing to finish.* What if she decided she *was* willing to finish it? She supposed that would depend on how big a glutton for punishment she really was.

She pushed away from the counter and walked across the room, turning off the overhead light when she reached the doorway. Then she stood there a moment, giving her eyes time to adjust to the sudden darkness.

As they did, she realized that she wasn't alone. Rafe was leaning against the wall of the hallway that led from the kitchen to the front part of the house.

"What are you doing?" she asked.

"Waiting for you to finish up down here and come upstairs."

Her heart rate had already begun to accelerate before she realized the reason he was waiting for her might have nothing to do with the sudden flare of hope those words had created.

"Why?" she asked.

"Because I don't intend to let anything happen to you."

"And you think something might happen to me here?" The tone of the question was almost derisive.

"I didn't like leaving you alone."

"Afraid I'll do something rash? Don't worry. If I were going to do that, I would have done it years ago."

"That's not what I meant."

"Good," she said.

She stepped through the doorway and walked toward him. Since this had been the servants' domain when the old house was built, the passage was narrow enough that they would be very close when she reached the spot where he was standing.

As she approached it, he straightened, she assumed to give her room to pass. Instead, his hand reached out to fasten around her upper arm.

She was so shocked by the unexpected contact that she made no attempt to pull free. Her forward progress halted as she turned her head to look at him.

"It had nothing to do with you," he said.

His leaving. *Nothing to do with you…*

"I wanted you to know that," he went on. "I changed, and because of that, nothing between us could ever be the same. I didn't want what we had to become…something less. Not for me. And whether you believe it or not, especially not for you."

"You just decided all that for both of us."

She had called him an arrogant bastard. If what he'd just said was true, it was verification of exactly how arrogant.

"I wasn't sure you'd make the right decision."

For the first time there was a trace of amusement in his voice. She waited, his hand still around her arm, but apparently he had said all he intended.

"I wouldn't have made *that* one. Not without giving it a chance. Not without giving me a chance."

"Elizabeth—"

"Do you remember what it was like? Do you?"

"More clearly than you can imagine."

"I don't know. My imagination is pretty good. Of course, I don't have to use it for that because my memory is even better. I've had *lots* of nights since you left to remember."

What the hell is wrong with me? she thought as the silence stretched unbearably after that confession. *Why can't I just leave it alone? Leave* him *alone? He's made it clear that's what he wants, no matter how much he's now trying to soften that rejection.*

"I did warn you, you know," he said softly.

The words made no sense in context. Before she could begin to figure out what he might mean by them, his fingers tightened around her arm, drawing her toward him.

And then, as it had when they stood together in her bedroom, his mouth began to lower toward hers. Even in the darkness she could tell that his eyes were closed. At the last possible second he tilted his head to align his lips over hers.

Firm and warm, they moved with the same confident possession she had remembered. When his tongue sought entrance, her mouth opened willingly. There was no pretense of denial.

Too much wine? she wondered. Or too long without this? Without him.

She had kissed other men, of course. Several since she'd last kissed Rafe. With none had there ever been this sense of rightness. Familiarity. *Homecoming.*

This was where she belonged, she acknowledged as his arms closed around her. He held her so tightly that the hard wall of his chest flattened her breasts almost painfully. Whatever had happened six years ago, he seemed as hungry for this as she had been.

And she *had* been. All along she had wanted him to do exactly what he was doing now. Kissing her with a thoroughness and a passion that belied any possibility of his disinterest.

He wanted her. She had known that yesterday when his fingers had grazed the curve of her breast.

Perhaps she had been wiser then, but she couldn't regret whatever had made her keep probing the open wound of their former relationship tonight. Not if this was the result.

His tongue caressed, its movements choreographed by experience. Nothing had been forgotten. Nothing had changed. Not about this.

His right hand left the small of her back to fasten under the fullness of her breast. As it did, his lips began to move as well, dropping a series of small, openmouthed kisses along the length of her throat.

She turned her head to accommodate his touch. Moving lower now, his tongue found the dark cleavage between her breasts.

He hadn't taken time to shave when he'd grabbed that predinner shower. The abrasiveness of a two-day growth of beard was incredibly sensual against her skin. It reminded her of those days when they had made love through most of the night, only to begin again as soon as they awakened. They had been insatiable, never tiring of giving and receiving pleasure.

His fingers began to work at the buttons along the front of her shirt, slipping them out of their holes with quick expertise. As he did, he lifted his head to look into her eyes.

Trying to judge her reaction to what he was doing?

Then, unexpectedly, he smiled at her, the same familiar slant at one corner of his mouth. And the years fell away.

Friends *and* lovers. Truly the best of both worlds.

His hand slipped inside her bra, lifting her breast free of its restraint. She could feel the calluses on his palm and fingers. Rough. Undeniably masculine. Exactly how a man's hand should feel.

He lowered his head, his lips fastening loosely around her nipple. His tongue rimmed it, painting the surface with moisture. Then he leaned back a little, blowing seductively over the dampness his mouth had left.

Heat ran through her veins like molten metal, weakening her knees. Causing a sweet, nearly forgotten ache to begin somewhere deep inside. An ache for which there was one relief.

Her fingers found the back of his head. Spread, they moved slowly through the dark strands of his hair, almost a caress. Blessing. Benediction.

Suddenly his mouth closed over the nub his tongue had teased to hardness. At the first hint of suction, her fingers tightened, grasping the silk of his hair. Anchored to reality only by the feel of it within her hand.

This *was* real. Not another of those tantalizing dreams from which she would awaken, cold and alone and still empty.

Don't start something you aren't willing to finish.

She *was* willing. No matter what happened tomorrow, she wanted this. She wanted his mouth on her body, trailing hot, wet kisses over her skin. She wanted his hands, hard and rough and masculine, moving possessively against all the secret places only he knew. She wanted him. She always had.

"Rafe," she whispered.

There was no response. Deliberately she tightened her

fingers in his hair, using them to urge his head up. After a moment his lips released. She felt the depth of the breath he took before he again lifted his head.

He didn't smile at her this time. His eyes seemed almost glazed. His mouth was open, his breathing audible.

"What's wrong?"

"Nothing's wrong," she whispered. She allowed her hand to sooth over the back of his head. "I just thought that before this went any further, we should probably go upstairs."

She didn't mention the reality that Griff might suddenly show up. After Rafe's call to the Phoenix yesterday, that had always been a possibility. After all, this was the place any member of the team would come if they were in trouble. If Griff wanted to look for them, he would start here.

Gradually awareness of time and place came back into Rafe's eyes. He closed his mouth, his lips thinning into a straight, taut line. Without comment he released her, stepping back so that their bodies were no longer in contact.

Although she knew from his face that something had changed, she smiled at him, lifting her hand to lay it against his cheek. Before she could complete the motion, he took another step back, the movement clearly meant to thwart her intent.

"Rafe?" she questioned, feeling a growing unease. She tried to think what she might have said or done that would have precipitated his withdrawal.

"Forgive me," he said, his voice very low. "I know you'll think I'm running away again, but I don't believe that would be good for either of us."

"Going upstairs?"

"It seems to me we have a more pressing agenda. This would prove a distraction we can't afford right now."

A *distraction?* He was right about that, of course, but still…

"I see," she said, trying to gather pride as an armor against the pain of this newest rejection.

One minute he had seemed as eager to hold her as she was to be in his arms. The next he was again almost a stranger.

"Whatever you think—" he began.

"Spare me," she said, cutting off any explanation he wanted to make. "You started this. I didn't, despite that business about warning me. I don't know what the hell kind of game you're playing, Rafe, but whatever it is, I should probably mention I'm not enjoying it."

"Do you think I am?"

Maybe he wasn't. All she knew was that she was too tired to deal with him. Or to deal with this.

"I don't know. I don't know you anymore. All I know is that for a moment at least, you wanted me. Maybe not what we had before. Maybe for nothing more permanent than what's left of tonight, but you *did* want me. And I don't know what I said or did—"

"It wasn't anything you did."

"Just…the press of business," she mocked.

"I shouldn't have touched you."

"More mea culpas?"

"If you need to hear them."

"I don't suppose I do. They really don't change anything, do they?"

"For what it's worth—"

"Don't," she ordered softly. "Just…don't."

Awkwardly adjusting her clothing to cover her exposed breast, she stepped by him, moving through the darkness of the narrow hall. Before she reached the bottom of the stairs, the tears had begun.

She fought them as she had before, although no one would know this time if she had cried. Crying not for what had happened tonight, of course, as humiliating as that had been, but for what once was and apparently would never be again.

That was a lesson she had finally learned. That she hadn't learned it the first time was entirely her fault. After all, Rafe had done his best to tell her that just because she still loved him didn't mean he felt the same way.

Chapter Eight

Rafe's hand was on her cheek. She turned her face against it, pressing longingly into the caress. Seeking to deepen the contact between them.

"There's someone downstairs."

For a second or two she tried to make the whispered sentence fit into her dream. It was disturbing enough to pull her from it instead.

She opened her eyes to find Rafe leaning over her bed. In the faint moonlight that seeped into the room through its sheer draperies, his face was shadowed, almost sinister.

And even after she was awake, the dream images that lingered in her brain were almost as powerful as this reality. Certainly more pleasant.

"Downstairs?" she repeated, whispering as he had.

"Come on," he ordered.

By that time, she was far enough out of the web of the dream to sense his urgency. She began to sit up. As soon as she did, he straightened, moving across the room to stand beside the open door.

He seemed to be listening to something she couldn't hear. Something that had obviously been loud enough to wake him.

She threw back the covers and slipped her legs off the side of the bed. The resultant series of squeaks from the mattress were loud enough to cause Rafe to look at her over his shoulder. Warned, she took greater care in easing up off the bed.

She tiptoed across the carpet, stopping behind him. For the first time she realized that he held the Glock he'd brought into her bedroom in his right hand.

Maybe this would prove to be nothing but a false alarm, as that episode had been. Maybe what had awakened Rafe were simply the normal sounds an old house makes settling for the night.

Then, coming from the darkened rooms below, she heard a noise that could not in any way, shape or form be dismissed as normal. Not in a supposedly empty house at midnight.

Someone had opened a door. The house's proximity to the ocean caused most of the hinges to creak. She had noticed that last night. The same unmistakable sound she had just heard.

She put her hand on Rafe's shoulder, squeezing with her fingers. He nodded in response. He had heard it, too.

And of course, he'd heard something from downstairs before this. Whatever it was that had caused him to come to her room.

He had needed to know exactly where she was before he went wandering around a dark house with a loaded gun. Until he told her otherwise, she decided, that would be exactly where she was right now. Pretending to be his shadow.

"Stay here," he whispered.

She felt him move, pulling free of her fingers and stepping through the bedroom door. He held his weapon in both hands, leading with it.

Heading downstairs? Or would he wait for whoever was there to come up here?

The danger in doing that was all too evident. They had

no way to know what was going on down there. Whoever this was could be setting a fire or rigging an explosive. They could be busy filling the place full of booby traps, assuming that the two of them were still sound asleep up here.

As she had been. As she would still have been if Rafe hadn't awakened her.

But just because she hadn't heard the original noise didn't mean she had no role in this. She might not have a weapon, but she had training and experience. Not as much as Rafe, but that didn't mean she was going to be content to remain a bystander in whatever was about to happen. No way in hell.

He couldn't know how many of them were down there. Despite being unarmed, she would help even the odds.

Decision made, she took a breath and then followed Rafe into the hall. He was already edging along the wall toward the top of the stairs. She ran along the carpeted passage until she caught up to him, again stopping at his shoulder.

He turned his head and suddenly they were face-to-face. Eye-to-eye. Breath-to-breath. The moonlight was strong enough out here to allow her to see his features, but not to read what was in his eyes.

Get back, he mouthed, gesturing with a movement of his chin toward the room she'd just left.

She shook her head and watched his mouth tighten in frustration. He couldn't afford to argue, not out here, and they both knew it.

He began to move again, slanting across the hall at an angle that would bring him to the top of the stairs. Without allowing herself time to think about the wisdom of what she was doing, she followed, once more positioning herself behind him. He glanced back at her, giving it one more shot.

"Stay here," he hissed.

To listen and wonder what was going on? Not likely. Besides, if something happened to Rafe, she'd be left without a weapon. Then whoever was down there could do whatever they pleased, and she wouldn't have any way to stop them. Given those options…

She shook her head.

He didn't try again to convince her. Instead he started down the staircase. Back against the wall, weapon extended, he went down sideways, one slow, infinitely careful step at a time. She followed, praying that none of the risers creaked.

If they did, it wasn't enough to give them away. They reached the bottom, and before Rafe stepped off the bottom step, he paused to listen again.

Elizabeth had heard nothing on the way down, concentrating on any noise they might be making. Now she listened as well. There were no more noises from the darkened rooms to give away the location of whoever was down here.

Apparently they weren't going to be that lucky. They were going to have to play hide-and-seek in the dark with some unidentified intruder.

For the first time she wondered how he'd gotten in. Rafe had reactivated the security system as soon as they were inside. Maybe the alarms had already gone off at whatever firm Griff employed to guard his property. Maybe while they were sneaking down the stairs, help was already on the way.

As that comforting thought formed, Rafe stepped off the bottom step. His bare feet made no sound on the hardwood floor, but her heart, which had already been beating too rapidly, lodged in her throat.

Truth or dare time. They had entered enemy territory. And they had no idea who that enemy might be.

Rafe moved silently through the moon-touched rooms.

The faint, silvered light made everything ghostly, even furniture that she recognized from the time they'd spent here before they'd gone upstairs.

He stopped in the doorway of each room, the Glock held in front of him. His gaze and the weapon moved in unison, sweeping the perimeters. Searching for whoever had opened that door.

One by one they covered the rooms until the only area that remained unsearched was the kitchen. Maybe the intruder had gone out through the back door, she thought, and down the exterior stairs off the deck. Or maybe he'd gone into the basement. That entrance was also in the kitchen.

Despite the need to understand who this was and how he'd gotten in, she wouldn't be disappointed if they found no one. Who had been in the house was a mystery she could live with. As long as they both got out safely.

Feeling useless, she trailed Rafe down the narrow hall that led to the kitchen. He seemed to be taking more care now, easing along it as slowly as he had down the stairs.

When they reached the doorway, he turned his head, looking back at her once more. The kitchen's wrap-around windows, which had allowed that unimpeded view of the ocean while she'd cooked dinner, also provided enough moonlight so that she could see his face for the first time since they'd left the upstairs.

His eyes held hers for maybe five seconds. There was something within them that made her expect him to speak to her, in spite of the obvious danger of doing that.

Then, turning back toward the kitchen, he stepped through the door. And everything seemed to happen at once.

She heard Rafe shout. Someone answered, although whatever words he said were unintelligible, sounding on top of Rafe's.

Suddenly the lights in the kitchen came on and Rafe shouted again. This time something that made sense.

"Drop it, you bastard, or I swear I'll shoot you."

She waited for gunfire. Rafe's or whoever he'd ordered to drop his weapon.

"Sinclair? Rafe Sinclair?"

The tone of that question wasn't what she might have expected from an enemy who had just been disarmed. But if he were disarmed…

She moved far enough into the doorway to see part of the kitchen. Rafe was still in a shooter's stance, knees bent, the Glock pointed at a target she couldn't see. Not until she took another step into the room.

On the other side of it, hands raised in the classic gesture of surrender—although one of them still held a weapon— was the intruder.

Not Gunther Jorgensen, she decided. Tall and broadshouldered, with dark hair and eyes, this man looked nothing like the grainy photograph in the terrorist's file.

Those intense eyes had been drawn to the doorway by her movement. Rafe must also know she was here, but he didn't look at her, his entire concentration on the man in front of him.

"I'm behind you," she warned unnecessarily.

"Weapon on the counter," Rafe ordered, ignoring her.

"Ms. Richardson?"

Whoever the intruder was, he knew her name. And the name he had just called her was not the one that had been created by the CIA when the team disbanded. It was her real name.

"Who the hell *are* you?" Rafe demanded, recognizing, as she had, the significance of that.

"John Edmonds. We talked yesterday. I took your call at the Phoenix. I have identification. If you're familiar with the—"

"Put the goddamn gun down," Rafe interrupted. "Do it."

This time, after a brief, assessing interval, the intruder obeyed. He leaned to the side, moving carefully, with his hands still held high. Slowly he brought the one that was holding the weapon down, laying the gun on the kitchen counter.

"Now move away from it," Rafe said.

As the intruder obeyed, Elizabeth skirted behind Rafe. She edged along the counter toward the weapon, staying well out of the reach of the man who'd put it there.

When she was close enough, she reached out and picked up the gun. It was a Beretta, the weapon of choice for a lot of operatives.

Despite the length of time since she'd handled a gun, it fit comfortably into her palm, just as her own agency-issued firearm had. She had to admit that she felt better with it there.

Despite Rafe's continued vigilance, she trained the gun on the man who claimed to be a member of Griff's new organization. The problem with that claim was that everyone in the Phoenix had once been a member of the External Security Team.

"You know him?" Rafe asked.

Rafe had left the team before she had. Maybe he was thinking Edmonds had been a late addition.

They had lost people through the years. It was the nature of what they did. And so there had been, of necessity, replacements. This man hadn't been one of them.

"I've never seen him before in my life."

"You sure?"

"Absolutely."

She was. Whoever John Edmonds was, he hadn't been a member of the team prior to the time the CIA had ordered it stood down. She couldn't imagine, therefore, why he would have been invited to join the Phoenix.

"I contacted Griff when I heard what he was doing," the intruder explained.

"When you *heard?*" Rafe repeated, emphasizing the last word. "How the hell would you hear about the Phoenix?"

"We have…mutual acquaintances."

"In the company."

It was what most of the CIA's operatives called the agency among themselves. It was certainly a term Edmonds should be familiar with. *If* he were telling the truth.

There was a slight movement of the intruder's mouth, almost a tightening. "I wasn't CIA. I was with the NSA."

The information seemed to be reluctantly given. That could be an act, of course, but if what he'd just said were true, he *might* be reluctant to reveal it. An entity more secretive than the CIA, much of what the National Security Agency did was shrouded in mystery, even from the intelligence community.

"That doesn't explain why you're here," Rafe said.

"Griff thought you might come to the summerhouse. He asked me to check it out."

"So…believing we might be here, you break in in the middle of the night? That seems like an invitation for disaster."

"I didn't *break* in. Griff gave me the codes. And I had no way of knowing who was inside. Considering what happened in Mississippi yesterday, I didn't feel I could take the chance that someone else might have the same idea as Griff about your destination."

It was plausible enough. After all, he knew their names. He knew about Rafe's call to the Phoenix. And he had the security codes for the summerhouse.

"Why didn't Griff come himself?"

"He's in Moscow. When I finally got in touch with him

to tell him about your call, he asked me to do some ground-work in trying to locate you before he gets back.''

That didn't sound like Griff. If Cabot believed one of his people was in trouble, it wouldn't matter what he was do-ing. He would come.

''And now that you've located us?''

The tone of Rafe's question reflected her own doubts about what they were being told.

''I'm supposed to offer you my assistance.''

Rafe laughed.

Surprised by the harshness of that sound, she took her eyes off the man who claimed to be part of the Phoenix long enough to glance at him. His eyes still on his captive, Rafe's expression was as mocking as his laughter had been.

''Did you give Griff my message? Did you tell him I'm not going to play this game?''

''There is no game, no matter what you believe. As a friend, Griff passed on to you a legitimate security alert, issued by the CIA's new antiterrorism unit. As far as he's aware, nobody from the agency knows he's spoken to you. And nobody's trying to manipulate you into doing any-thing.''

''What do you know about Gunther Jorgensen?''

Edmonds's eyes narrowed slightly. ''The German terror-ist?''

''Griff didn't tell you that's what the alert was about?''

''I know he's been dead for years,'' Edmonds said with-out bothering to answer the second question. ''Somebody blew him away. Paris, I think. Maybe…five years ago. At least that.''

''The CIA in their wisdom has decided he's still alive.''

There was virtually no response. No reaction at all in the dark eyes. Elizabeth wasn't sure what that might mean.

''That's what the alert was about?'' Edmonds asked.

Rafe nodded.

"Then you must have had something to do with his death."

"Griff sent you here without bothering to make you aware of how I'm connected to Jorgensen? Is that what you're saying?"

"He sent me here in hopes you'd show up," Edmonds said patiently, ignoring the sarcasm. "He wants a meeting. You and whoever he can round up from the Phoenix on such short notice."

"A meeting here?"

"At Griff's estate in Maryland."

"What do you think?"

It took a moment for Elizabeth to realize Rafe's question had been directed at her. Another to realize she wasn't sure what she thought.

Whoever this man was, he was incredibly well informed. And the information he had was not the kind that would be readily available to anyone outside Griff's immediate circle.

"I'd like to see the identification he mentioned," she said. "Something from the Phoenix."

"Of course," Edmonds said. "If you'll allow me..."

He made a gesture with his right hand, moving it toward the breast pocket of his dress shirt. Both of them reacted, fingers tensing over the triggers of the weapons they held. The motion stopped, his hand turning, palm toward them again.

"I *did* ask permission," he said, sounding amused.

If nothing else, Elizabeth thought, he has guts.

"Slowly," Rafe said.

Her mouth had gone dry, but Edmonds couldn't have much in the way of lethal weapons in a shirt pocket. Despite that reassurance, her eyes remained trained on the long fingers that dipped into the pocket of the blue Oxford cloth he wore. They came out with only a business card, which he held out to Rafe.

"Get it," Rafe instructed her. "Stay at arm's length."

She didn't need the reminder. If she hadn't been so eager to see what Edmonds was holding, she would have told him so.

Instead, she reached out for the card, her fingers never making contact with those of the man who held it. As soon as it was in her hand, she lowered her eyes to study it.

The card was nondescript enough to meet even CIA standards. Edmonds's name, the Phoenix, and a phone number. At the top center was a logo of a stylized bird rising from the flames.

"Elizabeth."

Rafe. She turned and found his hand extended. She walked back to him and laid the ivory-colored rectangle on his palm.

"Watch him," Rafe ordered her.

"I believe you have one that Griff gave you when he invited you to join," Edmonds added. "A comparison of the two might remove any lingering doubt."

She glanced at Rafe's face for confirmation, wondering how Edmonds could possibly know about that other card unless Griff had told him. Rafe nodded almost imperceptibly before he examined the card Edmonds had handed her.

"He didn't give you anything else?" Rafe asked.

"I suppose he thought that should be proof enough."

She wasn't sure it was. Not for her.

She knew it wouldn't be for Rafe. His eyes lifted from the card to focus on the man whose arms had gradually lowered until his hands were now below shoulder level. Rafe's face was closed and tight, so that it was hard to tell what he thought.

"Name them," he said, his voice very soft.

"Name...who?" Edmonds seemed puzzled by the request.

"The members of the Phoenix. Name them."

Edmonds laughed. "If I did that, I'd expect you to shoot me," he said, his voice perfectly relaxed. His face, in contrast to Rafe's, seemed on the verge of breaking into a smile. "I'd deserve it."

It was a request any of them would have refused. The ultimate betrayal, and Edmonds hadn't made it.

"One name," Rafe pressed.

"Go to hell."

Genuine refusal on the grounds of security? Or a convenient out?

Her gaze went back to Rafe. His eyes were on Edmonds as if he were attempting to evaluate him.

"I'm no Jake Holt," Edmonds said softly, "but other than that I don't have any other proof to offer you. Whether you trust me or not is up to you."

Jake Holt had been a member of the EST from the beginning. He had also been the only traitor the team had ever had to deal with. That this man would know his name seemed particularly telling. And convincing evidence that he was who and what he claimed. At least it was to her.

And for Rafe?

"Right now," he said, "I don't suppose I have much choice."

Chapter Nine

"You drive," Rafe said.

Maybe it was nothing but paranoia, but he'd be more comfortable if he were situated so that he could keep an eye on Edmonds during the trip to Maryland. Despite the proof the man had presented less than an hour ago, Rafe would be a fool to trust someone he didn't know. Not in this situation.

"My car or yours?" Edmonds asked. He didn't seem insulted or surprised by the order.

"Yours."

"You riding shotgun?" Edmonds asked.

"I'll be in the back."

"Then…Ms. Richardson?" John Edmonds's words sounded like an invitation.

Hearing them, Rafe turned to find Elizabeth standing in the doorway. She had just come down from the upstairs bedroom where she had gone to dress and repack her suitcase.

"She'll sit in back with me," he said.

He was sure that's what Edmonds expected. His suggestion that Elizabeth might do otherwise could not be taken seriously. Rafe even wondered if it had been a form of taunting.

More paranoia? Or the result of the way Edmonds had

looked at Elizabeth earlier in the kitchen? Granted, there were few men who would have had the self-control necessary *not* to look. He didn't, despite the lecture he'd given himself after he'd made the mistake of kissing her last night.

Her nightgown had been virtually transparent under the fluorescent lighting. What the sheerness of the material didn't expose, it hinted at, clinging to every curve of her body. It was no wonder John Edmonds couldn't keep his eyes off her.

Rafe didn't blame him being interested, but he didn't have to like that he was. Actually, there wasn't much about Edmonds being here that he did like. Not even if Griff *had* sent him.

Actually, he admitted, his dislike was probably based more on the fact that Griff *had* sent him than on anything the man had done. It implied Cabot didn't trust Rafe to keep Elizabeth safe.

And Griff had never before questioned his ability to handle any situation. Because Rafe had left the team as soon as the effects of the trauma associated with the Amsterdam bombing had become apparent, he had never before had reason to.

"Then…whenever you're ready," Edmonds suggested easily.

He reached out for the suitcase Elizabeth was carrying, his hand fastening over the handle beside hers. For a moment it seemed as if she were going to refuse to hand it over. Edmonds must have thought the same thing because he smiled at her again as he virtually pulled it from her grasp.

"I'm very trustworthy, I promise you," he said lightly.

"And *I* promise *you* that I'm very capable of carrying my own bag."

"I'm sure you are," he agreed, his smile widening attractively. "I, however, seem to be incapable of watching you do that. Early lessons are seldom forgotten. My mother was of the old school."

"Are you suggesting that chivalry isn't dead?" Elizabeth responded, her lips relaxing into a smile.

"Not in the South, in any case."

"You first," Rafe said.

The conversation was verging too close to flirtation for him to be comfortable with it. Elizabeth's eyes lifted, questioning the tone of the command.

Let her, he thought. Despite his determination to keep his hands off her, he'd be damned if he were going to stand around and watch Edmonds hit on her.

John's expression was slightly quizzical as well, as if he weren't quite sure what he'd done to offend. Rafe didn't care what either of them thought. All he knew was that the sooner they got to Cabot's place and got Edmonds's role in this resolved, the better he'd feel about what was going on.

No matter Griff's intentions, Rafe didn't like being saddled with an unknown factor on a mission as dangerous as this was turning out to be. He had enough to deal with without having to worry about where Edmonds was every minute and what he was doing.

"I parked a few hundred yards down the drive. If there *was* someone else waiting up here," John said, "I didn't want to give them any warning."

In that case, Rafe conceded, it might be smarter for them to take his car. He had pulled it into the enclosed garage under the house when he and Elizabeth had arrived.

Then, to be on the safe side if anyone was trying to track them, they should move Edmonds's car inside the garage. Which meant someone would still have to make the trek down the road to bring it back up here, he realized. That all seemed more trouble than it was worth.

"Lead the way," he said as soon as he reached that conclusion. "Elizabeth will follow you. I'll bring up the rear."

"Fair enough," Edmonds agreed.

His eyes were drawn to Elizabeth again as she opened her purse and took out the Beretta that Rafe had confiscated.

"I don't suppose I could talk you into giving me back my weapon," Edmonds asked.

"No," Rafe said uncompromisingly.

"I was afraid of that." Edmonds's concession didn't seem to contain any trace of anger or disappointment. After all, he had probably expected that answer, too. "You know how it is. After all these years I feel naked without it."

"Elizabeth is more than able to guard your back."

"And you'll guard hers. I guess all we'll have to worry about then is a frontal assault."

Without waiting for a reply, Edmonds opened the door that led to the basement stairs and stepped through it. Elizabeth glanced back at Rafe, her expression again questioning. Mouth tight, he shook his head, trying to warn her silently that he still had his doubts about Griff's messenger.

She nodded her understanding before she turned to follow the supposed Phoenix agent. Taking a quick look around the kitchen, Rafe put both hands around the grip of the Glock, and followed them down the stairs.

When he reached the midway point, he saw that Edmonds had stopped at the door leading from the basement to the outside. Dawn had broken. In its pale, watery light, the unpaved road that stretched before them, little more than a private drive, seemed very exposed.

"Through the woods," Rafe said.

No one argued, although with the long summer's heat and moisture the undergrowth beneath the trees that sheltered the narrow lane appeared so dense as to be impenetrable. As Rafe had surveyed their surroundings, he'd decided that wasn't a bad thing. Not for what he needed to accomplish.

Edmonds led the way, seeming as comfortable with the trailblazing as he had been flirting with Elizabeth. Periodically he would hold a branch or a vine back to allow her an easier passage through a particularly difficult spot. As soon as she cleared whatever obstacle he was protecting her from, he would again assume the lead.

The insects had come to life with the first rays of the sun. From the woods around them came a steady hum of activity, broken by the occasional birdcall.

After less than fifteen minutes Rafe could see the roof of Edmonds's car ahead of them through the trees. During their journey, they had skirted the road. By keeping within the cover of the woods, he hoped they'd be shielded from view of anyone who might be out there waiting for them.

The floor of the forest would have been less dense farther in and easier to travel through, but they would have been more visible. The thickness of the vegetation along the drive, where the undergrowth was exposed to sunlight, suited Rafe's purposes exactly.

As he neared his car, Edmonds stopped and looked back. He seemed to be waiting for instructions, apparently having accepted Rafe's command of this expedition with grace if not enthusiasm.

Rafe's first inclination was to signal him to move out into the lane. He'd seen nothing out of the ordinary since they'd left the house. Nothing had set off any of his well-honed instincts for danger. It all seemed as peaceful as any stretch of country woods anywhere.

Elizabeth had halted, too. Both of them were now turned toward him, awaiting his decision. Before he made one, he listened. In the early-morning stillness he couldn't hear anything beyond the low, almost mesmerizing murmur of the insects.

Slowly he scanned the area around the car. The broken patterns of light and shade, created by the overhanging branches that partially filtered the thin sunlight, could in themselves be a form of camouflage. But there seemed to be no unnatural shapes or colors in the surrounding woods. Nothing suspicious. Nothing, he decided, that demanded this much caution.

After all, there was no reason to expect there might be. No one had followed him and Elizabeth here from Mississippi. No one but the members of the team knew this location. Unless someone had been able to trail Edmonds...

Not at night, he told himself. Not over the isolated back roads that led to this house. Edmonds would have known. Anyone would.

His gaze had completed the slow circuit of their surroundings, and he'd seen absolutely nothing to be concerned about. Finally he met John's eyes and nodded permission.

Edmonds started forward, but because the brush thickened along the road, he had to force a path through it. After he had, he held the foliage back to ease Elizabeth's passage.

Even with his help, she struggled through the undergrowth. Once she used the hand holding her weapon to push back a branch impeding her progress.

Rafe, following a few feet behind them choked back a warning. Edmonds seemed oblivious to the opportunity she'd given him, appearing more concerned with helping her through to the road.

Consequently, Elizabeth was the first to step out into the open. By then, of course, the weapon she carried was back in position. Edmonds cleared the last of the brush almost immediately, stepping out onto the roadbed beside her.

He should have told them to check out the car before

they unlocked it, Rafe realized belatedly. He began to hurry in case neither of them remembered who they were dealing with and took that necessary precaution.

The crack of a high-powered rifle echoed through the dawn stillness. Adrenaline had already been pumping through his bloodstream, both from exertion of the walk and the need for constant wariness. Its effects, along with the unmistakable sound of the rifle, ricocheted him back to the last time he'd heard that distinctive crack and whine.

Instead of viewing a mixture of dappled light and deep shadow in a Virginia woods, the scene before him was the brilliant noonday heat of a Parisian street. Like an echo of the current shot, he heard the sound of the rifle he himself had fired and watched the bullet explode at high velocity into the skull of the man he'd targeted.

The flashback seemed to last only a second or two. He couldn't be sure of that, because by the time it was over and the present had reformed before his eyes, neither of the people who had been standing at the edge of the roadway was there.

Mouth dry, he eased up from the low crouch he'd automatically dropped into at the sound of the shot. He couldn't even be sure if there had been one shot or a barrage.

The woods around him were as quiet as a tomb. Even the ubiquitous buzz of the insects had been silenced.

He fought the urge to call out to Elizabeth. And the far stronger one to go plowing through the corridor of scrub vegetation that lay between his current position and the last place he'd seen her.

She's fine, he told himself. She and Edmonds were doing exactly what he was. Lying low, trying to get some idea of the shooter's location, and trying not to call attention to themselves in the meantime.

Of course, the gunman obviously knew where she and

Edmonds were. That shot had been taken as soon as they'd appeared on the roadway.

Whoever was out here must have found the car during the night and banked on them doing exactly what they had done this morning. He had been waiting for them to show up. And they hadn't disappointed him.

Elizabeth and Edmonds were pinned down, which meant it was up to him to do something to get them out of this, Rafe decided. He tried to mentally recreate the sound of the shot, in order to judge distance or direction.

He couldn't. The flashback, triggered by its sound, had distorted his perceptions. He couldn't be sure what was real and what was memory. Certainly not sure enough to use his impressions to fix the shooter's location.

And his need to get to Elizabeth was becoming more urgent. He needed to know she was all right. If he didn't, the building anxiety about her safety was likely to have additional side effects he couldn't afford right now.

He began moving toward the last place he'd seen her, making no attempt to hide the noise he was making. If Jorgensen wanted a target, he'd give him one. It was only after that thought formed that he realized the concession he'd just made.

Jorgensen was dead. He had watched him die.

And he had done it again in that flashback. Although the people who had been with the terrorist had rushed to his aid, there was no way that head shot had left him alive. No way.

Almost in answer to that mental assertion, a bullet slammed into the trunk of the tree above him, sending splinters of bark down on his head. It was immediately answered by the deep cough of Edmonds's Beretta. He hoped like hell Elizabeth was the one firing it.

He glanced up at the damaged wood above his head.

Whatever ammo the bastard was using, he didn't intend for anybody to walk away.

As the last echo of the two shots faded, their sound lost within the canopy of trees, Rafe changed direction, angling back the way he'd come. The bullet hadn't come from beyond the parked car, as he had expected. The shooter seemed to have established his stance a couple of hundred feet back down the lane. Toward the house.

Which would have given him a clear line of fire on anyone coming down the road. As well as a line of sight on anyone doing what they had done—using the woods as protection until they'd had to step out of them and onto the roadway beside the car.

The whole time he was thinking about the setup of the ambush, Rafe was moving toward the area from which the second rifle shot had been fired. This time he concentrated on making as little noise as he could.

The guy was obviously across the road. To get to him physically, Rafe would have to expose himself by crossing its narrow, open expanse.

Unless he could get the man with the rifle to expose himself first. Thinking about the possibility of doing that, he stopped at the barrier of undergrowth fronting the drive.

He studied the opposite side, eyes probing the shadows. Looking for any anomaly in the natural patterns that might indicate his enemy's location. Again there was nothing.

As he paused to make that appraisal, he heard a telltale rustle in the vegetation to his right. He took one last scan of the other side of the road, watching for some reaction to the noise he was hearing.

Then he turned his gaze, as well as the muzzle of the Glock, in the direction of the sound. Given the location of the shot that had struck the tree above his head, whoever was approaching him through the undergrowth on this side of the road couldn't be the man with the rifle. It didn't necessarily follow, however, that it was a friend.

There had to be some explanation as to how they'd been discovered, because he knew no one had followed them here from Mississippi. He would stake his life on that. It was all he knew right now with any degree of certainty.

That and the fact that someone had set up an ambush at the place where John Edmonds had abandoned his car before he'd stolen up to the house. The question now was whether that ambush had been set up with or without Edmonds' contrivance.

The third rifle shot was unexpected, causing him to duck instinctively. He heard the bullet strike something off to his right, very near where he had heard the rustle in the bushes a moment ago.

There was no outcry, but there also seemed to be no more movement. Or maybe whoever had been there was now taking pains to ensure his approach was silent.

Rafe's eyes again considered the opposite side of the road. Nothing moving there, either.

They could play this game all day, each of them hunkered down and protected by the density of the foliage around them. And unless their attacker had planted some kind of trap in or around the car—

"It's Edmonds." The whisper came from his right, very nearby. "Elizabeth's hit."

The words were like a fist in Rafe's gut. For a split second he wondered if they might be some kind of trick. Even as he considered the possibility, he knew he had no choice but to react as if he believed them.

Especially when he remembered the damage that second shot had done to the tree over his head. The shooter had chosen his weapon with the clear intent to maim, if he didn't kill. The realization of the kind of injury one of those slugs could do to the slender body he'd held in his arms last night made him physically ill.

If she'd been hit, they had to get Elizabeth out of here. That was their first priority. To get her someplace where she could be treated. And every second was critical.

He turned his head, concentrating on keeping his voice as low as Edmonds's had been. There wasn't time to try to coordinate a plan.

"Get her into the car. I'll cover you. Then get the hell out of here. Get her to a hospital."

"What about—"

"Do it," Rafe ordered, his voice too loud in the stillness. He took a breath, determined to stay in control. "Just get her in the car and then get her out of here."

There was no response, but before he had to issue the order again, he heard Edmonds moving back the way he'd come. As Rafe waited, allowing plenty of time for him to reach the edge of the road where he'd left Elizabeth, a dozen unanswered questions bombarded him, the most important, how badly she'd been hurt.

It was too late to ask. Too late for everything but what he intended. Without allowing himself to think of anything but the feel of Elizabeth's mouth trembling under his as it had last night, he stood, presenting himself as an alternate target for the shooter.

Chapter Ten

As soon as he was standing, he pumped two quick shots into the location he believed was the most likely place for the shooter to be set up. They drew an answering fire, but it wasn't directed at him. The bastard was still targeting Elizabeth and Edmonds.

The return fire did give him a more precise location, although by now the ambusher should already be moving. On the off chance that he wasn't, Rafe put two more rounds into the thickly shadowed area from which the rifle had spoken.

As he squeezed off the last, he began to force his way through the undergrowth, headed toward the road. There was only one way to make sure the next round would be aimed at him. He had to present a threat the man with the rifle couldn't ignore.

When he cleared the barrier of vegetation on this side of the road, he was relieved to hear movement on his right. It came from the direction in which Edmonds had disappeared. Apparently the Phoenix operative was doing what he'd been told.

As soon as Rafe's feet hit the smooth surface of the road, he began to run, charging across the lane toward the area from which the last series of shots had come. There was an immediate reaction. A bullet nipped the sleeve of his shirt a fraction of a second before he heard its report.

He didn't slow, but his next step, taken at a dead run, was a leap to the left. He continued a randomly zigzagging pattern as he crossed the open expanse.

Down the road a car door slammed. Despite his concentration on reaching his target, despite the roar of adrenaline running through his veins so strongly now that he felt invincible, he knew what the sound meant. Edmonds had gotten Elizabeth into the car.

He heard the second door close, followed by the sound of the engine starting. He felt a sense of triumph that nothing, not even the bullet that hit the ground in front of him, spraying dirt and gravel against his shins, could destroy.

He leaped into the brush on the far side of the road, blindly firing off another round into the vicinity he'd been targeting. There was no answer, but he had expected the shooter would move as he advanced on his position. He had counted on him doing that to give Edmonds a chance to get Elizabeth into the car. The question was: In what direction would that movement be?

From the road behind him, the car horn bleeted. Intent on scanning the area around him, his eyes searching patches of light and shade, Rafe didn't stop to respond.

He assumed that was Edmonds's way of letting him know he'd succeeded in carrying out the task he'd been given. That was all that mattered. Getting Elizabeth to a hospital. Whatever happened next—

The horn sounded again, a long impatient blast that pulled him out of his single-minded focus on the shooter. What the hell was Edmonds doing? He should be out of here by now.

Distracted, he slowed, shooting a glance over his shoulder. From where he was, he couldn't see the car. The horn sounded again, this time as another series of staccato beeps.

Ignoring them, Rafe started forward, moving more cautiously as he approached the area where he believed their attacker had been hiding. There was no one there now, but as he searched, expecting another shot at any moment, he discovered a shell casing lying beside an uprooted tree. The metal shone against the black loam of the forest floor.

Still alert, he knelt behind the fallen trunk, near where he'd found the casing. As he'd expected, there was a clear line of sight across it and through the woods to the road.

This was where the bastard had been set up. He scrutinized the surrounding area, but there was nothing here now. No one moving through the undergrowth. No sound but the insistent demand of Edmonds' horn.

Was it possible that despite Elizabeth's injury the idiot was waiting for him? If so, continuing to search for their ambusher would only delay the treatment she needed.

And, Rafe admitted, unless the shooter chose to reveal his location by taking another shot, which he didn't seem inclined to do, he had little chance of finding him. There were too many places here where an attacker could conceal himself, like that behind the fallen tree he'd chosen for his original ambushcade.

The next time the horn sounded, Rafe responded. Giving up the search, he began to make his way back to the road, moving cautiously, making use of whatever cover he could find.

Either his charge into the woods had frightened their attacker away or, more likely, he had accomplished what he'd intended. As with the explosion back in Magnolia Grove, Rafe believed that Elizabeth had been his target from the first. This time he had had more success.

He broke through the fringe of vegetation, stepping out onto the shoulder of the road. Apparently that was what Edmonds had been waiting for. He gunned the engine, sending the car skidding down the dirt road. It pulled up beside him, the passenger side door opening before it had stopped.

"Get in," Edmonds yelled.

"I told you to get out of here," Rafe said, but he was scrambling into the front seat as he said it.

Before he could close the door, Edmonds had the car moving again, this time in reverse. Almost reluctantly, anxiety twisting his guts, Rafe turned to look in the back seat.

Straight into Elizabeth's eyes. Although they were widely dilated, the dark pupils eating up most of the color, they seemed focused and alert. And clearly furious.

"What the hell was that about?" she demanded.

Ignoring the question as rhetorical, he examined her face instead of answering. It was far too pale, the faint freckles across her nose again starkly prominent.

His eyes fell to her right arm, which she was holding crossed over her breasts. She was pressing Edmonds's Oxford cloth dress shirt, haphazardly folded, over the upper part of the left. He could see a spreading bloodstain on the cloth beneath her fingers.

"How bad?" he asked.

"Not bad enough that you needed to play kamikaze. What the hell did you think you were doing?"

The tirade sounded remarkably normal. *She* sounded normal, and for the first time since Edmonds had told him she'd been hit, the coil of fear inside his stomach began to unwind.

She was losing blood. In and of itself that could be life-threatening, but she seemed to have all her faculties about her. Given the time that had passed since the first shot, that probably meant nothing major had been hit. No arterial bleeding. Anything else they could deal with.

The car swerved wildly. The hand of Elizabeth's injured arm, the one that was not applying pressure to her wound, came up as she tried to keep herself from being thrown sideways by that sudden change of direction.

When her fingers grabbed at the back of the seat, she breathed an expletive he'd never before heard her use. It was low, but it was definitely heartfelt. Smiling a little, despite the gravity of what had happened, he turned his head to look out through the windshield.

Edmonds had backed the car into a small turnoff. Before Elizabeth had a chance to right herself, he pressed the accelerator again, sending the sedan squealing back onto the road. This time heading away from Griff Cabot's summerhouse.

"FAR ENOUGH," Rafe said. He didn't have any idea how far they had come or how much time had passed since they'd left the dirt road and pulled onto the state highway. Long enough for him to be certain no one was following. "Take the next turn."

"I'm not sure—" Edmonds began.

"I want to look at that wound. Then we can decide where we go from there."

"We go to meet Griff," Elizabeth said. "Like he told us."

"That needs to be tended to."

"It's a graze," she said.

"A graze that's bleeding like a stuck pig."

"Thanks for the image," she said, "but it's still just a graze."

"That's accurate," Edmonds offered. "The bullet tore a chunk of flesh off her upper arm. As long as she keeps pressure on it—"

"I want to see for myself," Rafe interrupted, working to keep his fear-driven anger in check.

He still couldn't get the picture of the hole this same type of bullet had gouged in that tree out of his head. He couldn't seem to separate that damage from the memory of the unbroken smoothness of Elizabeth's skin.

"There's a turnoff ahead," he directed. "Take it."

"Rafe," Elizabeth protested, but thankfully the car had already begun to slow.

Rafe took one last look out the back window. There was no traffic. No tail. Wherever their attacker had disappeared to, it wasn't to come after them.

When he turned back to look through the windshield, he saw that the road they'd pulled off on, although paved, was almost as narrow as the drive leading up to Griff's. About a hundred yards ahead on the right was a small frame church.

"Behind the church," he said.

If they had to, they could break into it. The building would be unoccupied this time of the week, but it would undoubtedly have some kind of rudimentary kitchen. Maybe even a nursery with clean crib sheets ready for the next service.

Edmonds obeyed his instructions without argument. Before the car had come to a complete stop, Rafe had his door open. As he walked around behind the sedan, he checked out their surroundings. There was nothing here to alarm him, but he remembered that he had felt the same way just before Elizabeth stepped out of the woods and onto the drive at Griff's.

There was a cemetery beside the church, its gravestones old and weathered gray-green. The area was shaded by a couple of pin oaks. In close proximity to one of them, within a few feet of the last of the graves, someone had built a children's play area using two-by-fours and old tires.

The whole churchyard was deserted. There didn't even seem to be a parsonage nearby.

Satisfied that they would be undisturbed for the few vital minutes he needed to assure himself that they weren't mistaken about the seriousness of Elizabeth's wound, Rafe opened the back door on the driver's side, slipping into the seat beside her.

She slid her suitcase over to give him room, but her eyes were still angry and cold. He wasn't sure if that was because of what he'd tried to do back in the woods or because he'd demanded they stop here despite her repeated assurances that she was all right.

Not that he cared. All he cared about was seeing for himself whatever damage lay under that bloodstained shirt.

Without thinking, he touched her arm, slipping his fingers under it, right above the elbow. His intent was to lift it to get a better look at the injury.

An involuntary intake of breath brought his eyes up to her face. She had smothered the sound by the expedient of closing her mouth and setting her teeth tightly into her bottom lip.

Without warning, the features of the burned woman, her mouth opening in that terrible, silent scream, superimposed themselves over Elizabeth's. The smell and the heat of the fire were all around him. He could hear someone screaming, but he didn't know who it was.

As quickly as the flashback appeared, it faded. Once more Elizabeth's face was before him. His hand was no longer around her injured arm, although he couldn't remember removing it.

Instead of the anger he'd seen in her eyes, they were full of shock. He wondered if he'd said something or if he'd only jerked his hand away from her arm, hurting her in the process.

"I'm okay," she said, the words thready. "It only hurts when I laugh. Or move. Or breathe," she added shakily. "The truth is it hurts like hell."

"Take it off," he ordered, steeling himself for what lay beneath the cloth. He knew by now that this had been another mistake. He had no idea how he would react to the sight of Elizabeth's flesh, torn and bleeding.

He had cut himself a couple of times in the workshop without any psychological aftershocks, but that had been his own blood. His own pain. This was entirely different.

"Are you all right?" Elizabeth asked, her eyes puzzled and concerned.

Suddenly he knew with the clarity of one of those chilling flashbacks that he should get out of the car right now. He could go into the church, using the need for water and a clean bandage as his excuse.

Only the accusation Elizabeth had thrown at him last night held him immobile. He might make a fool of himself, finally exposing to her what he'd left six years ago rather than reveal. But if he did...

He repeated the phrase mentally, recognizing the significance. *If he did,* then she would finally understand why he'd walked out on her. She would know that what he had told her last night was the absolute truth. It had nothing to do with her.

"Move the damn shirt," he said, his voice hard with a tension she couldn't possibly understand.

Her teeth released her bottom lip, and her mouth opened slightly. Her right hand, the one holding Edmonds's shirt, lifted the fabric away from the wound.

Immediately blood began to seep out of the torn flesh. Seeping and not pumping. Which was a very good thing.

Edmonds's description of the injury had been accurate. The bullet had cut a furrow across the outer part of her arm. It was a raw, ugly gash and she was still losing blood, but it was exactly what they'd told him it was. Nothing more than that. Nothing worse.

"Okay," he said, almost light-headed with relief. Relief that the injury was relatively minor *and* that he hadn't gone off the deep end while viewing it. "Keep the pressure on it until we can find something to make a better pad. When we do, we can tie it on so you won't have to hold it.''

''There are some things in my suitcase,'' she said, putting the bloodstained shirt back over the wound. She winced as the cloth touched the gash, but she held it down tightly, ignoring the pain.

''Something cotton?'' he asked, remembering that sheer nightgown.

''There's a clean T-shirt in my bag in the trunk. I'll get it,'' Edmonds offered.

He climbed out of the car, closing the door behind him. Leaving them alone. Neither of them said anything for a moment.

''Rafe, what's wrong?'' she asked finally. The coldness had been wiped from her voice. And he knew *this* question wasn't rhetorical.

''Nothing,'' he said, and then, realizing how stupid that sounded, he amended it. ''I was worried about you.''

She held his eyes, but she didn't question what he'd just said. ''I thought you'd decided you're too old to play hero.''

''Me, too.''

''Don't you ever do anything like that again,'' she said, unshed tears shining in her eyes. ''Promise me, damn it. I don't need you to try to take a bullet for me. I don't need to have to worry about that.''

''You don't.''

''Then promise me.''

He thought about it for a couple of seconds.

''I've never lied to you. I'm not going to start now.''

''Damn you—''

''I don't remember you cursing so much.''

He had deliberately lightened his tone, but she wasn't buying the distraction. Her mouth tightened with frustration, and, seeing it, he smiled at her.

"Would you take a bullet for me, Elizabeth?"

Definitely a rhetorical question. And she made no attempt to deny what they both knew.

"How the hell did we get into this?" she asked, her voice plaintive.

"Since I'm not sure what 'this' is, I can't answer that. Maybe Griff can."

"I like him," she said, glancing down to adjust the makeshift bandage.

Him? Obviously not a reference to Griff, which left...

"You trust him?" A far more important question.

Her eyes came back up and after a moment she nodded. "I liked the way he handled himself back there. I especially liked that he wouldn't leave you behind."

Now that it was over, Rafe could admit he wasn't averse to being here rather than wandering around the woods, locked in combat with an adversary he couldn't see. An adversary armed with a very powerful rifle.

"That's what he was supposed to do. I *told* him to leave me."

"I don't think he recognizes the chain of command."

There had been a quirk at the corner of her mouth as she said it. Although he had understood the words were a gibe at his tendency to assume control of every situation, that subtle movement of her lips had lessened their impact.

His reaction to it was an urge to press a kiss over that exact spot. He didn't, of course. He had already revealed far more of how he felt than he'd ever intended.

Instead of getting better at hiding his emotions, he seemed to have gotten worse. At least where Elizabeth was concerned.

"Don't let your guard down just because you think he's one of the good guys," he warned. "He may not be."

"Is that what we are? Are we still the good guys?"

"As opposed to whoever that was out in the woods."

"And whoever set off that explosion."

"You think they're two different people?"

She shook her head. "Not really. But...there could be more than one person involved in this, couldn't there?"

She was right. Jorgensen had had a lot of followers. A lot of people as dedicated to the concept of violence as a political weapon as he was.

Or maybe that should be as he *is,* Rafe admitted, although he didn't want to even consider the possibility that Jorgensen could be alive.

The front door opened and Edmonds got back into the car. He turned, handing Rafe the T-shirt he'd taken from his suitcase in the trunk.

"I couldn't find anything I thought was really suitable," Edmonds said, "but she'll be more comfortable with a sling."

It was a good idea. The arm would be less painful if it were stabilized.

"Why not use John's shirt," she said. "Unless you want it back." The last was directed to Edmonds.

"You need it more than I do. I like the James Dean look," he said, glancing down at the snow-white T-shirt he was wearing.

"I'm afraid it's ruined."

"I'll buy him another one," Rafe said, his tone reflecting his impatience with the whole conversation. What the hell did it matter if Edmonds's shirt was damaged?

Elizabeth turned to look at him again, that same movement at the corner of her lips. It was too subtle to be called a smile, but it indicated amusement nonetheless.

He lowered his eyes, concentrating on folding the T-shirt Edmonds had handed him into a small, tight square. He couldn't blame Elizabeth for being amused. He'd made such a frigging deal yesterday about how it had been better for them both that he'd walked away six years ago. Now, faced with the reality that Edmonds was interested in her, he was acting like the proverbial dog in the manger.

Elizabeth wasn't his. Once she had been, and he had chosen to leave because he couldn't handle what had happened to him after Amsterdam.

And he could tell himself until he turned blue in the face that it had been the right thing to do. He had been telling himself that since the day last week when Griff Cabot had walked into his workshop.

He'd said it again when Elizabeth had appeared in the doorway of her dining room, demanding to know what the hell he thought he was doing back in her life. And when he'd taken her into his arms last night, giving in to what he had wanted to do from the minute he'd seen her again.

Six years ago he had surrendered any rights he'd ever had to make love to this woman. Unless he wanted to explain why he'd left and to give her a chance to decide if the man he was now was someone she still wanted.

I thought you'd decided you were too old to play hero, she had said. That decision had been made a long time ago, and it hadn't been a matter of age or lack of desire.

Griff Cabot had forged him into a weapon. After Amsterdam, he was as flawed as the dueling pistol he'd inherited. He gave the appearance of being the same person he had once been—controlled, efficient, deadly. He knew what a sham that was.

"I'll need something to tie this on with," he said.

"The belt of my robe?" Elizabeth suggested. "It's in my bag."

He reached behind her and unsnapped the suitcase, fumbling around in it until he located the belt. He pulled it free from the loops of the bathrobe, stuffing the garment back into the bag and refastening the locks.

Then he touched the fabric of Edmonds's shirt, signaling that she should release it. Elizabeth turned her head, refusing to watch what he was about to do. She knew as well as he did how much tying the pad into place tightly enough to stop that slow seep of blood was going to hurt.

Edmonds put his hand over the back of the seat, reaching out for hers. "It helps to have something to squeeze," he said, smiling at her. "It's like biting the bullet."

"You speak from experience?" she asked.

"You don't want to know."

"I thought you guys just listened in on the occasional conversation," she said, gripping his fingers gratefully as she talked.

Rafe was aware of the breath she took, preparing herself for the ordeal. He laid the pad over the gouge, which had begun bleeding again as soon as she'd removed the original bandage.

"Some of the things we got involved in were…a little more challenging," Edmonds said, his voice relaxed, almost teasing. "Nothing like the excitement you CIA types manage to generate, of course."

"Not anymore," Elizabeth said as Rafe tightened the knot.

The last syllable was almost a gasp. As she had before, she cut it off by catching her bottom lip in her teeth. Her fingers gripped Edmonds's almost spasmodically.

"That's it," Rafe said.

Let go of her hand, you bastard.

"Thanks," she said, sharing a smile between him and Edmonds. Her relief that it was over was almost palpable. His probably was, too.

"How about the sling?" Edmonds reminded him.

Elizabeth released his fingers, handing over the bloodstained shirt that had been lying in her lap. He took it, folding the tail of it back over the body. Then he leaned through the opening between the front seats to tie the ends of the sleeves around her neck. As he did, his face was very near her hair.

Too damn near.

As soon as that knot had been secured, Edmonds leaned back. There was nothing in his expression that Rafe could take exception to. They watched as Elizabeth carefully eased her injured arm into the cradle of the sling he'd made.

"Better?" Edmonds asked.

"I think it will be," she said, making minor adjustments to the shirt that was now supporting her arm.

"That's it then," Rafe said.

Both of them looked at him as if what he'd said made no sense. Maybe it didn't in the midst of what was obviously a mutual admiration society.

"We've been here long enough," he warned. "We may have lost our attacker, but we don't want to give him an opportunity to pick up the trail."

Edmonds nodded. "You riding back there?"

The smart thing to do would be to get out of the back seat and walk back around the car to the front passenger side where he'd started out. Of course, he hadn't done the smart thing since Cabot had asked his question: *Do you know where she is?*

He didn't do it now.

"I'll stay back here for the time being," he said.

Edmonds made no comment about that decision. He turned around and started the car.

Rafe was aware that Elizabeth was looking at him. As a form of self-protection, he didn't allow his eyes to meet hers. He focused them through the front windshield instead. And finally, after a long moment, she did the same.

Chapter Eleven

"Almost there," Edmonds said. "How's she doing?"

Rafe looked down at the woman who was sleeping in his arms. He wasn't sure how that had happened. They certainly hadn't discussed it, but at some time during the long drive, he had ended up holding Elizabeth. As she breathed, her breast moved gently against his chest.

He had thought a couple of times about waking her to make sure she was all right. Her breathing was slow and regular, however, and, given the amount of blood she'd lost, her color looked pretty good. He had finally decided to let her alone, more than content to hold her as the long miles ticked off the odometer.

"I think she's okay," he said, watching her face.

Her eyelids hadn't fluttered at the sound of his voice. He wasn't sure how significant that was, considering that neither of them had had a decent night's sleep since all this had started.

"I tried Griff again," Edmonds said, "but there's still no answer. There may be nobody there when we arrive. I'm not sure they were expecting us this soon."

Rafe wasn't convinced *anybody* was expecting them. In spite of Elizabeth's willingness to trust John Edmonds, in spite of his actions at the summerhouse, Rafe was still wary of his role in whatever was going on. The question that bothered him most was why, considering all the people involved in the Phoenix that he knew, Griff would send a stranger to make contact.

"Everyone else was on assignment when your call came," Edmonds said, almost as if he had read Rafe's mind. "It may take a while to get in touch with the people Griff wants in on this."

"You *weren't* on assignment?"

"I'd just finished something. I'd gotten back into Washington the morning before you called. That's why I was in the office so late. I was trying to catch up on things that had been accumulating on my desk."

"You work out of the Washington office?"

Rafe knew Phoenix had two centers of operation, one in D.C. and the other in New York. He had never known who was assigned to each.

"Most of the time," Edmonds said. "When I'm in the office. Which isn't as often as you'd think."

Rafe didn't comment, letting the silence settle back around them.

"You never considered joining?" Edmonds asked.

Rafe couldn't deny that the thought had crossed his mind when Griff invited him. Considering the nature of the typical Phoenix case, as Griff had described it, he had realized very quickly that those unexpected flashbacks would place anyone he worked with in danger.

"No," he said shortly.

"I know Griff thinks highly of you."

At one time he supposed that had been true. It wasn't conceit to believe he'd been valuable to the team. His success rate had been exemplary, and he'd never lost a partner. That record alone was enough to keep him from wanting to spoil what he'd accomplished.

When he'd heard that rifle shot today, instead of being able to lay down a protective fire, he'd been thrown back into the middle of an event that had occurred years ago. Maybe if he hadn't been...

He looked down on Elizabeth's face. Without his conscious volition, his fingers found an errant strand of short, sun-streaked hair and brushed it away from her cheek. She stirred, turning her head restlessly. He removed his hand at once, holding it slightly away from her face until she'd settled back into the sleep from which his unthinking action had been in danger of awakening her.

He had sworn he wouldn't let anything happen to her. Within a day of making that promise, he'd allowed whoever was behind this put a bullet through her arm.

Mea culpa. There were now far too many of those in their relationship. More than they could possibly overcome.

"Griff thought highly of everyone he selected for the team," he said aloud. "Since he was the one who chose us, however, maybe he had a built-in bias."

"And a success rate that was legendary. He didn't make many mistakes."

He hadn't. None of them had, or they wouldn't have been around long enough to tell about it.

Griff had chosen his weapons with care, and then he had trained them hard, holding his agents to the same rigid standards to which he had always held himself. They had served him, and their country, well.

But when a weapon becomes flawed, when it cracks under pressure, it's useless. Worthy only of being discarded. That hadn't been Griff's decision six years ago, but it had been his.

Given the events of the last few days, it was one he didn't regret having made. And the sooner he could put Elizabeth under someone else's protection, the better off they all would be.

Maybe then even Edmonds would get what he wanted.

"YOU NEED SOME HELP with her?" Edmonds asked after he'd pulled the car around to the back of the Maryland estate and parked it.

"I can manage," Rafe said.

He would have to relinquish his care of Elizabeth soon enough. He wasn't going to do it voluntarily one minute before he had to.

He had begun to slide across the back seat of the sedan when she opened her eyes. For an instant they were sleep-fogged and unfocused. As soon as she realized he was holding her, they widened. And then they held on his face, examining it as if she had never seen it before.

"We're here," he said softly.

She nodded, struggling to sit upright.

"You don't have to do anything," he said. "I'll carry you inside, and then we'll—"

"We're at Griff's?" When he nodded, her lips tightened with determination. "Then I'll walk in under my own steam, if you don't mind."

"I do mind," he said, beginning to move across the seat again, still holding her.

"Don't do this to me, Rafe," she said, pushing against his chest with the palm of her hand.

"You're in no condition—"

"I worked too hard to be accepted on equal footing with everyone else on the team. I'm not going to spoil it now by being carried inside that house like some kind of damsel in distress. Would you want to be?"

She had a point. He would have fought tooth and nail against any such suggestion if he had believed he could possibly make it on his own. Without another word, he released her.

SHE ALLOWED RAFE to help her out of the car, his fingers reassuringly strong and steady under hers. Despite everything she could do, her knees trembled with weakness when she stood. She was forced to put her hand against the top of the door to control the vertigo.

Rafe didn't hurry her, obviously understanding what was going on. After a moment she met his eyes and nodded. He put his hand under the elbow of her good arm. In spite of what she'd said in the car, she was grateful for the support.

"Our instructions were to go in through the back," John said. "Through the famous rose garden."

She had known Griff came from a moneyed background, but she had never before been on the Cabot estate. It was damned impressive, she admitted, as they followed Edmonds across the carefully manicured lawn and through the extensive collection of hybrid teas.

After a few steps she freed her elbow from Rafe's hand and eased her good arm under the injured one, holding it against her body. Even while she slept, she had on some level been aware of the growing pain from the wound. Now every movement seemed to send an electric shock through her body, each step an unwanted reminder of the bullet that had grazed her.

"Still okay?" Edmonds asked as she approached.

He was holding open the door that led inside from the garden, allowing her to precede him into the house. She was aware of Rafe behind them, taking a last look around the grounds before he joined them.

The room Edmonds ushered her into was obviously Griff's study. It was dominated by a huge desk, covered with computer equipment. On the far side of it, under the windows, was an equally outsize couch. It was there John directed her.

As rocky as she was feeling, she didn't decline the invitation. She walked over to the sofa and lowered herself by careful stages down onto the butter-soft leather cushions.

By that time Rafe had come inside. His eyes assessed her face, but he didn't ask how she was feeling. She would have been reluctant to tell him.

"Now what?" he asked, the question addressed to John.

"We wait. Unless you can think of anything else we should be doing before Griff gets here."

"Then I'm taking Elizabeth upstairs," Rafe said. "Griff will have some kind of antibiotic salve and aspirin in the bathroom cabinets. Those will be better than nothing."

"I'm fine," she said, refusing to be shuffled off upstairs and away from the decision-making.

She understood Rafe was only trying to take care of her. If their roles were reversed, if he were the one who'd been injured, she would probably be doing the same. And he'd react with the same denial she'd just made.

"We can do it up there or we can do it here," he said uncompromisingly. "The choice is yours."

Rafe had apparently decided Edmonds was trustworthy enough to leave alone. She agreed, based not only on her instincts, but also on the depth of the man's knowledge about Griff's operations, not the least of which was how to get into both of Cabot's very secure houses.

And she wouldn't object to having a shower and getting out of these bloodstained clothes and into something clean. Rafe had thoughtfully brought her bag into the house with him.

"I'd like a shower," she said, giving in to his ultimatum without saying the words.

"That can be arranged. *After* I take a look at your arm."

He walked over to the couch and held out his hand. Her first inclination was to refuse to take it, despite knowing how ridiculous that would be. As deep and soft as the sofa was and as weak as she felt right now, it would probably be impossible to stand without his help.

She put her fingers into his and allowed him to pull her

to her feet. Then, as he had outside, he put his hand under her good elbow, guiding her toward the door on the other side of the room, which led out into a wide hallway. Without hesitation, Rafe directed her to the left.

"You've been here before," she said.

"Once or twice."

She hadn't been. Not here. Not at the summerhouse. Had the agency's old boys' network been alive and well, even among the team?

She was beginning to sound like one of those bitter feminist types who looked for sexism under every rock, she acknowledged in amusement. Not that it couldn't still be found, but the fact that she'd never been invited to either of Cabot's homes might be nothing more than coincidence. Lack of opportunity or need. It didn't equate to some antifemale bias.

As they climbed the stairs, that exclusion became the least of her worries. Either she was more out of shape than she'd realized or she'd lost more blood. The climb exhausted her, so that by the time they entered one of the bedrooms, she was leaning against Rafe openly.

The distance to the bathroom door on the other side of the suite seemed overwhelming. And the king-size bed between was incredibly tempting. She was determined, however, to make it all the way to the bathroom, already anticipating the heated spray of the shower pounding out the tension at the back of her neck and washing the cobwebs from her brain.

"How about if I take my shower first? I'm pretty sure this has stopped bleeding," she said, touching the thick pad of the makeshift bandage with her fingers. "If I clean it up a little, you should be able to tell more about it."

It was a reasonable offer, one that gave them both what they wanted. Whether or not Rafe would be reasonable about accepting it was another question.

"You sure you're up to a shower?"

"It will help more than that aspirin you mentioned," she said truthfully. "Not that I'm turning those down, mind you."

"I'll give you fifteen minutes," he said, putting her suitcase on the bed and thoughtfully popping the locks. "I'll look around for first-aid stuff while you shower. I might as well start in there."

He disappeared into the attached bathroom. As she one-handedly selected clean clothing from her bag, she could hear him rummaging through the medicine cabinet. After a few minutes she heard the shower enclosure door slide closed and water start in the shower. She silently thanked him for the thoughtfulness of that gesture as well.

By the time he emerged from the bathroom, she had managed to select a set of underwear, a pair of slacks and a cotton knit sweater, which she had laid out on the bed. His gaze examined them briefly before it lifted to her face.

"I better untie that for you."

She turned, allowing him access to the bandage he'd fashioned from her T-shirt and the belt of her robe. Actually, she should probably lay out the robe as well, she decided. Especially if Rafe was planning to show up here in fifteen minutes to reexamine her injury.

She watched as his fingers loosened the knot he'd tied, unconsciously remembering the pleasantly abrasive feel of them against her skin. She wanted to reach out and put her hand against his cheek, despite his withdrawal the last time she'd done that.

It had now been almost three days since he'd shaved. The blackness of the resulting beard along with the sun-darkened skin gave him a ruthless, cut-throat appearance, at odds with the concern with which he was unwrapping her arm.

That dichotomy had always been a part of who Rafe

Sinclair was. As an operative, he had been as ruthless as the situation demanded. It was only as her lover that she had become aware of the other side of his nature. The contrast between the two had fascinated her from the beginning.

"This may hurt," he warned.

His eyes rose from the bandage to fasten on her face. Set within that darkly weathered skin and surrounded by long coal-black lashes, they seemed incredibly blue.

And they were filled with compassion. The same emotion she had seen within them when she had begged for some explanation of why he'd left.

He had never given her one. At least not one she had been willing to accept.

Perhaps the only explanation really was the one he had offered. He had changed, and in the course of that change, he had discovered there was no place for her in his life.

"It's okay," she said, realizing that he was waiting for a response while she had again been lost in fruitlessly re-examining their past.

His lips flattened slightly. His eyes remained on hers as if he were wondering what she'd been thinking. Then they fell, as he pulled the pad away from the torn flesh.

He did it quickly and without warning. And it *did* hurt. This time, thank God, she had managed to prevent any audible expression of that pain.

Together they looked down on the wound. She held her breath in anticipation of that slow seep of blood. Despite the tearing from the bandage, it didn't happen.

"Looks like it's finally stopped," Rafe said, sounding as relieved as she felt. He touched the bruised skin around the furrow, his hands gentle enough not to cause additional pain. "This may leave a scar."

She laughed, which brought his eyes up again.

"Maybe Griff knows a good plastic surgeon," she said,

still amused that he thought she might be worried about something that minor. She was far too grateful to be alive.

"If not, Steiner does," he said, releasing her arm.

A reference to the agency's destruction of the identities of the members of the EST. In some cases that had included measures like plastic surgery, intended to change facial features that had become too well known to the enemy.

"I don't think I'll be asking for Steiner's advice on anything," she said.

"He did pass on the alert."

"You aren't feeling grateful, are you? Whatever those bastards do, it's for a reason. *Their* reason. You're the expert on Jorgensen. And now, due to their own stupidity, they don't have anybody capable of going after him. They figured they could get to you by going through Griff. So they did."

"Except this isn't Jorgensen," Rafe said. He didn't look up at her, which made her wonder what she was missing.

"Then we're back where we started," she said. "And frankly, I'm too tired right now to even think about what that means. All I know is that I need a shower, a change of clothes, and something to eat. In that order. Other than that..." She hesitated, knowing if it were up to her, right now there wasn't anything other than that. "I guess the only thing we can do is wait for Griff."

"Fifteen minutes," he said.

She nodded, wondering if she was up to the plan she'd just outlined. Rafe would stay and help her into the shower if she asked him. As tempting as that was in one respect, however, it was also the last thing either of them needed right now.

RAFE TAPPED on the door of the bedroom where he'd left Elizabeth almost twenty minutes ago. After he'd finished rounding up the things he needed to dress her arm, he had realized there were still ten minutes left of the fifteen he'd promised. That meant there was time enough for a shower of his own, along with a much needed shave. And he had to admit he was feeling more human.

When there was no answer to his second knock, he put his ear against the wood panel, trying to decide whether the water was still running. He couldn't hear anything, but that might be due to the thickness of the door.

He could always open it without permission, but he hesitated to do that. Especially when he remembered what had happened the day he'd burst into her bedroom. He wasn't sure he was up to a repetition of that kind of temptation.

He knocked again, and when there was no response this time, he turned the knob, allowing the door to swing inward. The bedroom appeared to be deserted, although Elizabeth's suitcase was still on the bed.

The door to the bathroom was standing open, and there was a thickness to the air that testified to its high moisture content. He listened again before he stepped inside the room. There was water running somewhere.

"Elizabeth?" he called.

She appeared in the open doorway of the bathroom. Her hair was still damp from the shower. It had been combed straight back from her face, which was bare of makeup. She was already dressed in the short-sleeved cotton sweater and slacks he'd seen on the bed.

"Sorry. I was brushing my teeth," she said.

"How's the arm?" he asked, breathing in the fragrances of soap and shampoo that had accompanied her into the room.

"Not as gory, at any rate."

"Ready for me to put a dressing on it? I found some antibiotic salve."

She nodded, walking over to the bed to sit on the side.

"Or had you rather do this in the bathroom?" she asked, looking up at him. "It's still a little steamy in there."

Her eyes seemed clear and very green. There was a becoming flush of color along her cheekbones, probably caused by the heat of the recent shower. If he hadn't seen the amount of blood she'd lost, he might be willing, as she seemed to be, to dismiss her wound as minor.

"This is fine," he said.

He laid the materials he'd gathered on the bed and put his hand under her upper arm, bending over it to take a closer look. It was less gory, the path the bullet had taken clear.

"Any problems with mobility?" he asked.

She opened and closed her fingers and then she turned her wrist back and forth. "It hurts, but everything seems to work."

She'd been lucky, he realized as he examined the gash. Discounting the possibility of infection, which the salve he'd found should prevent, this would heal within a few days.

He released her arm to twist the top off the tube of ointment. Then he squeezed a thin thread along the line of the wound. Next he tore open the packaging that held one of the gauze pads and placed it over the gash, letting the salve hold it in place until he could tape it.

When he'd finished, he straightened, stepping back. The combination of Elizabeth and a bed had always been dangerous. It was especially so right now, given his gratitude that she was alive.

The injury was a graphic reminder of the fragility of human life. One he hadn't thought he'd ever need after Amsterdam.

"That should do it," he said unnecessarily.

"Thanks," she said, putting her palm lightly over the

bandage and smoothing the tape with her thumb. Then she looked up at him again.

"Are you going to do what they want?" she asked. "Are you going to go after whoever this is?"

His eyes fell again to the square of white gauze he'd just taped over a bullet wound the bastard had inflicted. As much as he hated the idea of doing what Steiner and his crew wanted, it didn't seem as if he were going to be given an option.

Whoever this was had made it personal. And he had used the only weapon that would ensure that Rafe would come after him.

"Griff's here."

They both turned at the interruption. John Edmonds was standing in the door of the bedroom, his eyes moving quickly from one of them to the other. Finally they settled on Rafe.

"He's found something he thinks you ought to see."

"About Jorgensen?" Rafe asked.

"You could say that. Come downstairs when you're through. He and Hawk are waiting for you. He wants to tell you about this himself."

Chapter Twelve

"I thought you should see this," Griff said, laying a folder on the table in front of Rafe. "We can't make a definitive connection with what's going on now, but we have to concede that the possibility exists."

Surprisingly, Rafe found himself reluctant to view the material he'd just been handed. If this were proof Gunther Jorgensen was alive, not only had he wasted a year of his life, but it also would represent a massive failure of his abilities as an operative. Something he had once taken so much for granted he had never even thought about his competency.

He put his hand flat on its manila surface, drawing the folder toward him. Involuntarily, he raised his eyes, focusing on Elizabeth's face. She seemed almost as anxious about what this contained as he was.

"You were right, by the way," Griff said, bringing his attention back to him. "Jorgensen *didn't* survive Paris."

A kind of vindication, Rafe supposed. He had gone to France to execute a multiple murderer. It was comforting to know that despite the effects of Amsterdam, he had succeeded.

"Then...who is this?" Elizabeth said. "And why?"

"I think that may provide part of the answer to your

questions,'' Griff said, nodding toward the folder that lay, still unopened, on the table between them.

Emboldened by the information that whatever was going on now, at least he hadn't been mistaken about what had happened in Paris, Rafe finally lifted the cover. Inside were documents he recognized as having come from CIA files.

It was obvious they had been heavily redacted, but based on what Griff had told him, he knew that the information he needed to unravel the mystery must be in them. It came down now to recognizing what was pertinent.

"You want to give me a clue what I'm looking for?" he asked, running his thumb along the edge of the stack to point out its thickness.

There seemed no reason to reinvent the wheel. If Griff had found something he considered significant, Rafe was willing to concede it probably was.

After all, Cabot had more experience with this kind of search and discover than he did. His own expertise was more in the nature of the kind of searching he'd done during the year after the embassy bombing.

"Jorgensen had a brother," Lucas Hawkins said. Once the team's expert marksman, Hawk, as he was more commonly known, had become Griff's right-hand man within the Phoenix. "He was only a kid at the time you took out the brother. And according to agency sources, he was there that day."

"The day Rafe killed Jorgensen?"

Even as Elizabeth posed the question, Rafe was mentally back at the scene. Looking down on that same Paris street, mercilessly lit by a noonday sun. Not a flashback, but a deliberate recreation of an event he had seen far too often in one of those fractional, distorted images. The view of the exact second when his bullet had struck the German terrorist.

Now he concentrated on the people who had been around

Gunther Jorgensen. His entourage had converged on their leader as soon as they realized what had happened.

There would have been little they could have done to prevent Jorgensen's death, not given the precision of planning Rafe had devoted to this attack. In the aftermath, however, their consternation over their failure to protect him had been obvious even from the top of the building from which Rafe had fired his shot.

At that distance he hadn't been able to distinguish their features or even their ages. He couldn't now. He shook his head slightly, the gesture unconsciously acknowledging his failure to do so.

"How old?" he asked aloud. "You said he was a kid."

"Adler Jorgensen was fourteen that day in Paris," Griff said quietly, his tone devoid of censure.

"My God," Elizabeth breathed. "Fourteen and he watched his brother die?"

Rafe didn't regret killing Gunther Jorgensen. Not with the man's unquestioned record of death and destruction. Not with his stated commitment to continue that reign of terror against innocent people like those who had died in Amsterdam. He *did* regret that an impressionable child had been witness to the very violence at which his brother had been a master.

"You think *he's* responsible for the latest bombings?" Rafe asked. It made sense, despite his youth. He had suspected a protégé or admirer. This boy had obviously been both and more.

"It seems…feasible," Griff said.

"We know he turned his dead brother into an object of worship," Hawk added.

"And Jorgensen's organization was more than willing to use the kid as a rallying point to keep their cause alive," Griff said. "With the financial backing of the same ideological groups who supported his brother. The bombings in Madrid and Greenland were undoubtedly their work.''

''And the one in Mississippi?'' Elizabeth asked.

She sat huddled in her chair, arms crossed over her breasts, as if she were cold. The hand of the uninjured arm was cupped over the bandage Rafe had applied to the wound only minutes before. The posture seemed almost self-protective.

Why wouldn't it be? Rafe thought. She had been a target from the first.

''The agency, working with the international intelligence community, has made serious inroads in breaking up Jorgensen's cell, arresting several prominent members in the last few months as well as cutting off their funding. The noose is definitely tightening. We believe that's what set the boy off. A feeling it was now or never.''

''Hardly a boy,'' Rafe said. ''Not with that record.''

''Nineteen,'' Griff agreed. ''He entered this country on a student visa. If it's any comfort, he seems to have entered it alone, perhaps because there's no one else left in the organization's inner circle.''

''Did you know about this when you contacted me? Did you know Jorgensen's brother might be involved?''

''If I had, I would have told you. You saw and heard everything I was given. The security alert and Steiner's notation that they believed it had merit.''

''And all along the agency had access to these,'' Rafe said, lifting the stack of papers the folder contained. ''Are you telling me they couldn't take them, like you have, and put two and two together?''

''You should probably be warned that I'm not exactly an unbiased observer when it comes to Steiner's capacity for duplicity,'' Hawk said. ''I think they *did* put it together. I think that was their express purpose in passing on the alert.''

"To get me to go after this kid?" Rafe asked. "Using the pretext that it was Jorgensen himself?"

"I don't think they were trying to get *you* to react."

"Then… What the hell was the point of passing the information on to Griff?" Rafe demanded, at a loss about where Hawk was going.

"Steiner wanted *Jorgensen* to react," Hawk said.

For several heartbeats no one said anything.

"Are you suggesting he *knew* Griff would contact me?"

"Perhaps hoping I would," Griff confirmed.

"So he could track you?" Elizabeth asked. "So you would lead him to Rafe?"

"I think you're the one they needed," Griff said, turning toward her. "You were the key to bringing Adler Jorgensen out of hiding."

"Me?" she repeated in disbelief.

"Part of what those documents contain is his promise to find the people who killed his brother *and* hurt them in the same way he himself had been hurt," Griff said. "By having to watch someone he loved die."

Someone he loved… There was a cold sickness in the pit of Rafe's stomach, but after all, this was nothing new. Elizabeth had been a target from the beginning.

The only thing that had changed was that now his enemy had a name. And Rafe understood his reason in targeting the one person he might truly say he loved.

"But…" The sentence faded as Elizabeth shook her head, obviously thinking about what Griff had just suggested. "That can't be right. He was there *before* Rafe arrived. I felt someone watching me all that week."

"Someone," Rafe repeated. "Not necessarily Jorgensen."

"I don't understand," Griff said.

"Did Steiner order that explosion in Elizabeth's office?

Was that somebody's bright idea of how to get me involved?''

''Despite Hawk's assessment of Steiner's motives, I can't imagine he or the agency would sanction anything like that.''

''Did *you?*'' Rafe asked quietly.

It was a legitimate question. Griff had been the one who had implied Elizabeth might be in danger. The fact that it was legitimate hadn't made it any easier to ask.

''Steiner reminded me that the elder Jorgensen had no compunction in targeting the families of his enemies,'' Griff said. ''It was well known in terrorist circles that the EST had made him a priority. I thought it was reasonable that Carl would want me to pass on the information contained in that alert to the people who had been in on that operation.''

An operation that hadn't been successful. The CIA hadn't gotten Jorgensen. His death had been the result of a one-man crusade. A personal vendetta that had consumed a year of Rafe's life.

''So you're telling me that as far as you know, whoever blew up Elizabeth's office wasn't working for the agency?''

''As far as I know,'' Griff said evenly.

''And not for the Phoenix?''

''I've been willing to make allowances,'' Hawk said, ''considering how you feel about Elizabeth. I'd probably be paranoid, too, if someone had been targeting my wife. But you should think about who you're accusing. If you think Jordan or Drew or any of the rest of us would put Elizabeth in danger, then you've gone farther off the deep end than I thought.''

''Hawk,'' Griff warned.

''Nobody at Phoenix is involved in this except in trying to figure out what's going on,'' Hawk said.

''*I'm* the one who suggested the possibility that the Phoenix might be involved,'' Elizabeth said. ''Whoever set that explosion seemed to have arranged it so that he could be certain I *wouldn't* be inside the building. And then there was this.'' She glanced down at the dressing on her arm.

''Are you saying whoever shot at you was trying to graze you?'' Hawk asked.

That wasn't anything Rafe had considered, but he could understand, given their speculation that the bomb had been keyed to her car's remote, why Elizabeth had said it.

''I'm not sure even I would try that,'' Hawk said.

The tension eased with Griff's laughter. If Lucas Hawkins wasn't willing to attempt that shot, few others would be.

''We weren't involved,'' Griff assured them. ''I can imagine that up to this point it's felt like the two of you against the world, but that isn't the case. That's why I sent John to Virginia. I wanted you to know that whatever's going on, we are trying to help. Maybe we were too slow in understanding what was happening, but...we're here now.''

''To do what?'' Rafe asked bluntly. ''If Adler's targeting Elizabeth in order to get at me, how do we stop him?''

''I'm not sure that's what he's doing,'' Griff said.

''But the bomb—''

''Was one way he could be sure of flushing you out,'' Griff interrupted. ''Somehow he found Elizabeth. And we're still trying to figure out how. I think the explosion, which made most of the national broadcasts, by the way, was simply his way of bringing *you* to *him*. I don't believe he had any idea when he set it off that you were already there.''

It made a kind of sense. Rafe had known he wasn't followed, and Elizabeth had thought someone had been watching her all week. Instead of arranging the explosion so Rafe would be there to see it and fear Elizabeth had been hurt, maybe it *had* been set off so Rafe would come to Magnolia Grove. Where Jorgensen would be waiting for him.

If that were the case, then the message on Elizabeth's answering machine had been more than a taunt. It had been Jorgensen's way of ensuring she knew who had set off the bomb. After she'd listened to it, she was supposed to contact Rafe and tell him exactly who was responsible.

Thanks to Griff's warning, he had already been there to receive the call himself. It was ironic now that he'd come so close to missing it. Frantic to get Elizabeth out of town, he had almost left before the terrorist's communication arrived.

"What about the attack at the summerhouse?" Rafe asked, trying to fit all the pieces of this puzzle into some kind of pattern that made sense.

"Right now, that's as much a mystery as how he found Elizabeth," Griff admitted.

"Yet you refuse to believe Steiner's involved."

"I can't imagine the agency would allow a terrorist to go after their own people."

"But we're no longer *their* people," Elizabeth said softly. "And that was their choice, if you remember."

"A choice they have since regretted, I assure you," Griff said. There seemed to be a hint of satisfaction in the comment.

"It's a regret that comes too late to mean much to any of us," Rafe said. "Or to the people who have died since."

"If the agency's *not* involved," Hawk asked, "then where did Jorgensen get the information about Elizabeth's current location and the safe house?"

Hawk had admitted his distrust of Steiner. That didn't lessen the validity of his question. Rafe had left the CIA on his own, but for the rest of the team, including Elizabeth, the agency had created the identities they'd assumed.

"If you're implying Jorgensen gained access to that information through Steiner—" Griff began.

"He couldn't have. I moved three years ago," Elizabeth said. "I was careful not to leave any forwarding address. Rafe said *you* didn't know where I was. I don't see how Steiner could."

There was a silence, prolonged enough to be revealing. Rafe's accusation broke it.

"You *did* know where she was."

"I never told you I didn't."

Do you know where she is? Griff's question in the workshop that day might have implied he didn't have Elizabeth's address, but technically he was right, Rafe realized. He had never said that.

"So all the information Jorgensen needed to do what he's done was available from within the agency."

"There's another possibility besides thinking Steiner's been manipulating this for his own ends," Griff said. "A little more than a year ago our encryption software was compromised. We can't be sure who's had access to any information in the databases. No matter how it was originally classified."

"However he acquired the information he's using, there's still only one way to put a stop to this," Rafe said.

He didn't have a problem going after the younger Jorgensen. Gunther's little brother had proven himself an apt pupil when it came to copying his sibling's murderous modus operandi. He had at least three bombings to his credit. That the one in Mississippi hadn't added to the body count was only because it seemed to have had a different purpose.

"I think I can safely promise you'll have the full support of the agency this time," Griff said.

"Tell them from me what they can do with their support," Rafe said. He closed the folder and pushed it back across the table.

"You're going after him on your own?" Hawk asked.

"I won't have to. He'll come after me."

Even as he said it, Rafe hoped he was right. He couldn't afford the year he had devoted to the search for Jorgenson's older brother. Then he had been a faceless, nameless nemesis. The man he sought probably hadn't even known he was being hunted. At least not by Rafe.

This was something very different. This time Rafe, and through him Elizabeth, had been the terrorist's prey from the very beginning. And the longer this madman was allowed his freedom, the greater the danger he represented.

"What about Elizabeth?" Griff asked.

"That's your job. You take care of her, and I'll give Steiner what he wants."

"Thank you both for including me in your plans," Elizabeth said, her voice edged with sarcasm. "I'm afraid I've become too accustomed to making my own decisions to go along with them."

"I can't do both," he said, meeting her eyes for the first time since he'd noticed her self-protective posture.

During the time they had been talking, that had changed. Her body was now upright, her chin tilted in challenge.

"No one's asking you to," she said. "I don't believe I've asked any of you for anything."

She hadn't. Just as she had vehemently resisted being carried into this house, she would resist his trying to hand her over to the Phoenix for protection. And to be fair, no one had ever been less "damsel in distress" than Elizabeth.

"You're a target," Griff said. "Like it or not, Adler Jorgensen will try to use you to get to Rafe."

Rafe expected her to protest. To argue that there was nothing between them. Or that sentiment shouldn't have a role in something like this.

She did neither. Her mouth tightened as she considered

what Griff had said. Then she turned, looking at Rafe directly.

"Let him."

It took a second to sink in. "Use you?"

"You want him to come to you. Right now, I'm the best bait you've got."

Chapter Thirteen

She could tell by their faces what they thought of the idea. And her immediate response to the disbelief she saw there was anger that *these* particular men would react that way. After all, she'd worked with all of them before. Her performance on those occasions hadn't provided justification for keeping her out of the action now.

"You asked me a question in the car," Rafe said. "Maybe you should try applying that same standard to this situation."

She had asked how he'd feel about having to be carried inside. Was he suggesting that she should consider how she would feel if *he* were used as bait to catch a madman?

While she acknowledged the validity of the comparison, she wasn't buying into it as an excuse for excluding her. Neither would he if the situations were reversed.

"You use whatever they give you," she said. "You're the one who taught me that."

"You don't use other people."

"Why not? If it's for the greater good."

"Because that's what separates us from them," Griff said.

"What separates us from them is that *we're* trying to save lives," she argued, "and they're trying to take them.

That's the only moral consideration that has any meaning in this.''

"No," Rafe said.

"Because you think I can't take care of myself?"

"Because it isn't necessary. You aren't the one Jorgensen wants. There's no reason for you to be involved."

She understood the refusal was the product of his concern for her. The cold rejection, not only of her offer to help, but also of the reality of her involvement from the first, still hurt.

"How can I *not* be involved?" she demanded, her eyes on his. *How can I not be involved in something that threatens you?* "Jorgensen has been targeting me."

The truth of that briefly prevented further protest. Then Rafe shook his head, rejecting that argument as well.

"It's not an option."

"Then maybe it should be," Hawk interjected. "The agency has been trying to get a handle on this guy for almost a year. You aren't going to find him unless he wants to be found. And the only thing we're fairly sure about is that he wants you to watch Elizabeth die."

"So you think I should make that *easier* for him? You're beginning to sound like Steiner," Rafe said, his voice sharp with anger.

"Don't compare me to that bastard," Hawk said.

"Then quit thinking like him," Rafe said. "Would you agree to use your wife for bait?"

"Elizabeth isn't your *wife*. She's an agent. And a damn good one."

"That's enough," Griff broke in.

The authority in his tone was probably enough to put an end to the increasingly hostile exchange. Or maybe, Elizabeth acknowledged, that had more to do with the relationship these two men had once shared.

Both responded to the command, looking at Griff rather

than continuing their debate. And it was to him that Rafe spoke.

"I'll do this, but only on one condition. I do it alone. You'll be responsible for keeping Elizabeth here and for keeping her safe. If anything happens to her, I'll hold both you *and* Steiner personally liable."

"I'm not yours to dispose of," she said.

He couldn't have it both ways. He couldn't profess disinterest and then attempt to arrange her life.

Of course, he hadn't seemed all that disinterested. Despite her moving without a forwarding address, he had known where to find her. When Griff issued his warning about Jorgensen, Rafe had not only known where to deliver it, he had brought it himself.

"That doesn't mean you're free to throw your life away," he said.

"Of course it does. It means I'm free to do whatever I want."

He held her eyes for perhaps ten seconds before he turned back to Griff. "I'll leave it to you to talk sense into her."

"It's *my* life," Elizabeth reiterated. "And if something happens to me because I want in on this, that's my business. My choice."

He refused to look at her, his eyes still focused on Griff.

"Your decision," Rafe continued as if she hadn't spoken. "It all comes down to how badly you want him."

"I didn't contact you with the intention of sending you after Adler Jorgensen," Griff said. "I was only passing on the agency's warning."

"That may be true, and I'd like to believe it is, but we both know that's why Steiner came to you. You agree to keep Elizabeth out of my way, and I'll give the agency what they want. If she's in on this, then I'm not."

"I don't believe what I'm hearing," Elizabeth said. "Who the hell put you in charge?"

"Adler Jorgensen," Rafe said.

Without glancing her way again, Rafe stood, pushing his chair back so violently that it teetered. He crossed the room, slamming the door behind him. There was a moment of stunned silence.

"You aren't going to give in to that blackmail, are you?" she asked Griff.

"Exactly what Rafe's accusing *me* of. Emotional blackmail. And maybe I'm guilty," Griff conceded. "I'm the one who brought up your name. He wouldn't even be considering going after Jorgensen if you weren't involved."

"This has never been about me. It's always been about Jorgensen trying to avenge his brother's death."

"And doing it in a way guaranteed to cause the most pain. For Rafe, you're that way."

She wanted to tell him he was wrong, that Rafe didn't care. Somehow she couldn't bring herself to give voice to a lie of that magnitude. Rafe still refused to explain what had driven him away six years ago, but she no longer believed it had been indifference. That had been evident in every encounter she had had with him since he'd showed up in her living room.

"You're telling me to let him do this alone?" she asked.

"I'm telling you to stay out of his way," Griff said. "For everyone's sake. Because of his concern for you, he's undertaken to do a job that desperately needs to be done. One that will be hard enough without the additional stress of having to worry about your safety."

"You think he's agreed to do Steiner's dirty work because of me. I think it's just as likely that he's missed the rush. Rafe's an adrenaline junkie like the rest of us."

The silence that followed her assertion was strained. She replayed the last words of what she'd just said in her mind, wondering what had produced the emotion she couldn't quite identify in Griff's eyes. After all, they had been addicted to those alternating peaks of fear and elation. That addiction probably had as much to do with the formation of the Phoenix as anything else, despite their genuinely altruistic motives.

Or was that sour grapes? she wondered. Because she hadn't been asked to join? Suddenly she was ashamed, not only of what she'd said, but of what had prompted it.

"I didn't mean that," she said quickly. "I know that what Rafe is trying to do—"

"Has he told you about Amsterdam?" Griff broke in to ask.

Acknowledging that he hadn't would be hard. In light of her comment, however, she supposed she deserved Griff's rebuke.

"Not really. I know that what he did there was incredibly heroic."

"And incredibly costly."

She'd never known how long Rafe had spent in the hospital. Like a fool, she had respected his wishes against her flying over to be with him, forced to rely on Griff for information instead. Rafe had never answered any of her letters or calls.

She had believed that he needed time. Time to recover. Time to put the horrors of what he'd experienced behind him. She had never dreamed that eventually he wouldn't let her help him do that.

He hadn't. And it had hurt. Only much later had she acknowledged that he wasn't coming back to her, no matter how much time and space she gave him.

"I wanted to help," she said defensively. "He wouldn't let me."

"He wouldn't let *anyone*. He was completely focused on

finding Gunther Jorgensen to make him pay for that atrocity he'd committed.''

"He succeeded."

She hadn't known for sure until she had asked him the night he'd eaten dinner at her house. Two strangers discussing without outward emotion what was probably the seminal event in their relationship.

"He succeeded in killing Jorgensen," Griff agreed, "but if you want to understand why he feels so strongly about your not being involved in this, get him to tell you about Amsterdam."

"Do you really think he would?" she mocked.

"He needs to tell someone," Hawk said.

Ironic, she thought, that the most uncommunicative of all of the fairly closemouthed members of the team should offer that observation.

"Then maybe he'll tell *you*," she said bitterly. "He hasn't told me anything in the past six years. I don't think he's going to start now."

"Ask him," Griff urged.

And be rebuffed again? Even she wasn't that great a glutton for punishment.

"I take it I'm free to go," she said without verbally committing to what they'd suggested. "Or should I consider myself under house arrest?"

"Don't make this any harder than it is," Griff said.

"Harder for who? Surely you aren't referring to your role in this. You got what you wanted. So did Rafe. Don't lecture me on how to deal with having my own freedom of choice curtailed by the two of you."

"Rafe's only concern is your safety."

"And what's yours? To see how high you can jump when Steiner says boo?"

"My concern is the same as it's always been," Griff said, his voice calm, despite her mockery. "To keep my people safe. As safe as they can be, given the difficulty of the mission we undertook for this country.''

"In case you hadn't noticed, it isn't *our* mission. Not any longer. You can thank Steiner for that.''

"The mission and the need for it never changed. We've always known that, even if the CIA didn't. This one, however, has become...personal,'' Griff said. "On both sides.''

"Well, I've been warned off the personal enough times that the message has finally sunk in. If you think Rafe needs to talk to someone about Amsterdam,'' she said to Hawk, "maybe you should ask him. I'm following Griff's advice. I don't intend to make this any harder for him *or* for you than it already is.''

"I TAKE IT everything's decided,'' John Edmonds said.

He had been sitting on one of the benches in the rose garden when she came through the French doors. Unless she wanted to chance running into Rafe in the inner hallway, they had seemed the only viable exit from Griff's office.

"You could say that.''

"Anything I should know?''

"That I'm not going to be allowed to be involved.''

"When Rafe goes after Jorgensen?''

"*Alone.* It's what he wants.''

Edmonds's eyes conveyed his surprise. "None of you could convince him that might not be the wisest course of action?''

"I couldn't. They didn't try,'' she said. "They made a deal with him.''

"What kind of deal?''

"They keep me out of the way while he tries to lure Jorgensen to come after him.''

"How?''

"I don't know. They didn't let me in on their plans.''

"And that angers you."

It wasn't a question. Obviously he could read that emotion in both her tone and her attitude.

"I think it's stupid. Jorgensen chose the players. He came after me before Rafe had any idea what was going on. It seems I'd be the logical lure to get him to come out of hiding again."

"Rafe doesn't see it that way," Edmonds said, a subtle movement at one corner of his mouth.

"Obviously not."

"If you hurry, you can probably catch him."

"What?"

"Rafe. He went to get his things from my car."

He tilted his head in the direction of the drive, which was hidden by the thick foliage of the crepe myrtles that had been planted to screen it off from the garden.

"You expect me to go chasing after him?"

"If you want to talk to him before he leaves. I got the feeling he was in a hurry."

"I don't believe his departure is imminent. I think he and Griff have some unfinished business." The unthinking phrase seemed to echo with personal significance.

"Look," John said, "I know this is none of my business—"

"That's right. It isn't."

Edmonds's quick grin made him look almost boyish. She realized that she had been so focused on what was going on between her and Rafe that she almost hadn't noticed how attractive he was.

"You won't ever regret trying to talk to him," he said. "If you don't, however..."

Rafe was about to go after a man who had sworn to kill him. Someone who, though young in years, was old in bloodshed. Someone who had learned hate at the hands of a master.

"What do you know about what happened in Amsterdam?" she asked.

Edmonds shook his head. "Nothing beyond the fact that the bombing there was what sent Sinclair after Jorgensen. Is there something else I should know?"

"I don't know. Hawk suggested I make Rafe tell me about it."

"I wouldn't think that would be a suggestion he'd make lightly. That memory can't be pleasant."

Rafe had never talked about what had happened the day of the embassy bombing. And for Hawk to suggest to her that he should...

"Maybe you're right," she said.

"About the memory being painful?"

"About regrets. I really don't need any more of those."

SHE MET RAFE on his way back to the house. Actually, she almost ran into him as she rounded the row of tall shrubs.

When he found her blocking his path, his expression hardened, becoming almost grim. She expected him to step to the side and go past her without speaking.

He stopped instead, waiting with ill-concealed impatience for her to say whatever she wanted to say to him. She knew he was probably already thinking about what lay ahead, his mind totally focused on the mission. She was nothing more than an unwanted distraction right now, so she decided to make this short if not sweet.

"Griff said to ask you about Amsterdam."

It was apparent by the widening of his eyes that it had caught him off guard. "What about Amsterdam?"

"I don't know. That's what you're supposed to tell me."

"People died. Jorgensen was extremely efficient."

"Ever the meticulous planner."

He said nothing in response, his eyes so shuttered now that she wondered if he even saw her.

"You were able to save some of them," she went on, determined that if Griff and Hawk thought this was so damned important, she would finish it.

And if she did, despite what was in his eyes, maybe finally there would be no regrets. Not for things that had been left unsaid or undone. Not this time.

"A few," he said. "Is that what you want to talk about? The few people who somehow managed to escape that inferno."

"I don't *know* what I want to talk about. Griff seemed to think it was important that *you* talk about it."

"Let it go, Elizabeth."

"Let *you* go," she said. "Isn't that what you mean?"

"Nothing has changed. I shouldn't have come to your house. If I hadn't, none of this would have happened."

"The bomb? You heard Griff. That was Jorgensen's way of attracting your attention. It would have happened whether or not you were there."

"And this?" he asked. He touched the gauze and tape he had applied to her arm. "Would this have happened if you hadn't been with me?"

"I don't know. I don't know how madmen think."

"I know how this one thinks."

"He isn't his brother."

"I haven't been able to see much difference. That's why I don't want you there."

"Because you're afraid for me? Or afraid I'll get in the way?"

"I don't doubt your competence."

There had seemed a slight emphasis on the pronoun. Not enough to cause her to comment about it, but enough that she would remember it later.

"Then let me help," she begged. "Despite what you suggested inside, I have a stake in this. That bastard targeted me, no matter what the reason. I have a right to go after him.''

There was a hesitation before he answered. Long enough that she knew he had considered what she said.

"I'll do better without you," he said.

"Why, Rafe? Give me one good reason why you're so determined to do this alone. We've never worked this way."

Griff had always insisted on backup. No one on the team went into a situation alone if they could figure out any possible way to avoid it. Now he seemed to be sanctioning Rafe's determination to do exactly that. And it made no sense.

Even if Rafe didn't want her with him, Griff could still have sent Hawk or John. The decision not to provide backup was a departure from the standard operating procedure Cabot had always insisted upon.

"There is no *we*," Rafe said. "Not any longer."

He meant the External Security Team. She understood that, but again the words seemed to resonate with personal meaning.

"If that's true, then we've let Steiner win."

"Steiner won a long time ago. This country paid the price of his victory in being unprepared for terrorist actions on our own shores. We can't do anything about what happened then, but I have the opportunity now to do something about one particular terrorist. And this time, I don't need Steiner's approval to go after him."

"They *want* you to go after him," she said. "They're using you. Griff knows that, and so do you. But this time... This time, Rafe, you don't have to do it alone."

He held her eyes a long time, reading in them, she hoped, her need to be by his side. She hadn't been there six years ago, and through each long, dark, empty day since, she had lived with that regret.

He lifted his hand, laying his fingers lightly against her cheek. His mouth moved, slowly tilting upward at the corners as he continued to study her face.

"I couldn't ask for a better offer," he said. "Or for a better partner."

Her heart quickened with the flare of hope those words produced. And then, as he continued, it settled back into the same despair she had felt when Griff agreed to Rafe's conditions.

"I *have* to do this alone, Elizabeth. There's no other option. Believe me, if there were—"

He seemed to bite off the words, stopping the flow before he said more than he intended. She waited through the silence, hoping he'd finish.

When he didn't, she knew there was still one question she had to ask. No matter the answer.

"And when it's over?"

He knew what she meant. She could read that in his eyes.

"This isn't a business that allows people to make promises," he said. "You know that. We both know it."

As he said the last, his thumb moved to trace across her bottom lip, pulling against the thin, sensitive skin. Her mouth opened, her breath catching like a sob as his denial snapped the last thread of hope she had foolishly clung to.

She nodded, stepping back so that there was no longer any contact with the warmth of those dark, calloused fingers. It seemed, however, that she could still feel them against her skin.

His hand hesitated briefly in midair, and then, lips tight, he stepped around her. Without looking back, he rounded the hedge of crepe myrtles and disappeared, leaving her as alone as she had ever been in her life.

Chapter Fourteen

Rafe couldn't think of anything else that needed to be done before he left. Everything related to the mission had been set into motion. He already had the keys to one of the cars Griff kept in the garage here in his pocket. All he had to do was throw his bag into the trunk and head out.

The only thing stopping him was the knowledge that too many things had been left unsaid. He hadn't apologized to Hawk for the ridiculous accusation he'd made. He hadn't explained to Griff the fear that was the basis for his determination to do this alone. More importantly, he had treated Elizabeth as if she weren't entitled to be told the truth.

It wasn't that he intended to tell her now. It was simply that he hated to leave things as they were between them. As melodramatic as it sounded, this might be the last chance he'd ever have to make them right.

Maybe Griff and Steiner had conspired to send him to her house, but the ultimate responsibility for going there had been his. At any point along the way, he could have refused.

He hadn't, because he couldn't. As soon as Griff had made the suggestion that Elizabeth might be in danger, providing him with a legitimate excuse for contacting her, he had leaped at the chance.

They had had a long time to deal with the loss of what

had once been between them. Now, thanks to his inability to stay away, they were again being forced to deal with those same painful emotions.

He had told himself a dozen times that anything he tried to say could only make it worse. A clean, surgical break is always best. He had known that six years ago. Nothing had changed.

He picked up his suitcase, into which he'd tossed the clothes he'd changed out of, and walked out of the bedroom. As he clicked off the light, the upper story of the house was plunged into darkness.

The others were still working in the study downstairs. They had spent hours there using Cabot's computer and his connections within the international intelligence community to gather as much information as they could about Adler Jorgensen and his organization.

Elizabeth had been right about that. You use anything an enemy of this kind gave you to bring about their destruction. *Anything except those you love.*

He reached the top of the staircase leading to the lower level and stood in the darkness a moment, knowing that Elizabeth was sleeping in the bedroom across the hall. He could almost feel her nearness, a physical connection that remained as strong between them now as it had ever been.

He closed his eyes, picturing her face when he'd seen her this afternoon. The strain of the previous two days had been etched on her features, and in her eyes had been all the questions he had never answered.

If he hadn't been able to bring himself to answer them before, when it might have made a difference, there was no point in trying to now. After all, he didn't want disgust to be the last emotion he would ever see in her eyes. Or, and the thought was more unbearable, he didn't want to see pity in them. Either would be infinitely worse than what was already there.

He lowered his foot to the first step. Then, as if his body possessed a will of its own, he brought it back to the top again. He set down the suitcase and in a couple of strides crossed the hall to the closed door of Elizabeth's bedroom.

He hesitated, drawing a deep breath before he allowed his fingers to close around the knob. He turned it, the door opening soundlessly, but he didn't enter.

He allowed his eyes time to adjust to the level of light inside the room. After a few seconds he could identify the various pieces of furniture by their shape. The bed was before the windows, the small mound in the center drawing his gaze.

As exhausted as she had been, Elizabeth would be sleeping too soundly to know he was here. He stepped inside, his footfall reassuringly silent on the thick carpet. He reached back and pulled the door almost closed behind him, giving them some privacy. He paused, again listening.

Thankfully, there was no reaction from the sleeper on the other side of the room. Now that he was here, this close to her, he realized that the last thing he wanted was to talk. Or to explain. He preferred that she think of him—if she ever did—as the cold, uncaring bastard he had pretended to be rather than to have her understand what he really was.

All he wanted, he decided, standing in the black silence, was to look at her before he left. Something to remember besides the strained, bitter lines into which her face had been set when she'd confronted him this afternoon.

Then he would disappear from her life again, just as he had before. And no matter the outcome of the mission he was about to undertake, she would be safe.

He slowly crossed the room, stopping beside the bed. Here, finally, he could hear the slow, regular breathing he had listened for at the door.

Elizabeth lay on her side, one hand folded under her chin. She was wearing the same clothing she had worn this afternoon, as if she had lain down to rest for a few minutes and fallen asleep.

Gradually, in the filtered moonlight, he was able to discern her features. The strain that had been so evident this afternoon was gone, hidden by the lack of light or dissolved by the relaxation of sleep. She looked at peace. She looked exactly like the woman she had been before Amsterdam. And if he were the man he had been then...

But he wasn't. The difference that one event had made in his life was the crux of the estrangement between them. An estrangement that couldn't be changed by any explanation he might try to make.

He had no doubt that if he told her what had happened to him, she would respond with the appropriate platitudes. And she would mean them.

It was what would happen through the days and weeks, or perhaps, because this was Elizabeth, through the months that followed that he feared. Her gradual realization that what he had told her in the kitchen of the summerhouse was nothing less than the truth. He wasn't the man she had loved. He could never be that man again.

She turned her head against the pillow, brow furrowing. Fearing that she might awaken, he took a step away from the bed, the carpet disguising his movement, but he couldn't make himself leave. Not yet.

Instead, as soon as her features relaxed, he moved toward the bed again. As he had in the car today, he allowed his fingers to touch a strand of hair that lay against her cheek, dreading and yet also anticipating that she might yet awaken to his touch.

Her breathing had slowed, however, evincing a return to a deeper level of sleep. Reluctantly he lifted his hand, holding it a long heartbeat above the curve of her cheek. Resisting the impulse to allow his fingers to brush against the smooth skin beneath them. He had never known such temptation.

Or such certainty that to do so would be the biggest mistake of his life. Far better to leave it as they had this afternoon. No promises. None that he would ever have to break.

He took a step back, putting distance between himself and the enticement Elizabeth had always been. Still she slept, the slight rise and fall of her breasts visible in the moonlight.

"There was no one else," he whispered, the words hardly a breath in the darkness. "No one who was ever like you. There never will be."

Then, before he lost his resolve to do what was best for her—all that had kept him from taking her in his arms— he turned. He re-crossed the room without hurrying, pulling open the door he had left ajar to step out into the hall. Without looking back at the bed, he eased it closed behind him.

As soon as he'd picked up his bag at the top of the stairs, he was almost running down the steps, his free hand trailing over the banister. Head lowered, he had reached the bottom before he realized someone was standing there. Startled, he looked up, straight into Lucas Hawkins' eyes.

And discovered, unbelievably, that his own were blurred with tears. He blinked to clear them, hoping the light was dim enough to hide that unwanted moisture.

"Good luck," Hawk said, holding out his hand.

"Better lucky than good," he said, his fingers closing over the skilled ones of the team's marksman.

"Are you sure you don't want one of us—"

"I'm sure," he said quickly. It was typical that this man, in spite of the angry words they had exchanged this afternoon, would offer to put himself into a danger they both understood far too well. "I wanted to apologize—" he began, only to be cut off.

"Don't," Hawk ordered. "You were right. I wouldn't allow Tyler to be used as bait. I shouldn't have expected you to feel any different about Elizabeth. I didn't realize you two were still…"

Hawk allowed the awkward sentence to trail. Neither of them was the kind of man who talked easily about emotions, particularly these.

"We aren't," Rafe said shortly.

He had already begun to move again when Hawk's question stopped him. "Any message you want me to give her?"

That I love her. That I always have and always will. And if I were a different man…

"No message," he said.

He stepped around Hawk and headed toward the waiting car. The first step on a journey that could end only in a death—his or Adler Jorgensen's.

As SOON AS the bedroom door closed, Elizabeth opened her eyes, wondering why she had let Rafe go with saying anything. When he had first opened the door, she had been unsure of his purpose in coming, so she had pretended to be asleep.

She had decided after this afternoon that the next move must be up to him. She had told herself that over and over during the long hours that had passed since their confrontation in the driveway.

Then, as always, he had thrown her surety about his feelings—and even about her own—into confusion by those whispered words. *There was no one else. No one who was ever like you. There never will be.*

An answer to the woman's question she had asked at the

summerhouse. And she couldn't doubt the quiet sincerity of them. And if she hadn't been such a coward...

As soon as the word formed in her consciousness, she sat upright on the edge of the bed. Rafe had come to find her, if only to say goodbye. An overture, which in her hurt and uncertainty she had refused to acknowledge.

She ran across the room, throwing open the door he had closed. There was no sign of Rafe.

She walked across to the bedrooms on the other side. The doors were open, but there was no one inside either of them.

She turned to the head of the stairs. She stood in the darkness a moment, listening. Although she could hear nothing moving below, there was something about the quality of silence on this floor that indicated it was empty.

She started down the staircase, but before she had descended halfway, she realized someone was coming up. A man, obviously, but there wasn't enough light to distinguish which of the four who were in the house tonight.

Then, given the events of the past few days, she felt a frisson of anxiety. What if this *wasn't* one of those four men? What if this was someone who wasn't supposed to be here?

"Rafe?" she questioned.

"You missed him by a couple of minutes."

Her throat closed, aching against the finality of Hawk's words. Knowing what lay before him, she had allowed Rafe to leave without bridging the gulf that lay between them. A gulf that had widened in the last few hours.

"Something wrong?" Hawk asked.

"I thought..." she began, and knew it was all too difficult to put into words. She had too many unanswered questions herself to attempt to make explanations to someone else. "Nothing's wrong."

"I know you'll think it's none of my business..."

Hawk was the second person today who had said that to her. This time her inclination was to listen.

"We're friends. You're Rafe's friend, too. I suppose in a way it *is* your business."

She couldn't see his face, not well enough to read those harsh features. Despite the permission she'd given, several seconds passed before he spoke. When he did, it didn't have anything to do with her relationship with Rafe.

"If you do what we've done long enough, it's bound to have an effect. For some of us that means we've become cynical about how we view the world. A deep-rooted, untrusting cynicism about every person and institution in it. For others..." He paused, seeming to search for the right words. "For others there's just a kind of...overload of evil. An exposure to too much of man's inhumanity to his fellow man."

"Are you talking about Rafe?" she asked, wondering where this was going. "About the bombing?"

"I think Rafe was already into that overload before Amsterdam. He lost a good friend when Paul Sorrenson died. And what those bastards did to him and Duncan—"

The words were abruptly cut off. Maybe because Hawk was remembering, as she was, exactly what had been done to Culhane by a terrorist cell in Basra.

"It brought home to all of us the barbarity of the people we were dealing with. Then, almost immediately after it happened, in the embassy bombing Rafe came face-to-face with the worst that human cruelty can devise."

She had heard a few of the horror stories that had come out of that day. None of them from Rafe, of course, but even secondhand, they had chilled her to the bone.

"And instead of getting help in dealing with what he'd seen," Hawk went on, "Rafe set out to get revenge. I would probably have done the same thing—I *have* done it—so believe me, I'm not criticizing. But...I think all he'd gone through festered inside him during the year he stalked Jorgensen. And since," he added. "He's *never* dealt with it."

"Words of one syllable, Hawk," she begged. "What are you trying to tell me?"

"The shrinks have a name for everything. Maybe it matters to them that they can call it something. That overload of evil. They named it Post-Traumatic Stress Disorder. A lot of guys who made it back from Nam had PTSD. Rescue workers in Oklahoma City and New York suffered the same symptoms, but by then everybody understood that they would. A natural consequence of being confronted with what man is capable of doing to his fellow man. Society was prepared to help *them* deal with the effects of those bombings."

More words than she had ever heard Hawk string together in all the years she'd known him, she realized. And the quiet compassion in his deep voice, echoing in the close darkness, made them even more poignant.

"At the time when Rafe should have had that same support, he was hunting down Gunther Jorgensen. Maybe having that focus held him together for a while, but the mind can absorb only so much horror before it breaks under the burden."

Post-traumatic stress. Everyone was familiar with the term. At least now they were. And yet ridiculously she had never once thought about it in connection to Rafe. Someone who was always in total control. Contained. Almost emotionless.

For the first time she realized something she should have known—even back then. Those aspects of his personality, the very ones she had most admired, were probably the worst possible combination for the kind of damage Hawk was talking about.

Rafe, who always had to be in control, had been faced

by a series of unspeakable human cruelties over which he *had* no control. Barbarities his very rational mind could find no way to rationalize.

"How did *you* know?" she asked, fighting a growing guilt that she hadn't.

"Griff kept track of us after the agency dissolved the team. It took him a while to unravel some of the identity puzzles the experts had created, but eventually he found all of us. All who'd survived."

"Are you saying...Rafe told *Griff?*"

Despite the darkness, she could see the quick upward slant of Hawk's mouth. "I doubt Rafe has ever told anyone. Griff is pretty intuitive. And don't forget, he's dealt with a few traumas of his own."

Griff, too, had survived a terrorist attack, this one aimed at Langley itself. His slight limp was a constant reminder of the incident.

"Did he suggest to Rafe that he get help?"

The smile had disappeared. Hawk's lips flattened as he hesitated over the answer.

"I don't know," he admitted finally. "Griff is also pretty good at keeping his mouth shut. I know he invited Rafe to join the Phoenix, and I know Rafe refused. Maybe in the course of that refusal... Maybe he said enough that Griff was able to figure out what was going on."

"What *is* going on?"

"Specific to Rafe, I don't know. But the symptoms vary only in severity. The longer they go untreated—"

"The more severe they become," she finished for him. That must be something she had read or heard after the New York attack, although she had no recollection of exactly where.

Hawk nodded.

"Flashbacks?" she asked, pulling out information she had apparently filed away in her brain.

As she articulated the word, she had a mental image of that strange incident after the explosion in Magnolia Grove. One second Rafe had been fully engaged in what was going on, obviously concerned with making sure she was all right. The next it was as if someone had broken the connection between them. His eyes were no longer focused on her face. Whatever he had been seeing, she realized only now, had not been the reality before him.

"One of the more common side effects," Hawk confirmed. "Nightmares. Assorted sleep disorders. An inability to feel. A tendency to isolation."

An inability to feel. A tendency to isolation. Including a rejection of those who cared about him?

"And you really think that Rafe…" She hesitated, still trying to come to grips with the idea. "All because of what happened at Amsterdam?"

It seemed incredible that an event that had occurred so long ago should still have such profound effects. She found that especially hard to fathom because of the kind of man Rafe Sinclair was.

"Amsterdam. Paul's death. Duncan's mutilation. Rafe was with the group that rescued him, remember. And maybe… Maybe even Jorgensen's death."

"But—"

"No matter how often you've done it," Hawk said softly, "there is always something personally damaging about ending another man's life. Even if it's necessary. Or just."

Lucas Hawkins was, she knew, more than qualified to make that assessment.

"If he knows this, if he only suspects it, then why would Griff even *think* about letting Rafe go after Jorgensen's brother alone? Why would he possibly agree to that?"

You don't use those you love as bait. They had all told her that. Except, apparently, when the bait was Rafe.

"That's the only way Rafe would let us play it. Believe me, we've both tried to talk him out of doing this."

That made no sense, either. That Rafe would want to go alone. Not if Hawk were right.

There had always been backup. That's the way they operated.

"Rafe isn't stupid," she said. "So why would he insist on doing this by himself?"

Despite what he'd tried to convince her of over dinner that night, Rafe would feel as great an obligation to take Adler Jorgensen out as any of them would. Maybe as great an obligation as he had felt about hunting down Adler's older brother. And in this case, the odds of succeeding would *not* be increased by working alone.

"For the same reason he wouldn't have anything to do with the Phoenix," Hawk said.

She shook her head, feeling as if she were too slow in figuring all this out. Of course she had never once considered that Rafe might be having psychological problems. He was the bravest man she'd ever known. As a member of the team, she had known a lot.

Rafe had always been the one least likely to be affected by fear or fatigue. The one who was up for whatever challenge was thrown at them, no matter how unexpected. The one in complete control of both the situation and himself.

And now he isn't.

From what little she'd read about flashbacks, she knew they occurred without warning, sending the sufferer mentally, and perhaps more importantly emotionally, into another time and place. And her understanding was that there was nothing that could be done to prevent them. No way to control when they might strike.

"He's afraid he'll leave someone else vulnerable," she said, voicing her sudden realization.

No partners. No Phoenix. No missions. No chance that Rafe's condition might get someone else killed.

"The primary trigger is always stress," Hawk said, "especially something reminiscent of the original trauma. But it doesn't have to be that. Any feeling of danger or vulnerability is likely to have the same effect."

Like the ambush in the woods outside the summerhouse. She had wondered about Rafe's delay in providing them with covering fire. In spite of being hit, she had gotten off a couple shots before he'd responded.

Because he had been thrown back to the scene of the embassy bombing? Or reliving any of a dozen other incidents in which he'd been pinned down by hostile fire?

"Then…*he's* the one who's vulnerable," she said. "What if he has a flashback at the moment Jorgensen comes after him? You and Griff can't let him face that madman alone. Not knowing this."

"I don't *know* it, but it seems to make sense of everything that's happened. Besides, we gave him our word."

"I *didn't* give him *mine.*"

As soon as the words were out of her mouth, she regretted them. She wasn't going to stand aside and let Rafe deal with this by himself, but she should never have telegraphed that intent to Hawk. He and Griff had promised to keep her out of it. That had been part of the deal.

"Don't take away what he has left, Elizabeth," Hawk said.

"What the hell does that mean?" she demanded, furious that the best he could come up with as a reason for letting Rafe face Adler Jorgensen alone was that cryptic bullshit.

"He wants to do this. Maybe he *needs* to do it. On *his* terms. He knows the odds are against him, but he isn't willing to put anyone else's life at risk. He'll get Jorgensen. Or he won't," Hawk added. "Either way, this is what he wants."

"To die?" she asked, her voice rising. "You think he wants to die?"

Hawk didn't answer, and his refusal made her almost as angry as his suggestion.

"You don't know him, Hawk. Not like I do. If you think Rafe is on some kind of suicide mission—"

Which was exactly what she had accused him of this morning. *Kamikaze.* The realization that Hawk was right cut her off in midsentence.

Rafe had ordered John to take her to safety, leaving him alone in the woods with Jorgensen. If Edmonds had obeyed, if he hadn't blackmailed Rafe into coming by refusing to leave without him, Rafe would have had both of them out of the way.

And then it would have been only Rafe and the terrorist. *Just as it was now.*

"Elizabeth?" Hawk's tone was concerned.

Maybe she could use that to her advantage, she thought, swaying slightly as if she were faint.

Use whatever they give you, Rafe had taught her. If she were going to try to outsmart Griff Cabot and Hawk, she would need every advantage and more. To carry that trick off, she would need every bit of intelligence, skill and daring she had ever possessed.

Chapter Fifteen

"Feeling better?" Hawk asked.

She nodded, elbows on the kitchen table, and her forehead resting against the heels of her hands. The bourbon he'd poured for her sat untouched nearby.

Without looking up, she said, "Just light-headed. I should have eaten something."

"We can fix that," he offered.

She shook her head. "I'll get something in a minute. You don't have to wait on me, Hawk. It's embarrassing enough to practically pass out in your arms. I'm *not* the fainting kind."

She glanced up as she said the last. She couldn't discern any skepticism in his features. Softened by concern, they didn't appear nearly as forbidding as they usually did. She felt a momentary guilt, which she ruthlessly suppressed.

Rafe's life was at stake. She would do anything she had to not to let him face Jorgensen alone. Anything, including lying to someone who trusted her.

"It's been a long day," Hawk said.

It had been. From the attack at dawn through the afternoon's bitter confrontation with Rafe to her missed opportunity to say goodbye. To cap it off, she had finally been given the key to understanding Rafe's rejection, without having an opportunity to act upon it.

To do that now, she had to make sure he survived an encounter with a terrorist bent on revenge. Assuming, of course, that she could escape Hawk's supervision. And that was a huge assumption.

"Can you at least tell me where he's going?" she asked.

For a split second the unexpected softness she had noticed before was back in his eyes. As quickly as it had appeared, Hawk cleared it, shaking his head.

"The less you know, the better."

"Better for who?" she asked. The resentment in her tone was too revealing, but then Hawk knew how she felt about Rafe.

"Better for all of us," he said simply.

She couldn't probe any more without making him wary. An alerted Hawk was an adversary she didn't need.

"Will you at least promise to tell me when it's over?"

He held her eyes for a long time before he nodded. The deal he had made with Rafe couldn't matter then. No matter *how* the mission turned out.

"Is this a private party?"

They turned to find John Edmonds standing in the doorway of the kitchen. She had no idea how long he had been there or how much he knew about what was going on. Maybe as little as she did. Or maybe...

"Not really," she said. "I took too long a nap, I guess. When I tried to come downstairs, I got a little ragged around the edges. Hawk came to my rescue."

"Rough day," John said, advancing into the room. "You're entitled to feel ragged. How's the arm?"

She hadn't realized that she was sitting with her hand held over the injury until he asked about it. "It's okay," she said. "A little sore."

"Want me to take a look at it?"

"Rafe—" For some reason her throat closed, preventing the completion of that sentence. If she didn't get a grip, she told herself, she was going to fail before she'd gotten started. "He changed the dressing earlier."

"That was before the planning session. Maybe we should—"

"It's okay," she said again, looking down at her hands. Apparently she was the only one who had been left in the dark about what they had in mind.

"Griff wants to see you."

Surprised, she looked up, only to realize the comment had been directed at Hawk. And then there was a spurt of adrenaline as she realized the implications for her plan. Edmonds might be an unknown quantity, but she had rather take her chances against him than Hawk.

"Now?" Hawk asked, sounding equally surprised.

"That's what he said. It's okay," Edmonds assured him. "I know what I'm supposed to do."

Which probably meant Griff had prepped John about their agreement. The excitement she'd felt at being left alone with him faded.

Hawk nodded, his gaze touching on her face. He pushed away from the counter he'd been leaning against and walked across the room. He stopped in the doorway, turning back to face her.

"Don't worry," he said. "I would never want to bet against Rafe Sinclair's chances of success."

That would certainly have been true once. With the information she'd been given tonight, however, she wasn't as ready to accept that positive assessment.

Don't take away what he has left, Hawk had advised. What if that were no longer enough?

"Thanks," she said aloud.

After Hawk had disappeared into the hall, John came over to the table and pulled out the chair opposite hers. His eyes examined her face.

"You know," he said.

"About the PTSD? Hawk told me. I can't believe I hadn't figured it out."

Even as she made conversation, her mind was racing, trying to think what she could do to get out of the house and be on her way to Rafe.

"He obviously did everything in his power to make sure you wouldn't."

"It just seems so foreign to who he is. I know something like that can happen to anyone, especially any one of *us*," she added, "but…" *Not Rafe,* she thought as she mouthed the empty words. *Anyone but Rafe.*

"You're finding it hard to accept."

"Hard to believe," she corrected.

"Why?"

"Because he's the strongest, bravest man I know."

"Which doesn't mean he's invincible," John said, his mouth relaxing into a smile.

"Then why are they letting him go after Jorgensen alone?"

There was a beat of silence before he answered. "Because it's what he wants."

"That doesn't make it right. Or smart. We've never operated that way. Why start now?"

"You'll have to ask Griff."

"I think it's because Rafe's expendable," she said, imbuing her tone with a bitterness she didn't have to fake.

"Expendable?"

She didn't blame him for that skepticism. It was an incredibly lame argument. It was all she could come up with on the spur of the moment.

"To the agency. The Phoenix. They get what they want, and none of their own people are put at risk."

"You don't really believe that's what Griff's doing."

She didn't, but maybe she could convince him it was possible, at least on the part of the agency. Edmonds had no loyalty to the CIA. He didn't even know Steiner. Of course, those who *did* know him—like Rafe and Hawk— were probably even *less* likely to trust him, she admitted.

Still, John was the only one here who hadn't given Rafe his promise. He was, literally, her last shot at making this work.

"I think the agency is using Griff, just like it's using Rafe. Carl Steiner is infamous for doing exactly that."

"Expediency above loyalty," he said.

Maybe he does know Steiner.

"Or in lieu of it," she said. "Only in this case, it isn't even expedient. Not if they really want Jorgensen dead."

"Whatever happened to Sinclair doesn't negate his skill or experience."

"It might. You had to be aware that it took him too long this morning to respond to that shot."

As she said it, she watched his eyes. And she could see the truth in them. He *had* wondered at Rafe's delay in reacting to the attack. That was probably why he had set off through the brush to find him.

"What if that happens when he's facing Jorgensen?" she demanded. "What then?"

At least he was honest enough not to deny the possibility. The silence expanded, but she didn't attempt to press her point. One way or the other she was going to leave this house. She would go through him, if there was no other way.

"There's nothing I can do," he said quietly.

"You can turn your back for thirty seconds."

"Even if I wanted to help, you're in no condition to—"

"*I'm* in no condition? I've got a scratch on my arm, while Rafe..." She shook her head, fighting an overwhelming despair at the hypocrisy. She took a breath, determined to control her anger. "Rafe is out there alone with a man who wants more than anything else in the world to kill him. And at any time—at the most critical time—he may be thrown back into some situation that happened years ago. And you're telling me you're worried about *this?*''

She touched the bandage Rafe had put over the graze. As she did, it was almost as if *she* were having a flashback. She was certainly back in *that* moment. Looking up into Rafe's eyes. Remembering.

"Don't do this," she begged softly. "Don't let Steiner win again."

She could tell that the phrase puzzled him. For someone who had not been part of the team then it was hard to explain. They had *all* been expendable. The difference was that they had been more than willing to give their lives to protect this country. And maybe, if the government hadn't tied their hands, they could have.

"All you have to do is look the other way," she said.

His eyes held on her face a long time. Then, without saying a word he stood, pushing his chair away from the table.

Her heart in her throat, she watched him. There was no way to tell anything about what he intended from his expression.

"He doesn't want you there."

The words were not encouraging, but perversely there had been something in his tone that gave her hope.

"I know, but…I also know that he wouldn't leave *me* to face Jorgensen alone. And I know that, despite what he'd told you to do this morning, *you* went back for *him*. That's the way it's supposed to work. Not like this. Not this… sacrifice."

John had called it expediency, but that was just another word for sacrifice. If there was anything she could do to prevent it, she wasn't going to let that happen. Not to Rafe.

She hadn't been aware that she was no longer watching

his face. Not until he laid something on the table in front of her.

Her eyes stung with tears as she realized what it was. Shocked that she had succeeded, she looked up in time to watch him remove the Beretta from its holster at the small of his back and lay it down beside his keys.

"If you let anything happen to you—" he began.

"I won't," she promised, fighting tears of relief. Her voice sounded betrayingly thick with them. "I swear I won't, John."

"You better go on," he said, his own voice husky. "They'd almost exhausted their sources when Griff sent me to get Hawk."

"What will you tell them?" she asked, standing and picking up the incredible gifts he'd given her.

"I don't know," he said. "I haven't had time to think about it. Maybe the truth."

If he did, it would probably mean the end to his association with the Phoenix. This was the kind of betrayal Griff would find hard to forgive.

She should be sorry for that, she supposed, but she wasn't. Right now all she felt was elation. And gratitude.

"Thanks," she said.

He nodded, that crooked smile moving only one corner of his mouth. She was halfway across the room before she remembered the vital piece of information she didn't have.

"Do you know where he's going?"

It had seemed from what Griff said this afternoon that they still weren't sure exactly how Jorgensen was getting his information. Or even what he knew. Obviously the location of her place and the summerhouse, since there had already been confrontations with him at both locations. It seemed reasonable that Rafe would have chosen one of those to start his search, but it would save time if she knew which.

"I know I'd choose the place where I'd have the most advantages," John said.

Familiarity with the terrain. Weaponry. Perhaps even somewhere without stress or unpleasant associations. And in this case...

"I'd go home," Edmonds finished, "and wait for him to come to me."

"I owe you," she said.

"Then you make damn sure you're still around when I decide to collect."

THE PLAN they'd devised had called for him to drive Griff's car to Dulles and leave it in short-term parking. From there he would fly to Jackson and rent a car to drive to Elizabeth's. Shortly after he left Cabot's Maryland estate, Rafe had decided against doing any of that.

After all, they didn't know how Jorgensen was getting his information. Not that he suspected Hawk or Cabot or even Edmonds of being the source, but he figured that if *no one* knew where he was, there was no way in hell Jorgensen could continue to be one step ahead of him.

His own car was sitting in the garage of the summerhouse. He could leave Griff's in its place and drive through the night, arriving sometime tomorrow in Magnolia Grove.

That wasn't the arena he would have chosen for this confrontation, but Elizabeth's house was the one place they had all agreed Jorgensen would continue to monitor. Especially since he seemed to have lost track of them after they'd left Virginia.

The terrorist should assume that Elizabeth would return home at some point. And since she had obviously been his target from the beginning, Jorgensen would eventually show up there. Only Elizabeth wouldn't be the one he'd find when he came.

THE UNPAVED ROAD leading to the summerhouse seemed more threatening in the middle of the night than it had at dawn. The car's headlights, reflecting off the overhanging branches, cast wavering shadows. As if something were moving through the woods bordering the drive. The sensation unnerved Rafe, making him wonder if this had been a good idea.

He thought about doing what Edmonds had done when he'd arrived this morning—stopping a mile or so from the house and walking in. Except, since the whole point of this exercise was to attract Jorgensen's attention, there seemed nothing wrong with announcing he was here.

His gut feeling was that he would be safe in doing that. Despite the method of his brother's death, he believed Adler Jorgensen would want a personal confrontation. Adler would arrange for it to be up close and personal, maybe even eye-to-eye, so there could be no doubt in Rafe's mind who was responsible for his death.

He pulled Griff's car to a stop in front of the door of the garage and turned off the engine, killing the lights at the same time. Then he sat in the darkness, listening to the small noises as the engine cooled.

After a moment or two he could also hear the familiar night sounds from the nearby forest. Gradually, away in the distance, he became aware of the rhythmic beat of waves breaking over the rocks on the other side of the house. There was nothing else.

After his eyes had grown accustomed to the near lack of light, he turned, still in the driver's seat, and made a visual survey of the area around the car. Nothing moved in the broken patterns of light the moon threw across the lawn and drive. More tellingly, he had no sense that there was anyone else on this isolated spit of coastline.

He reached over to the passenger's seat and picked up the Glock he had laid there. The cool surface of its grip against the heat of his sweating palm was pleasant.

Almost as an afterthought, he stretched his left hand toward the glove box, opening it and then feeling around inside. His fingers finally found what they'd been searching for, closing over the narrow, cylindrical shape of a small flashlight.

Straightening, he opened the car door with the same hand that held the light. And he listened again before he stepped out. After all, if he hadn't read Jorgensen right, this would be the most critical moment.

Maybe the terrorist was out there in the darkness, sighting through the nightscope on his rifle. Aligning its crosshairs on the exact spot at the base of Rafe's skull that would mean instant death.

If he *were,* Rafe told himself with the fatalism his former profession had instilled, then it would be over before he knew what had happened. Long before he had time to feel fear. Or regret.

Elizabeth. He allowed the image of her face as she'd slept to form in his mind as he slowly stood up beside the car. The sound of the ocean was clearer now, but there were no other noises in the stillness. Only the distant crash of the waves and the low murmur of the night creatures in the woods.

The hair on the back of his neck lifted. He waited for what seemed an eternity, but nothing happened. Because Jorgensen was no longer here.

He was sure of that now, a deep down, gut-level surety. And it grew with each step he took away from the car and toward the garage door.

He bent to lift it, and then hesitated before his hand closed over the handle. For an instant the roar of some fire—either the one at Elizabeth's office or at the em bassy—was in his head. He closed his eyes, willing his mind away from it.

After all, an explosion would be even more impersonal than a sniper shot. That wasn't what Jorgensen had planned for him. Gunther's brother had something far more diabolical in mind than blowing him to kingdom come.

Despite the assurances that both his instincts and intellect were providing, Rafe knew he couldn't afford to take any chances. Griff had trusted him to handle Jorgensen. He didn't intend to fail by being careless.

He clicked on the flashlight, directing its narrow beam slowly along the bottom of the garage door. Not satisfied with a visual inspection, he knelt, laying the flashlight on the ground and feeling along the entire length of the door. There were no hidden wires. No residue of any kind.

He slipped his fingers under the rubber strip and lifted. The heavy door slid upward, moving silently on well-oiled hinges. As it did, he straightened into a crouch. He shoved the flashlight into his pocket to put both hands around the butt of the Glock before he stepped into the garage.

Once inside he lifted his head, scenting the stale interior air like a hunting dog. There was no distinctive hint of plastique. Nothing but the expected smells of gasoline and oil.

And his car was still sitting exactly where he'd parked it. He squatted again, running his hand under the back bumper and then duck-walking along both sides and the front to do the same. When he finished, he straightened and opened the hood. A thorough inspection of the engine, using the flashlight he'd brought from Griff's car, revealed that nothing appeared to have been tampered with.

Still he hesitated, looking over the top of the car and out into the drive. He put the flashlight under his arm and fished in the pocket of his jeans for his car keys. His eyes remained focused outside, watching the play of light and shade caused by the slight breeze that disturbed the nearby trees.

When he'd retrieved the keys, he didn't use the remote, remembering what Elizabeth had said about the explosion at her office. Instead, he walked around to the driver's door and inserted his key into the lock.

Holding his breath, he turned it. There was a small click. And nothing else.

He opened the door, and the interior light came on. He had already started to slip into the driver's seat when he noticed something white lying on the dark dash. Something *he* hadn't left there. He halted, half in and half out of the car, trying to figure out if the object could possibly be what it looked like.

The bastard had left him a note. He could see the bold block marks on the inside of the folded sheet of paper. His eyes lifted again, looking out into the darkness once more.

Finally he took the flashlight out of his pocket and shone the beam along the open edges of the message. No filament.

He tossed the flashlight into the seat and reached out with two fingers, pulling the paper toward him. When he had it in his grasp, he hesitated a moment before he unfolded it, holding it up to the dome light.

Only then did he realize that what he was looking at wasn't a note, but a crudely drawn map. Not so rough that he didn't recognize the location. The landmarks, rural and virtually unknown to anyone not from the area, were infinitely familiar. For almost five years they had comprised the world in which he now functioned—the isolated mountain in North Carolina that bore his family's name.

Whatever Jorgensen intended, it seemed he had chosen his battlefield. One that Rafe Sinclair knew better than anyone else on the face of the earth.

Chapter Sixteen

Despite her eagerness to get to Rafe, her apprehension had been steadily increasing since she'd abandoned John's car among the trees along a side road. It was one of several that snaked off from the paved two-lane that came part of the way up the mountain. She had walked the rest of the way up.

Her hike to the ridge above the cabin reminded her of how long it had been since she'd done any really strenuous physical activity. Apparently her thrice-weekly aerobics class wasn't the ideal training for mountain climbing. And that wasn't the only inadequacy she felt as she studied the deserted clearing below, centered by the Sinclair home place.

She had been here half a dozen times during the years she and Rafe had been involved. They'd used the cabin for rest and relaxation after difficult missions. It was the one place they could be together and alone without being constantly on guard.

She had even come once after he'd disappeared. Hoping that if he could see her again in this familiar setting, the memories might be powerful enough that he would be willing to talk to her.

He hadn't been here. The signs of neglect had made her believe it had been a long time since anyone had.

Judging by the scene below, she had again come to the wrong place to find him. And as much as she'd like to, she realized she couldn't blame John for that.

When she considered his exact words, it was obvious that what he'd told her had been his best guess of where Rafe would prefer to face his enemy. Edmonds hadn't claimed any knowledge of the plan the others had devised. If she hadn't been so damned impatient to get to Rafe, she would have realized that.

In the long hours she had spent lying on her stomach, peering over the edge of the outcropping she'd chosen as her vantage point, she had seen nothing to indicate Rafe was down there. Nor had there been any indication of human presence on this mountain. Not here. Not during her trek up.

Which meant John had guessed wrong. It also meant, she was finally forced to admit, that she had wasted enough time on this wild-goose chase.

She could only hope that Rafe's confrontation with Jorgensen wasn't already being played out in Mississippi or Virginia. Locations that lay in opposite directions from where she was. And she had no way of knowing which of them would take her to the scene of the action.

She began to scramble back down to the base of the outcropping. Despite her conviction that she was alone on the mountainside, she tried to keep the noise of her descent to a minimum. Other than a few dislodged pebbles that tumbled down ahead of her, she thought she'd succeeded.

As soon as her toes touched the ground, she turned, eyes surveying her surroundings as she took a few seconds to catch her breath. Almost subliminally, she was aware of a slight noise behind her. Before she had a chance to react, a hand was clamped over her mouth.

At the same time she was jerked off her feet by a forearm around her chest, pulling her up into the muscled wall of a man's body. Her first instinct was to scream, but as cruelly tight as the hand was across her lips, all she managed was a muffled bleat.

"What the hell do you think you're doing?" Rafe whispered, his mouth against her ear.

She closed her eyes in relief. Rafe. Not Jorgensen. *Rafe.*

That he had caught her off guard was certainly embarrassing, especially since she had come here in what was obviously a misguided attempt to rescue *him.* Still, this was not the disaster she'd been imagining from the instant she felt that hand close over her mouth.

She tried to answer him, but his palm was still pressed so hard over her lips that nothing coherent emerged. Feeling those aborted movements, he loosened his hold.

The viselike grip of his arm around her torso also eased, although it was still in place. She closed her eyes again, willing her heart rate to slow. She wanted to explain what she was doing here without revealing the extent of that instant of terror she'd experienced when he grabbed her.

"I was looking for you," she said.

She could detect no quaver in her whisper, but her heart was still beating too rapidly. As closely as he was holding her, she suspected he could feel it.

She eased a calming breath, her breasts moving against his restraining arm. Despite the situation, her nipples hardened with the involuntary contact.

"Lying bastards," Rafe said, his mouth still against her ear.

Griff and Hawk. Although his accusation was unfair, her residual anger at the two prevented her from explaining that her being here was through no thanks to them. Not yet, anyway.

"Is he here?" she whispered.

Rafe removed his arm from her body and took a step back, freeing her. Despite the heat, she shivered at the loss of his warmth. There had been something very reassuring, in spite his fury, about the feel of Rafe's body once more fitted that closely against hers.

"Jorgensen?" he asked.

She resisted the urge to mock. *Of course, Jorgensen. Who the hell else are you hunting? Who else is hunting you?*

The effects of her shock at being captured were too near the surface to attempt that kind of flippancy. In truth, Rafe had scared the bejesus out of her. Not betraying the extent of her fear was presenting enough of a challenge without trying to pull off sarcasm at the same time.

Turning to face him, she nodded instead. As she did, she examined his face.

His eyes were rimmed with red. Shadows lay like old bruises beneath the dense bottom lashes. She wondered how long it had been since he'd slept.

Although he had shaved at some point during their long, harrowing ordeal yesterday, his whiskers were again dark enough to make the lean cheeks appear gaunt, almost hollowed. The beautifully mobile mouth was set and stern. He was obviously furious, and at the same time he looked totally exhausted.

With an unwanted insight, she realized that her being here would only add to the stress he must already be feeling. Hawk had been right. He and Griff had been right, and she had been wrong. Terribly, unforgivably, dead wrong.

"I don't *know* where he is," he said. Despite the softness of the words, his frustration that he didn't was clearly communicated. "When I heard you stumbling around up here, I thought *you* were Jorgensen."

"I wasn't 'stumbling around.'" An empty denial since obviously Rafe had heard her.

On the other hand, he had moved quietly enough that she hadn't been aware that anyone was in the vicinity.

Again the feeling that in coming here she had made a dangerous mistake, perhaps a fatal one, churned in her gut. Despite her genuine concern for Rafe, she knew that her presence had only complicated things.

Hawk had warned her not to take away what Rafe had left. What she had done was far worse. She had given him something else to deal with.

"Why would they let you go?" he demanded, ignoring that pointless denial. "We had a deal."

"They didn't. John did."

"Edmonds?" He controlled his surprise, quickly lowering his voice to ask the obvious question. "Why?"

She found she had no good answer. Replaying the conversation she and John had had over Griff's kitchen table last night, she couldn't remember a single compelling argument she'd made. She had said something about their always having operated as a team. Something cutting about Carl Steiner's motives. A lot about sacrifice and expediency.

"I know about the PTSD," she said.

The leap had seemed logical, at least until the words came out of her mouth. Maybe she couldn't make Rafe understand why Edmonds had let her leave, but she *could* explain why she'd felt it necessary to try to convince him to.

Rafe's eyes narrowed as if he were attempting to figure out the connection between his question about Edmonds' motives and her response. He shook his head, a small, almost considering motion.

"Are you saying Edmonds told you that?"

"Hawk told me," she admitted.

What was reflected in the tired eyes this time was clearly pain. They had seemed to physically flinch from the information. Rafe obviously considered Hawk's telling her about the post-traumatic stress a betrayal.

Why wouldn't he? she admitted. After all, it was something Rafe himself had gone to great lengths to keep from her all these years.

"That's why——" she began, and then knew, because she was still watching his eyes, that she couldn't tell him the reason she had been so determined to find him.

Don't take away what he has left, Hawk had warned.

Telling Rafe she'd been afraid he couldn't handle Jorgensen alone would do exactly that. He had volunteered for this mission. And Griff, far wiser than she had been, had agreed. Not because Rafe was expendable, but because he had recognized that Rafe *needed* this opportunity.

"That's why you came riding to the rescue," he finished for her when she stopped.

"We were a team," she said softly. *In every way imaginable.*

"We aren't anymore."

"You can't do this alone, Rafe. Not with——"

"I can do it a hell of a lot better alone than I can with you hung around my neck."

It hurt, even though she understood that he'd meant for it to. Maybe just to try to drive her away, but still...

"You didn't used to feel that way," she said, trying to keep emotion out of her voice.

"I didn't *used* to feel a lot of the things I feel now. And no, there isn't anything about what I feel that we're going to discuss. You need to find someone else to be the recipient of your good deed for the day."

She steeled her heart at the taunt and chose a weapon of her own. *A woman's weapon.*

"I heard what you said."

She hadn't intended to tell him that. It revealed too many things, including her cowardice in not responding.

She had found, however, that this rejection hurt as much as all the others had. There was no reason to let him get away with it when she knew the truth. A truth he himself had acknowledged.

"I don't know what you're talking about," he said, but he did. That, too, was in his eyes.

"I wasn't asleep when you came into my room last night. I knew you were there. I heard what you said."

"You really *have* changed, haven't you?"

The same accusation he had made that night at the summerhouse. Something to the effect that she was not the woman she had been six years ago.

She wasn't. And they both knew why.

"Only because you have."

He laughed, the sound without humor. "Mea culpa. How many times do you need to hear me say it?"

"What I need you to say is what you said in my bedroom last night."

She really did, she discovered. She wanted him to say it to her face. Here and now. Not whisper it in the darkness when he believed she was asleep. She wanted an open confession that he had loved her more than he had ever loved anyone else.

For a heartbeat she thought he might do what she'd asked. Instead he turned his head, looking into the woods. In the opposite direction from the cabin in which they had spent all those hours locked in one another's arms.

She refused to let her gaze follow his, keeping it fixed on his face. His profile, the angles sharpened with fatigue, was all that was visible. And she could never have said what she saw in it that told her something was wrong.

Or maybe it was something about his posture. A subtle straightening of his spine. A tenseness in the line of his shoulders. *Something.*

She turned her head in the direction he was facing. The shade-dappled sunlight filtering through the canopy of the forest seemed incredibly beautiful. Even as she listened, trying to hear whatever he had heard, it seemed as peaceful as it had when she had looked down on it from above.

"What is it?" she whispered finally, turning back to face him.

The Glock was suddenly in his hand, taken in one smoothly practiced motion from the same kind of holster Edmonds wore at the base of his spine.

"It is Jorgensen?" she prodded.

"Smoke."

As he spoke the single syllable, he turned his head so that he was facing her. In his eyes was something she had never seen before. An emotion she would never have associated with the Rafe Sinclair she had known so well.

"That son of a bitch," he said.

What had been in his eyes had disappeared, replaced, perhaps deliberately, by anger. And resolve.

"Where's your car?" he asked.

"Halfway down the mountain," she said. She turned her head, looking toward the smoke she could see beginning to waft toward them through the trees. And she could smell it now. Just as Rafe had. "In that direction."

"Mine's hidden on the other side," he said. "There are a couple of things I'd like to take with me from the cabin."

"We're leaving?" *Without confronting Jorgensen?*

"For now," he said.

He intended to take her down the mountain and to leave her there, she realized. The fire provided him with an excuse.

He had never wanted her here. He still didn't. She even understood why, although it had never been a deterrent to her determination to come. If Jorgensen got his hands on her, he would use her as a weapon against Rafe. A highly effective one.

If she hadn't heard what he'd whispered last night, she might not have been so sure of that. Now she was.

The best-laid plans, she thought, remembering the rest of that adage. A lot could happen between here and Rafe's car.

At least they were together, which was what she had wanted from the beginning. She took the Beretta Edmonds had given her from the pocket of her slacks.

"Okay," she said, signaling her readiness.

His eyes were on her face. The corners of his mouth moved, almost assuming an upward slant, but he didn't say anything. Maybe he felt, as she did, that there was nothing else to say. After all, she had already heard all that was important last night.

And she really *didn't* need to hear him say it again. He had said it, maybe not to her, but he had said it. If that was all she ever had, it would be enough.

"Keep close," he said. "Whatever happens, don't let him separate us."

He turned, moving confidently toward the clearing. Away from the acrid smoke that billowed from the woods at their backs. The ground was uneven, strewn with small rocks and boulders deposited by the glacier that had formed these mountains. She had to pick her way across them, trying to keep up with his longer stride without risking a broken ankle.

Because she was looking down, she didn't realize he had stopped so that she almost bumped into him. Surprised, she glanced up to find that he had turned to face her.

"There was never anyone else. Not like you. There never could be," he said.

Focused on what lay ahead, it took a second or two for her to grasp what he was saying. And more importantly, that, despite the threat that surrounded them, he had taken time to say it because she'd asked him to.

"I know," she said simply.

She did. What they had shared had been something very

special. For both of them. From the beginning, the possibility that any moment they spent together might be their last had made those times infinitely precious. And the passion they shared infinitely powerful.

Neither of them had ever before felt the need to articulate something they both understood. There wasn't any need now.

He nodded, holding her eyes a few seconds longer. Then he turned again, moving through the familiar terrain with an ease she could not hope to match.

As she followed, eyes once more on the ground, she discovered that although hearing those words had *not* been necessary, that he had finally said them was. And no matter what happened next, nothing could ever take that away from her.

THE SUMMER had been long and dry, especially for up here. Still, Rafe was shocked at how rapidly the fire had come roaring across the mountain. There were natural firebreaks that would normally have slowed its progress. Driven by a hot wind and the tinder-dry forest, however, the flames crowned in the top of the tall pines and then leaped the barriers nature had created.

There was no time for the kind of caution the possibility of Jorgensen's presence would normally have demanded. They would be lucky to reach the car ahead of the fire.

Maybe that estimation was the result of his fear, fed by the sound and the smell of the monster that followed them. Without slowing, he shot a glance over his shoulder, trying to estimate how close it really was.

His eyes automatically focused on Elizabeth, who was running only a few yards behind him. Her mouth was open, as was his, trying to draw enough of the smoke-charged air into her lungs to fuel their exertion. And beyond her, closer than he'd imagined, flames licked along the ground where they had been standing only seconds before. He could feel the heat of them.

Wildfire was the term for this kind of fast-moving inferno. He knew in his heart, however, this one wasn't wild. It had been deliberately set, intended to do exactly what it was doing.

From here, he couldn't tell how widespread it was. No matter how narrowly it had begun, under these droughtlike conditions it could easily sweep across and then down the mountain, destroying everything in its path.

He had taken comfort last night in the belief that Adler Jorgensen wouldn't choose some impersonal method of killing him. He hadn't. He had used the most personal means of coming after them he could have found.

Rafe wondered how the bastard had known about the effects of the Amsterdam bombing. *The same way he's known everything else,* he acknowledged bitterly. He had been one step ahead of them all the way.

He still was. Now he intended that they would be only one step ahead of the fire. One step ahead, and then ultimately...

He glanced back again and realized Elizabeth had fallen farther behind. He slowed, giving her a chance to catch up.

As she approached, he could hear air wheezing in and out of her mouth in harsh gasps. The thickness of the air around them was making it difficult to breathe. Despite that, she was moving as fast as she could over the rock-strewn ground. The running shoes she wore weren't nearly as well suited for this terrain as his worn hiking books.

Actually, they were a disaster waiting to happen. And if she fell, he'd never be able to carry her out of the path of the fire quickly enough. He slowed his pace even more, holding out his hand. His grip might provide some stability, at least enough to keep her from falling if she stumbled.

As her reaching fingers touched his, the fire behind them

gave a great *whoosh,* followed by a sharp crackling as it consumed another tree. The simultaneous assault of that sound and the feel of Elizabeth's fingers in his combined with the adrenaline already flooding his system to send him spiraling back to the bombing in Amsterdam.

Images he had never been able to force out of his memory invaded his consciousness, obliterating the present reality. He was no longer looking back at Elizabeth, but at the distorted face and open mouth of the screaming woman. The skin of the hand he held disintegrated under his touch, peeling away from the slender bones like every nightmare he had ever had.

The next thing he knew someone was screaming his name. He watched a mouth form the word at least twice before he knew whose mouth it was. And before he remembered why she was screaming at him.

He must have stopped running at the exact moment his mind betrayed him. No longer fleeing the real fire. Consumed instead by the sights and sounds of one that had happened six years ago.

Elizabeth was beating on his chest, her fists flailing at him. As soon as he knew what was going on, he reached out, his hands fastening around her upper arms, holding her away from him. He shook her once. Sharply.

"It's okay," he said. "It's over."

He raised his eyes to check on the progress of the fire. It was frighteningly nearer, and it seemed to be sucking the oxygen out of the air around them. A terrifyingly malevolent force with which he had too intimate a relationship.

There was no time to try for the cabin or the car, he realized. There was time for only one thing. Even as it occurred to him, he wasn't sure it would work. Elizabeth's fit of coughing destroyed that moment of indecision, bringing his eyes back to her face.

"We go down," he said. "It's our only chance."

She nodded, but he wasn't sure she understood what he was suggesting. Up to this point they had been fleeing across the mountain, running along a fairly gradual slope that would have taken them to the clearing. What he was proposing now was a sharper, much more treacherous descent. It would not only be more physically challenging, but it was without the promise of a car waiting to carry them to safety when they'd exhausted their limited physical strength.

They would have more than a mile to go down before they reached the narrow logging road that provided the only access to his property from this direction. If the fire cut down the mountain rather than across it...

No choice, he decided, his eyes lifting once more to the inferno. Without another word, he grasped her elbow and began to run, dragging her along with him.

After the first few steps she seemed to get her second wind, running almost effortlessly beside him. Whether it was the surge of adrenaline from watching him lose contact with reality or the brief rest the episode provided, something had made a difference.

Because he knew the mountain so well, he was aware that they were not yet into any of the tough spots. The downhill slope would eventually give way to granite outcroppings they would have to pick their way across.

Those very obstacles could also divert the mindless onslaught of the fire. And depending on the amount of rainfall upstream, the creek that meandered through the rocks and crevasses on this side of the mountain might contain enough water to give them protection. Whatever happened...

Whatever happened, he thought again, they had no choice. He put everything else out of his mind, concentrating on guiding Elizabeth down the mountain.

Chapter Seventeen

The creek bed hadn't been dry as Rafe had feared it might be. The depth of the water wasn't what he'd hoped for, but by the time they reached it, they could go no farther. Not at the speed with which they had been forced to make that harrowing descent.

Stumbling, sliding, picking their way down steep inclines, they had somehow managed to stay ahead of the flames. And he had fought off the threatening memories of that other fire as they did.

Now they had one chance. One chance at safety. One chance at life. He bounded over the rocks that bordered the stream, Elizabeth behind him.

Throughout the ordeal, she'd made no complaint, but he could tell that her physical strength was at an end. All that kept her on her feet was sheer, stubborn will.

"Get into the water," he shouted above the noise of the current, giving the instructions as they crossed the last few feet to their destination. "Get down on your hands and knees in the center of it. Find the edge of a rock on the bottom and hold on to it. When I tell you, take a deep breath and lie down flat on your stomach. Put your head under and keep it there until I come get you."

He didn't explain that would be when the fire had passed

over them. If he were still alive. Those were details it wouldn't be helpful to put into words.

He skidded to a stop on one of the flat stones beside the water. Elizabeth put her hands on her knees, bending forward at the waist and gasping for breath.

"Now," he ordered.

She straightened, her face contorted with the effort of breathing. Her eyes found his, saying what she had neither strength nor breath to express.

Then, without looking back, she waded out to the middle of the creek. She followed his directions, dropping to all fours, as he joined her in the water.

The current was stronger than he'd expected and so cold it took his breath. What he had left. And the water didn't come up to his knees. He waded out a few more feet, feeling his way carefully over the slick rocks that lined the bottom. Once there, he looked back to evaluate the progress of the fire.

Roaring through the pines, it was now louder than the swiftly moving stream. Much closer than it had been when he'd entered the water.

Because they would be able to keep their heads under for less than a minute, they would have to wait until the last possible second. In preparation for that moment, he stooped, reaching into the water with one hand, feeling for the edge of one of the submerged rocks to hold himself down.

He was still watching the leading edge of the blaze sweep toward the rocky slope that led to the stream, knowing that their lives depended on his ability to time its arrival. If he gave the signal too soon, they would run out of air before the fire had passed over them. If he waited too late...

He turned to check on Elizabeth. She was still on her

hands and knees, her eyes fastened intently on him. Her face was perfectly calm.

Trusting him to tell her when it was time. Trusting him to keep the flames from engulfing her, blistering the skin on her face and arms. Charring it, just as it had the skin on the arms—

Elizabeth's features began to change, becoming someone else's face before his eyes. He fought the flashback, the heat and the sound of the fire were all around him.

One second Elizabeth had been kneeling in the water. In the next, like some mythical shape-shifter, she had become the woman from the embassy, her mouth beginning to open in that terrible, silent scream.

"Rafe!"

That woman had never called his name. She hadn't known it. In some rational, still-functioning atom of his brain he knew that.

As if the heat from the fire were distorting the air between them, the image he had seen shimmered, trembled, and mercifully settled back into reality.

Which was terrifying enough.

He pulled his gaze from Elizabeth's face, forcing it to focus on the crimson maw of the conflagration. Willing himself to stay in the present so he could make that split-second decision that would mean life or death for them both.

The force of the heat was palpable now, overpowering, because the blaze had finally reached the rocks. *Reached the rocks,* he realized with a growing sense of wonder, *and was going no farther.*

The feeling of unreality left over from the flashback made him doubt what his eyes were telling him. In one of those inexplicable reversals, the flames that had been eddying over the downward slope were beginning to die.

Apparently the fire had burned so intensely it had consumed everything in its path. When it reached the rocky incline that led down to the creek, there was nothing to fuel its combustion. The very dryness it had fed on had ensured there would be nothing growing on this barren slope.

He could still hear the flames whipping through the tops of the trees to the east, but here... Here it had stopped, unable to jump the barrier created by the combination of rocks and crevasses and water to touch into flame the trees on the other side.

As he watched, the fire at the top of the incline died away, leaving a smoldering blackness behind. The smoke and the heat from it still parched the air. He felt as if the hair on his face had been singed, his staring eyes baked.

Yet he was afraid to close them. Afraid that if he did, he would awaken to some other reality. A reality in which he had failed Elizabeth again.

"Rafe?"

Except he had never failed Elizabeth. That had been someone else. Some other time. Some other place.

He swallowed. And heard his name again.

"Rafe?" Elizabeth's voice. He would have known it anywhere. "It's stopped."

Focusing on the smoking, blackened ground above the smoldering rocks, he realized she was right. He allowed his burning eyes to close, giving in to relief. Moisture stung behind the lids, and he wasn't sure if it was sweat or tears. He reopened them finally and turned to nod. The only answer he was capable of.

"What do we do now?" she asked.

He licked his lips, running his tongue around their cracked and painful dryness, trying to think what they did next. And even as he told her, he wasn't sure of his motives in making the decision.

"Cabin," he said.

He still believed the terrorist had set the fire. He just

wasn't sure if it had been intended to kill them. Maybe it
had simply been meant to do exactly what it had done. To
terrorize them.

"Is that...safe?" Elizabeth asked.

For over a year he had hunted Adler Jorgensen's brother
with a thirst for vengeance that had been with him every
waking hour, as well as through those during which he had
tossed and turned in anxiety-driven nightmares. He had
thought he would never hate another human being with the
same intensity he had felt then.

Today, believing that he was about to lose the only
woman he had ever loved, he had found he was not so dead
to emotion as he had once believed. Not either kind of
emotion. The hatred he felt now was no less than that with
which he had relentlessly hunted and then gunned down
Gunther. And his love for Elizabeth...

Not the time or the place for that, he told himself. First
things first. And the first thing was an answer to her question. *Is that safe?*

"Not for him," he promised softly.

"I CAN'T BELIEVE IT," Elizabeth whispered.

Neither could he, despite what he'd been hoping as
they'd made their way here. His cabin seemed untouched
by the conflagration that had swept down Sinclair Mountain, in spite of the direction in which it had been headed
when they'd veered off to flee downhill.

Of course, it was always possible that if they *had* tried
to come here, they wouldn't have been able to reach the
clearing before they'd been cut off by the flames. They *had*
survived by going down the mountain, as grueling as the
journey had been. In any case, second-guessing the decision
he'd made then was counterproductive now.

"The topography protected it," he guessed.

After all, the small log house had stood in this same spot

for more than a century and a half. This was certainly not the only wildfire that had occurred on the ridge during that time.

"Stay here," he ordered, starting to rise from the crouch he'd assumed when they'd hidden in the underbrush to observe the clearing.

Elizabeth put her hand on his arm, checking the motion. Surprised, he turned to look at her.

"I haven't done anything to deserve that," she said.

That. Being left behind while he went to find Jorgensen.

And she was right. He couldn't fault any of her actions to this point. Other than the one she had taken by coming here. If he were honest, he would have to admit he'd have done the same thing had their situations been reversed.

He would also resent like hell any implication that he wasn't capable of handling himself, no matter what situation he found at the cabin. And after all, he was the one operating under a disability.

As much as he hated the word, he acknowledged that what had happened back at the creek had put them both in danger. Only the sound of Elizabeth's voice had kept him anchored to the present.

Given the recent frequency of the flashbacks, he couldn't guarantee he wouldn't have another. That had always been the problem. He could guarantee nothing about his condition. Or when it would come into play. He couldn't argue that having Elizabeth as backup wouldn't increase the odds of success for this mission. It would, however, put her into danger.

And he had already made this decision back at Griff's. It was another one that didn't need second-guessing.

"You saw what happened back there," he said.

"All the more reason—"

"All the more reason for you *not* to be depending on

me. It should be obvious, even to you, that isn't a healthy pastime.''

She said nothing for a heartbeat, but her hand didn't release its hold. He thought about shaking it off, but the feel of those warm, steady fingers was more than comforting. It was nearly sensual.

He had held her hand through part of their headlong descent. He had not had time then to be aware of any sexual aspect of that contact. Now, incredibly, he was.

''I don't know about you,'' she said, ''but I didn't go into any of this thinking it was going to be particularly healthy. *Or* thinking of it as a pastime.''

This. The CIA. Covert ops. The External Security Team. Even the hunt for a terrorist who had made her a target from the start.

''I never know what will trigger it,'' he said, trying to keep his face expressionless. He hated talking about the flashbacks. Hated everything associated with his so-called disorder. ''It can be anything. Something totally unexpected.''

''I understand that,'' she said.

Her eyes hadn't changed. They remained on his, reflecting none of the emotions he had been terrified he would see within them.

Which doesn't mean she won't eventually feel them.

He had known all along that she would believe this couldn't make any difference to her feelings about him. He, on the other hand, had lived with this a long time. He knew all the subtle, and the not-so-subtle, ways in which it had changed him. Ways she couldn't possibly imagine.

''What kind of person would you be if all you've seen and done and experienced *didn't* affect you?'' she asked softly.

He shook his head, but for some reason his throat closed, tight and aching at what was in her voice.

"That's the person I wouldn't want to love," she went on. "Thank God he doesn't exist."

"You don't understand," he said, his voice low.

"Give me a chance, Rafe. You've *never* given me a chance."

"Elizabeth." It was clearly protest, but it didn't have the desired effect. He should have known it wouldn't.

"Just like you aren't giving me a chance on this," she went on. "We've worked together. I've never let you down. What makes you think—"

"I'm not worried about *you* letting *me* down." It was as if she hadn't heard a word he'd said. Or didn't want to hear it.

"And I'm not worried about you letting me down," she said. "I *am* worried about whatever Jorgensen is doing while we waste time arguing."

She was right, of course. They didn't have time to settle this now. And she wasn't about to let him dictate what she could and couldn't do. Besides, deep in his gut he knew she was right and he was wrong.

He had told Hawk he wouldn't let her be used as bait. He wouldn't. That was a different proposition from the one she was making now.

Elizabeth was a former operative, and a good one. She had the training, the experience and the intelligence to bring the terrorist down—even if something happened to him. In that case, getting Jorgensen had to take precedence over Rafe's desire to protect her. He didn't have the moral right to refuse her help.

Trying to hide that struggle to balance his feelings for her and his responsibilities to the mission, he turned to look up at the cabin again. Nothing about the scene there had changed.

It was always possible he was wrong in believing Jorgensen was waiting for him. The clearing might really be as peaceful as it appeared.

"See the line of trees that runs along the right side of the rise all the way to the house?" he asked, keeping his eyes on the cabin.

"White oaks and poplars," she said, her voice as calm as her face had been while she'd awaited his instructions at the creek. As ready now to do what he asked of her as she had been then.

"Use them to work your way up to the cabin. From there secure the front entrance. Don't let anyone in that way. And don't come in yourself unless I call for you."

"What if he's inside?"

"Then what you hear won't be me calling you."

"I hear somebody firing, and I'm in," she warned.

"Just use the front door," he cautioned. "I have to know where you are at all times."

He began to rise, preparing to make his way up the hill. Her fingers tightened over his arm. This time he turned his wrist, breaking her hold.

There was nothing else he was going to talk about. Not now. He had given her what she wanted. If they got through today...

Whatever else needed to be resolved between them would have to wait until after the mission had been completed. And if it didn't end in the way all of them hoped it would be, there would be no need for that discussion.

A DOZEN SCENARIOS played out in his head as he made his way up the rise. He climbed, choosing his cover automatically. He was not even thinking about the physical aspects of what he was doing. He knew this terrain better than he knew the contours of his own face, and he had participated in a dozen assaults like this during his days with the agency.

Jorgensen might hold the high ground, but other than that, the advantages here were all his. And they were pretty impressive.

Not only was this his home turf, but he had long ago prepared for someone trying to invade it. To some people, those precautions might merit his being labeled paranoid. Given his background, Rafe had considered them highly rational.

What kind of person would you be if all you've seen and done and experienced didn't affect you? Not the kind who worried about someone invading his property.

As isolated as this place was, however, there would be only one reason for someone to seek it out. The reason Jorgensen had come.

At the top of the rise, Rafe settled into the observation position he'd decided on during the way up. Shielded from the house by one of those glacier-deposited stones, he forced his eyes to examine every branch and bush and blade of grass that surrounded the cabin before he did the same to the windows and door.

Everything was exactly as he had left it. Not a leaf seemed out of place. None of the entrances appeared to have been opened or tampered with. And yet he knew, as surely as he had known anything in his life, Jorgensen was here.

He could feel him on some instinctive, almost primitive level. He couldn't have articulated a single proof that made him believe the terrorist was waiting for him, but still he knew it. And with as much certainty as he had felt that day in Paris after he'd pulled the trigger.

An eye for an eye. That's what it came down to. Both the political and the personal. This was all about vengeance, righteous or otherwise.

And no matter how this turned out today, he didn't regret what he'd done five years ago. There were plenty of things he *did* regret. Such as refusing to explain to Elizabeth why he'd left.

His eyes considered the stand of trees where she should be hiding. Then, tearing his gaze away from them, he shoved the Glock into the waistband of his jeans, the butt toward his right hand. Quicker to access it there than in a holster.

He melted back into the forest, slowly working his way toward the left side of the cabin where, by design, the woods had been allowed to encroach on the clearing. The branches of one massive oak angled over the roofline. Using as footholds several narrow, ladder-like strips of wood he had nailed into its trunk years ago, he climbed it.

Once he was standing on the lowest branch, which was as thick as his waist, he hesitated, back pressed against the tree. There were no sounds from inside the house, although the chimney would have been a natural conduit for them.

He stepped out on the limb, holding on to the one above with his left hand as he walked across. As soon as he was above the house, he stooped and, balancing carefully, lowered himself to the roof.

One step carried him to the rock chimney. Placing one hand on it, he squatted on the peak, leaning forward to lift a door that had been cut into the decking. The hand-hewn cedar shakes had been refitted so that they hid the opening when it was closed.

He paused to listen before he lowered himself into the attic. He walked across the ceiling joists to the interior access panel. With the same caution he'd employed since he stepped off the branch, he stooped again, easing it open.

The room below was a utility hallway that connected the cabin to his workshop. Its only furnishings were a stackable washer and dryer and a wooden clothes hamper. As he'd expected, there was no one in the room.

He lowered himself until he was standing on top of the

hamper. His eyes swept the narrow space as he completed his descent. Both doors, the one that led into the house as well as the one that led to the workshop, were standing open. And he hadn't left them that way.

He took the Glock from his waistband and climbed down off the hamper. His weapon in firing position, left hand supporting the right, he edged sideways toward the inside door, his eyes moving back and forth between it and the one leading out into the workshop.

The big central room of the cabin was empty. As soon as he had verified that, he began to ease back along the hallway, still throwing the occasional glance back at the interior door. Despite the continued silence, his instincts were all telling him that he wasn't in the house alone.

Still, perhaps because of the quality of that deep silence, he was totally unprepared for the scream. Clearly feminine and as clearly agonized, it echoed and then reechoed within the enclosed space of the workshop.

Elizabeth.

The thought like a knife in his heart, he was already charging at the door that would take him inside the shop when he felt the disconnect begin.

He was powerless to prevent it. The scream went on and on, catapulting him back to the day he had touched the woman in the embassy. The noise she had made had been exactly like this. Prolonged and hysterical.

And this time he not only saw her face, he heard the sounds she had made as he tried desperately to free her from the rubble. Because of the nearness of the fire, he knew that if he couldn't get to her...

He stumbled through the doorway, surrounded again by heat and smoke and flame. Something, perhaps a thing as simple as sunlight coming through the windows of the shop or the mundane familiarity of his surroundings, snapped the thread that had drawn him back to what had happened in Amsterdam.

As the scene from the past faded, his eyes focused on the tape recorder sitting on his workbench. There was a second or two to understand why it was there before the back of his head seemed to explode. He was unconscious before he hit the floor.

Chapter Eighteen

The stillness was eerie, Elizabeth thought, leaning back against the oak where she'd taken cover. So complete it seemed unnatural. Not a bird sang. There was no hum of insects. Holding her breath as she listened, she realized there was no sound at all in the small clearing.

Maybe the silence could be explained by the proximity of the fire. Although it hadn't reached this far, a pall of thin white smoke hung in the tops of the nearby trees.

Her shoulders still pressed against the trunk of the tree, she had eased far enough forward to be able to see the front door of the cabin. Her gaze lifted from the house to the woods beyond, searching for some sign that Rafe was also in place.

Even if he *were,* she knew she wouldn't be able to see him. He knew the land, and the opportunities for concealment it offered. She wondered if he had been able to track her progress up the slope and then put the thought from her mind. As long as Jorgensen hadn't, she didn't care. She wasn't hiding from Rafe.

Her eyes again surveyed the clearing around the Sinclair homestead. Nothing moved. Nothing seemed out of place. It was all as peaceful as a baby's nap.

Just as she decided that, she heard a single gunshot, and then two more in rapid succession. And she would have sworn they had all come from *inside* the cabin. Jorgensen shooting at Rafe on the other side of the clearing?

Which might mean that he didn't know she was on this side. While he was concentrating on Rafe, that would give her an opportunity to get in behind him. After all, that's why she was here. To provide backup.

She put both hands around the grip of the Beretta. When she had taken it out of the pocket of her still-damp slacks, she had felt a momentary frisson of anxiety. Too many old movies. Getting the powder wet wasn't a problem with modern weapons.

She looked across what now seemed the vast expanse between her position and the front door of the cabin. One step at a time, she told herself, estimating the distance to a small utility shed that stood midway between before she stepped out of the woods.

THE SOUND of the first shot woke him. His cheek was pressed against the floor where he'd fallen, but while he'd been unconscious his hands had been tied behind his back. Whatever had been used was tight enough that the pain in his wrists competed with that at the back of his skull.

He opened his eyes to a field of vision limited by the fact that he was lying on his stomach. He lifted his head, setting off a new chorus of agony right above his neck. It made the pain in his hands fade from consideration.

Almost immediately a foot was placed against the side of his head, pushing it down. The pressure wasn't brutal, but it was definitely controlling.

"Just lie still, Sinclair. It won't be much longer now."

The accent was the same one that had haunted his nightmares during the year of his search. The same one he had heard on Elizabeth's answering machine.

The man behind him, who he assumed was Adler Jorgensen, fired his gun again. And then once more. Fragments of wood rained down on Rafe's face.

The bastard was shooting into the ceiling. And as soon as Rafe realized that, he knew why.

I hear firing, and I'm there.

Adler Jorgensen wasn't going to bother seeking Elizabeth out. He knew she would come to him.

Lying here helpless, Rafe knew it, too.

He also knew there was no use appealing to the terrorist for her life. He had come here with the express intent of killing Elizabeth. More specifically he had come here to make Rafe watch as she died.

The controlling foot was removed, allowing him to move. He turned his head to the side as far as he could, straining until he could glimpse the face of the man standing behind him.

The first thing he noted was that the grip Jorgensen had on the Walther he held was completely professional. The second that its muzzle was pointed at his forehead.

When his gaze reached the terrorist's face, the familial connection to Gunther was obvious. A younger version, of course. Different haircut and clothing, both less sophisticated than the older man had favored.

The coldly murderous eyes, however, seemed exactly the same. Of course, he had never been forced to witness triumph mingled with the hatred in Gunther's. Both were evident in these.

A fuzz of pale whiskers covered his cheeks, and the equally fair hair on his head had been cut very short and brushed upward. He looked like the average European teenager, even to the black U2 T-shirt he wore.

It was hard to equate this boy with the deaths of more than three hundred innocent people. And despite the year he'd devoted to hunting down the older Jorgensen, Rafe found that he couldn't even remember the cause either of them espoused.

It didn't matter. Contrary to the popular sociological theories of cause and effect, he had always believed terrorists were born, not made. Like serial killers, they took their experiences, the same ones shared by thousands of people who *didn't* kill, and used them as excuses to justify what they did.

"She had nothing to do with your brother's death," he said, knowing he was wasting his breath, but incapable of not trying.

"No, you did that all by yourself," Adler responded. "I thought for a while that the CIA was behind his assassination. The more I learned about you, however... And believe me, I learned a lot. I studied you like a textbook. Who you are and what makes you tick."

He wasn't looking at Rafe, although the muzzle of the Walther hadn't shifted. His eyes moved back and forth, from the outside door of the workshop to the one that led into the house. Clearly he was waiting for Elizabeth to appear in one of them.

And since he knew which it would be, Rafe's own gaze focused involuntarily on the interior door, the nearer of the two. As soon as he realized what he was doing, he turned his head, looking up at the terrorist.

"Not exactly the way you slaughtered my brother," Adler said, smiling at him, "but I think your anticipation of her death is much better. Gunther's was so unexpected I didn't have time to dread it. You, on the other hand..."

The sound was slight, but instantly recognizable to Rafe. Someone had opened the door of the cabin, which despite everything he had done to it, still made a discernable squeak as wood moved against wood.

Not Elizabeth, he prayed, but he knew it was.

Maybe if he could goad the terrorist into shooting him

now, Jorgensen would decide there was no point in killing her. *Yeah, right,* he thought, discarding that hopeful notion in the face of the reality of who he was dealing with.

And there were far worse things than death. The memory of what had been done to Paul Sorrenson and Duncan had haunted everyone else who had been on that rescue team. It had never haunted him more than it did now.

This bastard wanted Rafe to watch Elizabeth die, but he had already passed up a couple of prime opportunities to make that happen. The most obvious explanation was that he was planning to make her dying as prolonged and as painful as he possibly could. Anything would be preferable to that, Rafe thought.

Certainly his own death would. He might not be able to save Elizabeth's life, but maybe he could prevent—

Jorgensen took a half step to the side, peering down the utility hallway through which Rafe had entered. The opportunity his distraction provided was probably the best shot he could hope for, Rafe decided. He flipped over onto his back, kicking up at the Walther as he did.

His foot didn't connect. More quickly than he would have believed possible, Jorgensen jumped back, putting himself out of range.

Instantly the muzzle of the gun steadied, again focused on the center of Rafe's face. The terrorist didn't pull the trigger, however, unwilling to give up his plan for the perfect revenge. Apparently he had nursed it too long to discard it unless he had to.

And beyond him, in the interior of the cabin, Rafe could hear someone moving. He knew time was running out.

Rafe's second kick missed the barrel of the gun by a hairsbreadth. It discharged, the bullet striking the floor beside his head. Close enough that he had instinctively closed his eyes to prevent the spray of splinters from blinding him.

He opened them just in time to watch the toe of Jorgen-

sen's boot, the heavy kind bikers favored, coming straight
at his jaw. He managed to jerk his head back and to the
side, but the toe of the boot connected solidly enough that
the air thinned and then darkened around him.

He fought to stay conscious. Combined with the effects
of the first blow to the back of his head this one seemed
to create a kind of detachment from what was going on.

He still knew where he was. He could see Jorgensen, but
it was as if he were looking at him through the wrong end
of a telescope. Everything seemed distant and distorted.
Even the urgency he'd felt only seconds ago seemed impossible to recapture. He closed his eyes, trying to clear his
head.

"Drop it. Do it now."

Elizabeth's voice. The one he would know anywhere.
And he did. He tried to find her, but when he moved his
head, turning in the direction of that shout, the room swung
in lazy, sickening circles. Bile climbed up his throat, thick
and sour.

"Let's try it the other way 'round," Jorgensen said.
"You drop yours, or I'll blow his head off. You ever see
someone's head explode, Ms. Richardson? My brother's
brains were everywhere. I would imagine that in a room
this size—"

"Shoot him."

Rafe's command was a croak. As he made it, he was still
trying to bring Elizabeth's face into focus. All he could
distinguish was her silhouette, limned by the sunlight coming down the hallway behind her.

"If you do, I'll still get off the shot. I'll take him with
me," Jorgensen warned. "I've waited too long for that not
to happen."

If that were true, what he was doing made no sense. All
Jorgensen had to do to have the revenge he claimed to want
was raise his gun and shoot Elizabeth. That he hadn't meant

Rafe had been right about the terrorist's need to prolong the moment. Just killing them, even making Rafe watch Elizabeth die, would be anticlimactic.

Over too soon, and not nearly enough to savor. It was an emotion with which Rafe could certainly identify. There had been that same void in his own life when he'd completed his quest for Gunther's death.

He had blamed the resulting emptiness on other factors, all of which had undoubtedly played a role. His loss of Elizabeth. The things he'd seen the day of the bombing. Leaving the agency because they wouldn't give him permission to hunt Jorgensen. The hated loss of self-control the PTSD represented.

Somewhere inside he had known the root cause of that emptiness was none of those. After a year of searching, he had killed his enemy, exacted his revenge, and it had changed nothing. It hadn't even changed him.

"Kill him," he ordered again.

No matter how reluctant Adler might be to end this in some way not in keeping with his personal vision of vengeance, eventually he *would* end it. The only chance Elizabeth had was to shoot first.

Because his vision had cleared or because she had shifted her position, he could see her face now. It was strained and white, but determined.

Her eyes had never left the terrorist. Not even when Rafe had spoken to her. And the weapon in her hand had never wavered.

"Your decision," Adler said, his eyes as firmly locked on hers. "You have three seconds to make it."

"Whatever he tells you," Rafe warned, "he's going to kill us both. Your only choice is whether he'll do it fast or very slow. *Shoot* him, damn it."

"One," Adler counted.

Rafe watched her swallow and knew she would never be

able to pull that trigger and bring about his death. He wasn't sure he could cause hers, not even if he understood, as she probably didn't, what was going to happen next.

"Remember what they did to Paul," he said, trying to explain that fear. "You can't let something like that—"

"Two," Adler interrupted, his count overriding Rafe's warning.

"No, damn it," Elizabeth yelled. The words were filled with such fury the shout stopped both of them. "No."

He had no idea what she meant. Apparently, neither did Jorgensen. They waited together through the last second the terrorist should already have counted off.

Waiting for her to shoot. Or to put the gun down, giving herself over to as slow and painful a dying as the German could devise. Hoping to keep Rafe alive a little longer.

Suddenly, something changed. Maybe because he knew her so well, Rafe understood that Elizabeth had made her decision. Something about her face or her body told him that she knew what she was going to do. He was terrified it was the wrong thing.

Maybe Jorgensen knew, too. He seemed to tense, the Walther moving a fraction of a millimeter. Swinging toward Elizabeth?

In response to the possibility, Rafe tried again what he had twice failed to do. He twisted, throwing himself to the side. Attempting to slam his body into the terrorist's legs. Attempting anything to disrupt his shot.

The gun went off, so close to his head it seemed to deafen him. He could smell the scent of burned powder. It threatened to fill his brain with memories. Pulling him away from *this* scent. *This* time. *This* struggle.

The room filled with the sound of gunfire, echoing and reechoing as the recorded scream had done. He lifted his leg again, swinging his foot sideways. Aiming at Jorgensen's groin.

He wasn't sure if he connected, but all at once the terrorist's body seemed to fold in two, collapsing onto his leg like a balloon someone had deflated. Uncertain what was happening, Rafe rolled in the opposite direction, carrying Jorgensen with him. The terrorist slammed shoulder-first into the floor, his head striking a split second later. It bounced slightly as it hit.

It was only then that Rafe saw the small, bluing hole in the center of Jorgensen's forehead. It was exactly between his eyes, which were still open. And just before the last spark of animation flickered out, there was within them a look of deep surprise.

Rafe pulled his gaze away from the dying man, trying to find Elizabeth. Trying to see if she was still on her feet.

She was standing where she had been, her legs slightly apart and bent. The Beretta, held out in front of her, was still pointed at Jorgensen.

"He's dead," Rafe said.

Her mouth had opened, but no sound came out. As he watched, her knees began to sag, her body lowering in slow motion. The gun came down with her, still focused on the terrorist.

"Are you hit?" he asked.

At the question, she finally looked at him. She closed her mouth, shaking her head as she did. "Oh, God," she whispered.

"It's okay. It's over."

"There's blood."

"Where?" he asked, a jolt of adrenaline shooting into his bloodstream. She had said she wasn't hit. Maybe in the heat of the moment she hadn't yet realized she was.

"Temple," she said.

He searched her face for the injury, but he couldn't see anything. No blood. No wound.

She laid the gun very carefully on the floor and began

to crawl toward him, avoiding Jorgensen's body. Rafe struggled to push himself upright. His hands, which were still bound behind his back, made the maneuver difficult. The vertigo he'd felt when Jorgensen's boot connected with his jaw had returned with a vengeance.

Elizabeth stopped directly in front of him, sitting back on her heels. After a moment she leaned forward, touching the side of his head. He flinched when her fingers brushed a raw place on his temple, realizing then why the terrorist's first shot had seemed so loud.

She brought her hand down, holding it out, palm up, to show him the blood. "A fraction of an inch—"

"That's all I needed," he said. "You can't waste luck."

Her lips moved, slowly tilting. "There's a quota? You think you can use it up?"

"Actually, I thought I already had."

"I guess you had a fraction of an inch left."

They were quiet for a moment. Maybe she was thinking, as he was, how close a thing this had really been.

"What were you going to do?" he asked.

No more unfair than some of the questions she'd asked him, he decided, but she didn't respond for a long time. And when she did, it wasn't an answer to what he'd asked.

"I need something to cut the rope," she said, gesturing toward his back with a small lift of her chin.

"There's a drawer full of woodworking knives behind you. Take your pick."

She stood, swaying a little. That was hardly surprising, of course, considering all that had happened.

She put her hand on the top of the workbench as she opened the drawer, taking a few seconds to make her choice. Then she stepped around him, bending to slice the rope Jorgensen had used to tie his hands. He closed his eyes against the sting of the blood flowing back into his fingers, bowing his head to hide the reaction.

He heard her lay the knife on the bench. When he opened his eyes, she was holding out her hand to help him up. As numb as his fingers were, he wasn't sure he'd be able to close them around it.

He put them against the floor instead, pushing tiredly to his knees and then climbing to his feet. The hand he'd ignored was still stretched out before him.

"I asked you a question," he said.

"I'll answer it one night when you're asleep."

"Pretending to be asleep," he corrected.

"You use what they give you."

"You did good," he said softly, looking down again at the dead boy.

He wasn't a boy, of course, but Rafe knew he would always think of him that way because he had been when he had watched his brother die.

"I had a good teacher," Elizabeth said.

Had. Past tense. And that was appropriate, he supposed.

Whatever she had decided to do, lay down the gun or shoot Jorgensen, Rafe knew he would be dead if she hadn't followed him here. And the surprising thing about that realization was that the only emotion it evoked was gratitude.

"Thanks," he said, acknowledging it.

"Pure self-interest. I had to make sure you stayed alive long enough for me to convince you of a few things. And since you're so damned stubborn..."

"Elizabeth—" he began.

"Why can't you see how...*ridiculous* this is?"

That was the last argument he'd expected her to make. He had thought she might say that whatever had happened to him, they would deal with it together. Or that it didn't matter. Just not that it was...ridiculous.

"No," he said.

"I don't care about the flashbacks. I don't care about any of it."

"You don't *know* about any of it," he said, sounding defensive. Maybe he was.

"I can learn. It hasn't changed anything about you that's really important."

"Elizabeth—"

"Stop *saying* that," she said. "How would *you* feel?"

"How would I feel? About what?"

"If it were me. If I'd been in the bombing. If I was the one having flashbacks."

If their situations were reversed. A standard they had both tried to impose lately. On a variety of situations.

"I'm not asking you for anything more than what we had before," she said.

Which was a whole hell of a lot more than he had now.

"No rings," she said. "And no promises."

"You deserve better than that."

"I'm not ruling them out, you understand. I'm just telling you I don't expect them as part of the deal." Her voice had lightened, sounding almost amused now at his resistance.

"Elizabeth—"

"Rafe," she mimicked. "I'm tired of being alone. I didn't know how tired of it I was until you showed up. There's been this huge, gaping hole in my life for the last six years. I guess that means I'm a failure as a feminist."

"You're a hell of an agent," he said softly.

"Lawyer."

"Whatever."

"Is that a yes?" she asked.

"Would you mind repeating the question?"

"I've forgotten what it was. If there was one, it isn't important. I just want to be with you."

"There's more than the flashbacks," he said, trying one last time to resist what she was offering. Trying to be fair.

"I figured there was. We'll deal with that, too. Or we won't. All I know is 'nothing ventured...'"

Nothing gained. And a great deal lost.

"Are you sure?" he said.

"There may be another Adler Jorgensen out there," she said, looking down at the man she'd killed. "Yours or mine. Nothing's *ever* sure. This breath. This moment. After what just went on in here, are you really considering wasting more of them?"

"Is there a quota on those, too?" he asked, smiling at her.

"I don't know. But there can't possibly be enough of them left. I'm all for grabbing those that present themselves."

The most rational thing anyone had said to him in a long time, he thought. And slowly, holding her eyes, he nodded his agreement.

Epilogue

Four months later

Rafe's fingers locked with hers, one on either side of the pillow beneath her head. Their hands intertwined as closely as their bodies.

His hips rose and fell, the movement unhurried. Their slow, powerful rhythm created an answering one within her body. A timeless duet in which they had always been perfectly matched.

Friends and lovers. Inextricably bound.

She had lost count of the number of times they had made love tonight. After a separation of three weeks, however, she knew how important it was for both of them to reaffirm their connection, both physically and emotionally.

She had put the trip back to Mississippi off as long as she could, but the house had finally sold. Darrell had even found some eager young lawyer, newly admitted to the bar, to replace her in the partnership. And the old man didn't seem to harbor any ill will, despite her sudden departure.

The only problem she'd encountered in Magnolia Grove was that it had all taken far too long. Unable to bear being away another day, despite the threat of bad weather she had started back in the middle of the morning, arriving at the cabin well after dark.

Rafe hadn't expected her until tomorrow. And the look in his eyes when she opened the door had been reward enough for the long journey.

They hadn't made it to the bedroom. They hadn't even paused to dispose of any article of clothing whose removal wasn't necessary to accomplish their goal. She had been surprised to find how little *was* necessary.

Their lovemaking the second time had incorporated the removal of the items that remained. Rafe's lips examined every centimeter of skin revealed as he discarded them. Then, once they were both unclothed, he had explored every curve and angle, each hidden recess, as if her body were something wondrous and unfamiliar.

They had napped, at least briefly, sprawled in a tangle of naked arms and legs. They had then awakened to eat, suddenly ravenous, and made love again with the remnants of that half-finished repast scattered around them.

Later—how much later she didn't know—Rafe had trailed openmouthed kisses over her bare stomach, his lips eventually moving lower. In response, her fingers had threaded through the dark, silken strands of his hair. She held to them like a lifeline, while his tongue and teeth and lips delicately, and yet deliberately, revived each sated cell of her body. Nerve endings, pleasured beyond endurance, were stimulated to new life. Finally, muscles that quivered in fatigue were soothed until her relaxation was so complete she'd again fallen asleep.

She had no inkling if hours or minutes had passed before his body lowering over hers awakened her. There was no doubting the hardness of his erection, however, pushing into her with the same control with which he had taken her the first time.

This had been nothing like that heated coupling, impatiently begun and as quickly ended. This was a slow, deliberate seeking. The joining of two bodies, so attuned that their responses were, if not simultaneous, then mutual.

The lift of her hips met the downward thrust of his. Her shoulder turned into the seductive brush of his lips, tracing over sweat-dampened skin. Her fingers stretched and then closed tightly over the calloused strength of his.

It would seem that the descent into mindlessness would be delayed, or at least prolonged, because of the intense sensuality of their previous encounters. Instead, she had been surprised by how quickly her body responded. How instantly ready she had been. Wet and aching from the first graze of his hand against her breast.

Now the spiral had begun, her breath panting with each downward stroke, his breathing as harsh as hers. His features, highlighted by the fire, seemed almost too finely drawn as he strained above her. It softened their harshness, however, smoothing the powerful line of jaw and cheekbone.

Even as she watched, unable to look away, his eyes closed, his chin tilting upward. The tendons in his neck corded as the shuddering release began. His seed jetted into her body, and as if she had never before felt that rush of hot moisture, hers responded.

A tremor, hardly more than a shiver at first, grew and then expanded. Moving outward, sensation spread like the circles generated from a pebble tossed carelessly into a still pond. It ran, liquid and molten, through veins and arteries to crash and foam against the relentless, rocklike strength that drove within her. And when it was over, feeling ebbed, streaming away into eddies that trickled again to nothing. To stillness.

Rafe raised his upper body, propping above her on his elbows. The air, cool despite the banked fire, brushed over the film of perspiration on her breasts.

"Cold," she whispered.

He lifted their still-joined hands, bringing them toward her face. The sides of his thumbs smoothed over her forehead, starting in the middle. He lowered his head, slowly kissing each eyelid in turn. When he raised it again, she opened her eyes to smile at him.

"I missed you," he said.

"I could tell." Her smile widened.

"I used to think I liked the quietness up here," he said. "The isolation. I thought that's why I'd come."

She waited, but disappointingly, he said nothing else.

"It wasn't?" she asked finally.

"I don't know. I can't really remember. All I know is that now it isn't isolated. It's…lonely. At least when you're not here."

Not really a declaration of any kind, she supposed, but it was more of one than he had made in the four months since she'd been here. And he had said it while she was awake.

She nodded, holding his eyes. After a moment his lips tightened. Then he dropped a kiss on the end of her nose, freeing his hands from hers at the same time. He rolled to the side, pulling her with him.

He held her against his chest, her head fitted on his shoulder, the curve of her hip over his. She felt his breathing gradually slow, becoming deep and regular.

She didn't close her eyes, however, staring out into the fire-touched darkness. Watching the play of shadows the firelight painted on the rough-hewn walls and thinking about the words he had whispered.

I missed you…

It's lonely. At least when you're not here….

There was no one else. No one who was ever like you. There never will be.

And she thought, too, despite everything she had promised herself, about the others. All the ones he had never said.

"YOU AREN'T SUPPOSED to be the one who doesn't sleep."

She turned to smile at him over her shoulder. He walked up behind her, wrapping the patchwork quilt he'd brought with him around her body, enfolding her in his arms as he did. She leaned back against his chest, thinking that she had never been more content in her life than here.

Which made the strange sense of ennui that had kept her from sleeping all the more inexplicable. There was literally nothing that should keep her awake.

"It's snowing," she said, looking up at the night sky.

It was the snow that had brought her outside. She had slipped out of bed, pulling on her nightgown, to stand on the small front porch of the cabin. Despite the steady shower of flakes, which had increased in the short time she'd been out here, she could still see stars. So clear in the thin mountain air she felt as if she could reach up and touch them.

"It does that this time of year," Rafe said.

The teasing note didn't bother her. Actually, she welcomed it.

"What's wrong?" he asked.

Typical male question, she thought, smiling to herself.

"What makes you think something's wrong?"

"You getting out of a warm bed in the middle of the night to stand in the snow."

She turned, still enclosed in the cocoon of quilt and his arms, to look up at him. His expression was far more serious than his voice had been.

She reached up to touch his cheek. "Nothing's wrong," she said truthfully. "I can't remember a time in my life when things have been *less* wrong."

There was a small silence.

"The whole time you were gone," he said, "I kept wondering what I'd do if you didn't come back."

She felt guilty she had been away so long. More guilty that he still didn't understand there was nothing he could ever do that would make her *not* come back.

She stretched on tiptoe, putting her cold lips against the warmth of his. For less than a heartbeat, they were unresponsive. Then he bent, his mouth opening over hers with the same hunger the long hours of their lovemaking had not, apparently, assuaged.

Not for either of them, she discovered. She answered each demanding movement of his tongue, relishing the knowledge that he still wanted her this much.

It was Rafe who broke the kiss, raising his head to look down into her face. His eyes were shadowed, the line of his mouth set. Unsmiling.

"I'll always come back," she said. "This is my home."

It was true. Each time he took her into his arms, she knew the same sweet sense of homecoming she had felt today.

"There's something I want to show you."

He released her, stepping back, but at the same time pulling the quilt more securely around her shoulders. She brought up one hand to hold the edges together as she shook her head, puzzled by his tone.

"Something to show me?" she repeated, unresisting as he took her elbow to urge her toward the door.

"I was going to save it for Christmas, but...maybe you should have it now."

"Something in the way of a bribe?" she asked, smiling at him as she entered the cabin.

"Or an insurance policy."

"Insurance against what?" she asked, following him across the central room.

The fire on the hearth provided enough light that she

hadn't turned on the lamp when she'd crawled out of bed. He didn't now. Not until they reached the dark utility hallway. There Rafe flipped the switch that controlled the overhead lighting, forcing her to blink against the brightness.

"In here?" she asked, still mystified.

"In the workshop," he said, opening the door.

Despite the quilt, she shivered as the cold air from the room was pulled into the cabin. She hesitated on the threshold, watching Rafe cross the workshop to turn on the lights.

She couldn't remember being in this room since the day of the fire. Involuntarily her eyes found the spot on the floor where Jorgensen's body had lain. There was nothing there now to mark it except memory. She pulled her gaze away, forcing it to focus on Rafe instead.

He was standing on the other side of the central workbench. On top of it was an object over which a sheet had been draped.

"It's not finished, you understand," he said. "You'll have to use your imagination."

"Okay," she said.

There was nothing remotely boyish about Rafe Sinclair, but there had been something in that disclaimer of a small boy who is about to show off a prized possession. Or some accomplishment.

And when he lifted the sheet, revealing what was beneath it, she knew that was exactly what this represented. An accomplishment.

Within a framework of elaborately turned spindles hung a cradle, intricately, beautifully hand carved.

"It's solid oak, but you can choose another color for the stain," he said. "Darker if you want."

Through a sudden veil of tears she looked up into the eyes of the man who had made no promises. And no commitments. Except, it seemed, this one. Shaped by his own hands.

"It rocks," he said unnecessarily, setting it into motion with the touch of one long, dark finger. The movement was noiseless, an effortless back-and-forth glide.

"It's a cradle," she said. The word sounded almost reverent. It was how she felt.

"I thought..." Rafe began before the sentence faded. His throat worked before he tried again. "We've wasted a lot of time. I thought you probably wouldn't want to waste any more."

"Babies," she said softly. Although technically, by inflection, that hadn't been a question, she wanted to be very sure she wasn't mistaken.

"That's generally what cradles are for." Thankfully the teasing note was back.

She took a breath, wondering what words she could possibly need to hear in the face of this. She crossed the room, coming to a stop across the workbench from where he was standing.

The workmanship of what he had made was even more apparent here. She touched the cradle into motion as he had, watching it swing for a moment before she looked up.

"Thank you," she said.

He nodded, blue eyes suspiciously bright.

"Are you sure, Rafe?" she asked softly. "This isn't exactly something you can change your mind about."

"This," he said, looking down at the cradle he'd built, "isn't a spur-of-the-moment endeavor. I've had lots of time to think about what I was doing."

"No reservations?"

"A thousand. All of them about the kind of husband and father I'll be. None of them about you. None about this."

All of them about the kind of husband and father I'll be.

Husband and father. For someone like Rafe, a man of honor, those roles couldn't possibly be separated. She had not dared to think beyond what the cradle represented. Now she realized she hadn't trusted him enough.

"Husband?" she repeated.

"You need to hear the words, I suppose."

"I *want* to hear them," she corrected.

"All of them?"

"As many as you want to say."

And only when he smiled did she know that whatever had happened to him at Amsterdam, whatever he had seen and done and experienced—none of it could destroy the core of decency she had recognized the day she met him.

"Husband," he said, sending the cradle gliding toward her.

When it swung back to his side of the workbench, he touched it into motion. "Marriage."

The third time, she knew the word that would accompany the push. "Baby," he said.

She caught the edge of the cradle, keeping it from swinging back. "Do I get a chance to answer?"

"I wasn't through."

"How many babies do you *want?*" she asked, laughing as she sent the cradle swinging toward him.

"Let's start with one," he said. "Isn't that how it's usually done?"

Long, dark fingers closed over the curved rim, holding the cradle motionless as she had. And this time when he set it into motion, his face was as serious as it had been on the porch.

"I love you, Elizabeth Richardson, soon to be Sinclair. I want very much to marry you and give you babies. As many babies as this cradle can last to rock to sleep through the years. And I probably should warn you…" he said.

The tears that had threatened before were back, making it difficult to see his face. It didn't matter, of course. Nothing mattered but the gift he had given her tonight.

Far more than she had ever asked for. And until he had offered it, more than she had even known she wanted.

She did, she realized. She wanted it all.

"Warn me?" she questioned.

"I may not be much of an operative," Rafe said. "Not anymore. But I am one *hell* of a carpenter."

* * * * *

Author Note

I hope you're still enjoying my Men of Mystery/Phoenix Brotherhood stories. I certainly want to do more of these in the future. My next Intrigue will be a little different, but something I'm very excited about. I'll be back in August 2003 with the first book of the Colorado Confidential series. Don't worry, though, that story has its own sexy and daring ex-agent. Please look for my story, the start of something dark and dangerous in Colorado.

Gayle Wilson

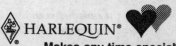

Steeple Hill Books is proud to present
a beautiful and contemporary new look
for Love Inspired!

HEARTWARMING INSPIRATIONAL ROMANCE

Love Inspired®

As always, Love Inspired delivers
endearing romances full of hope, faith and love.

Beginning January 2003
look for these titles
and three more each month
at your favorite retail outlet.

Steeple
Hill®

These are the stories you've been waiting for!

Based on the Harlequin Books miniseries
The Carradignes: American Royalty comes

HEIR TO THE THRONE

Brand-new stories from

KASEY MICHAELS

CAROLYN DAVIDSON

Travel to the opulent world of royalty with these two
stories that bring to readers the concluding chapters in
the quest for a ruler for the fictional country of Korosol.

Available in December 2002 at your favorite retail outlet.

HARLEQUIN®
Makes any time special®

HARLEQUIN®
INTRIGUE®

A royal family in peril...
A kingdom in jeopardy...
And only love can save them!

THE CROWN AFFAIR

Coming in December 2002...

ROYAL PURSUIT
BY SUSAN KEARNEY

Don't miss the exciting final installment in
THE CROWN AFFAIR trilogy. When an assassin
follows Prince Alexander to Washington, D.C., the royal
playboy hires stunning but icy private investigator
Taylor Welles—and goes undercover as her husband
to help track down a deadly traitor in their midst!

Look for these exciting new stories
wherever Harlequin books are sold!

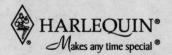

HARLEQUIN®
Makes any time special ®